THE
MURDER
HOTEL

A.J.A. GARDINER

i

Table of Contents

Part 1

1

When Miss McNee flings her spectacles across the desk, Daisy doesn't so much as flinch—even when they clatter over the melanine surface and drop into her lap. She merely raises a quizzical eye at their owner.

Daisy is difficult to rattle.

Unfortunately, I'm not—my insides are knotting.

Surely not another one?

We've had a string of them today—the "I can't see with my new specs" brigade. So far, they've all been cases of user-at-fault—wearing reading specs for distance (or vice versa), getting new pairs mixed up with their predecessors...

I'm helping someone choose frames at the other end of the shop, but have to intervene. As the optician who dispensed her glasses, sorting Miss McNee's problem is my responsibility.

Oh, joy

Before starting towards the fracas, I murmur an apology to my customer. She waves her hand at a stack of designer styles set aside for further

1

consideration. 'That's alright, Samantha. I've got plenty to keep me busy.'

Thus excused, I make my way across—breathing slow and deep in an attempt to quiet my thudding heart.

'Good morning, Miss McNee. Can I help?'

She glares, rather like Judi Dench did when she was mad at Daniel Craig. 'These won't do at all—everything's out of focus through them.'

The old lady smooths a faux-fur collar with gnarled fingers, then absently pats her blue-rinsed hair—it wobbles en masse, the sort of movement you'd expect a rigid jelly to make.

'But Miss McNee, when you picked them up yesterday, they seemed fine...'

'I didn't realise then how awful they are.'

She steps closer, a faint glow showing beneath several layers of Max Factor. 'They're so bad, I'm convinced you've mixed them up with someone else's.'

Which is patently impossible—I personally verify every pair of specs before they leave the shop. But I've enough battlefield savvy not to adopt an adversarial approach. Lifting the specs from Daisy's desk, I make a show of scrutinising them. 'Give me a moment, Miss McNee—I'll go and check them over.'

A sharp *Be sure and do it properly* follows me to the partial privacy of my workshop cubicle where I exhale long and hard. My pulse is ticking faster than a grandfather clock on speed.

Comments like that last (translation—you're clueless and incompetent) *used* to bounce clean off me—but not so much lately. Customers say that sort of thing all the time—every optician gets it—so what's changed? Are these displays of dissatisfaction increasing in frequency? (i.e. am I losing it professionally?)

Or has my skin thinned somewhere along the five years I've been doing this?

When did I start hating my job?

The thought startles me. I *don't* hate my job—do I?

'Sam?' Daisy's stage whisper nearly makes me drop Miss McNee's glasses, and I whirl to see her impish face keeking around the partition. I have to look down, too, because at 5'2" she's six inches shorter than I am. Somebody once suggested Daisy looks like Tinker Bell, from Peter Pan. Only once, mind—delicate little Daisy has a black belt in judo.

I raise my eyebrows. 'What?'

She steps inside a space barely adequate for one, squashing up against me and setting her mouth below my ear. 'You okay? You've been uptight all morning. Is it that waster you live with?'

Please don't remind me of Jake

'It's not just him   some of it is, but—oh, it's everything. I feel as though my life's out of control.'

I try not to flinch when her fingers close around my arm—Daisy grips like a Scotsman holds his wallet. 'Sort this one out, then it'll be lunchtime—you can tell me all about it in the cafe.'

3

I nod, and Daisy retreats to resume her lion-tamer role at the front desk.

"Sort this one out". If only it were that easy—has Miss McNee suffered a sudden cataclysm at the back of her eyes? Which would mean involving one of our optometrists, the management of which will probably nix my lunch hour.

The glasses aren't damaged—they're in pristine condition. It looks like we *will* need an optometrist, but let's whip through the motions first. Calling up Miss McNee's record on my built-in terminal and sticking her specs in the auto-focimeter, I flick between two sets of numbers. A digital readout of what power her lenses *are*—and the corresponding prescription details. (Or in other words, what power they *should* be.)

Expecting them to be identical.

Except they're different?

Absolutely nothing like one another

So this isn't an acute medical condition—she really *has* got the wrong glasses.

My head drops as I wonder...

Maybe I am, finally, losing it

These aren't Miss McNee's glasses—and I've no idea how that can be. Peeping out at the still fuming customer, agonising over what to tell her, my eye wanders to a cluster of plastic chairs comprising our waiting area and an elderly woman built like a sparrow who looks remarkably similar to Miss McNee.

Now I remember—that's her sister. Her *twin* sister. They're inseparable—even live together.

When I return to reception, Miss McNee squares up. She's ready for round two, but her face falls when I keep walking. The other lady glances up as I approach.

'Miss McNee,' I say, mustering an ultra-friendly tone. 'Are you just here with your sister, or can I help you too?'

The other Miss McNee leaps to her feet, face darkening. 'I should hope so,' she snaps. 'I can't see with *my* new glasses, either.'

MOST DAYS, DAISY AND I GO FOR A SANDWICH AT Maisie's—a friendly cafe down the road from Cosmo-Spex. Maisie's is bustling, as usual, and we have to queue for our sannies. Then we're lucky and get a table right away.

Daisy's still giggling. 'They were wearing each other's glasses?'

I nod, smiling despite myself. 'You see how closely they dress? So, of course, after their eye tests they insisted on choosing nearly identical frames. I remember now, telling them to be careful...'

'... not to mix them up,' she finishes gleefully. 'That's got to be one for the books.'

When I don't answer, Daisy's expression turns serious. 'Come on, then,' she says, unwrapping her cheese and pickle roll. 'What gives? You've been in a stotter of a mood all day—all week, actually.'

Gazing at a turkey wrap still in its cellophane and stirring my tea aimlessly, I automatically deflect. 'It's nothing in particular, Dais'.'

Then I realise—I don't want to "deflect" any more. Pulling my thoughts into some sort of coherence, I let it all out. 'It's everything. I'm sick of Cosmo-Spex and all the moanies we attract, and yes, I *am* fed up with Jake—he still hasn't found a job, and doesn't even give any impression of trying. Daisy, my last birthday was the big three-o, and it feels like all I've done so far is dug a hole too deep to climb out of.'

I refrain from mentioning the sudden death of my favourite aunt—Daisy was on holiday when it happened, just over a week ago, so doesn't know yet. A walk-on part in my list of reasons for feeling off isn't the eulogy Aunt Claire deserves.

'Tell me about it,' Daisy throws back, chewing at the same time. 'At least you've got qualifications. Me, I'm stuck in a minimum wage job, and I wouldn't even have got that without your help. Y'know what, Sam? I get fed up too, but I don't have your options.'

'What options?'

Shaking my head, I add: 'You never seem fed up.'

She grins, flicking a scrap of lettuce from her chin with a paper napkin. 'I'm a glass-half-full sort of girl—I can be miserable and still appreciate what I've got. You, though—dispensing optician living in a flat with no mortgage?—your glass is already full.'

'No, it's not.'

The denial came out sharper than I intended. My situation looks good when you put it like that, but the flat was paid for by an inheritance from my parents. Six years ago, a drunk driver collided head-on with our car. I lost both parents that night, along with my left leg from the knee down.

For a long time, I let the money moulder in a bank—paying peanuts in interest. It felt wrong—macabre, even—to profit from their deaths, until I came to my senses and realised mum and dad would want me to put their last gift to good use.

So, I invested in property—for instant, long-term security. Unfortunately, not having a mortgage is the only thing my flat's got going for it. Achieving finance-free ownership meant settling for a crummy one-bedroom in a run-down area and sometimes I can't help wondering how much my "property portfolio" has to do with Jake's continued interest. That, and the fact I'm keeping him since he lost his job—all of two months now.

My good leg jolts the table when Daisy snaps her fingers an inch from my nose. 'Daisy to Sam. We're supposed to be talking, and I'm not a telepath.'

'Sorry, what were you saying? Oh, yes—lucky me with all my "options". You know how I got the flat—I could have done without *that* particular piece of luck. As for being a dispensing optician, it's a dead-end job that pays too much to chuck—but not enough to compensate for the stress of dealing with miserable grannies and impossible-to-satisfy Elton John wannabees.'

'It's not dead-end. You could go the management route—'

'Like Callum, you mean?'

She slaps her forehead. 'On second thoughts, please don't consider management. And I'm sorry if I sounded insensitive. I know how you miss your folks, and I realise being an optician doesn't compare with the pro-tennis circuit.'

For a moment, in my head, I'm back playing at national level—feeling that so-familiar whack of nylon on rubber, with thunderous applause ringing in my ears. Wimbledon was within my grasp—before the accident forced me to swap tennis whites for the bleached jackets Cosmo-Spex insists we wear. 'It gets to me sometimes—after being in control of my own destiny, now I'm just another drone in the hive.'

She's listening, but also making exaggerated, sideways movements with her eyes. Following a miniscule tilt of her head, I see him. Mr Davidson—shuffling towards our table. (Not so much Elton John, but for miserable "granny" read "grampa".)

Daisy makes a face—Mr Davidson came in earlier to join the queue of complainants. He was easy to sort out, though—I simply pointed out he'd mixed up his glasses and was actually wearing the old pair.

So what now?

'My glasses are hurting me,' he wheedles, pulling at an earlobe.

Deep breath, Sam—remember, you've got two mouths to feed

He recoils when I look up, so my irritation must show. 'Mr Davidson, I don't know what you expect me to do in here. Anyway...' my voice rises—I can't help it '... you're *still* wearing the old glasses.'

'How can you tell?' he asks, sounding genuinely interested.

This is the problem—he insisted on choosing a frame virtually identical to his previous pair. (And wouldn't be talked out of it.) 'The old ones have dulled with age, and their sides bow out because they've been handled so much. So, if you just switch to the new ones, like I told you earlier...'

'It's the new ones that hurt my ear,' he interrupts, and I swear there's a sob in his voice. 'Terrible bad it is—that's why I've gone back to the old ones.'

'So, bring your new pair into the shop this afternoon and I'll adjust them—or maybe you'd prefer I come and do it straight away? After all, why should you care if I miss my lunch break?'

His face hardens. 'No need to be like that. I paid a fortune for them glasses—any more cheek and I'll put in a complaint about you.'

9

I feel Daisy's fingers circle my wrist—squeeze. She's right, he's not worth it. But my mouth's found a mind of its own. 'Go ahead, then. It'll give you something to do while I finish eating.'

Mr Davidson stomps out of the cafe.

Daisy lets go of me and covers her face, then peeks through splayed fingers. 'You really are down, aren't you? I've never heard you speak to a customer like that.'

'I didn't say anything out of order.'

'Mm. It wasn't so much *what* you said as the way you said it.'

A shiver of unease flutters through me. Maybe I shouldn't have... no, you've got to draw the line somewhere. I *could* have been more diplomatic—but then, Mr Davidson *could* have been more considerate when he decided to interrupt my lunch. Surely, no one would think he has valid grounds for complaint?

Oh, I'm sick of all this stress. I grab my cup for a slurp of tea and the teaspoon I left sticking out goes straight up my right nostril. '*Beggar.* There must be more to life than this.'

Daisy's elbows slide across the melamine tabletop, a sudden gleam in her eye. 'There *is* a way out—we've talked about setting up our own business. Haven't we?'

Here we go. Yes, we have, but it's cloud cuckoo land

'Daisy, you've got no cash and all mine's tied up in the flat. So we've no money to start a business,

10

and even if we did, the statistics say we'd be bust within a year.'

She taps the side of her nose—as always, insatiably cheery when faced with impossible odds. 'You could borrow against the flat—we've had some good ideas. Take dog walking—more and more people these days use a dog walker, and we both love animals. All we'd need is a van and some cages. As for statistics, they don't *all* go bust.'

I make a show of counting off on my fingers. 'Insurance, marketing, finance costs, plus all the rest—and we've still got to feed ourselves—it'd mean a huge plunge in income for the foreseeable future. Where's the fun in that?'

Daisy grabs her sandwich, crams what's left in her mouth, then speaks through it. 'You're such a pessimist, Sam. Well, if you don't want to talk about finding a way forward, I guess we're stuck with things the way they are. I'll see you back at the shop.'

She leaves Maisie's in a rush, and my vision shimmers before I blink away a sudden tear. Daisy's right—what's the point in complaining about everything then making no effort to sort it? Maybe I need to stop whining and *do* something. Anything's got to be an improvement on how things are now.

I still haven't touched my turkey wrap, and can't face it now. Sighing, unhooking my bag from the chairback, I stand. 'Except dog walking,' I add mentally.

My phone beeps, and I pull it out to read the text. Straight away, I see it's from Jake. Which reminds me—he'd better not forget about the shopping I asked him to do.

Sorry babe - gonna b busy all day. Andy needs help with stuff. Can u pick something up for tea? Jake X

2

Dipstick Davidson must have been true to his word. Fire erupts at the back of my throat (looks like that wrap I denied its destiny is getting the last laugh) when Callum, our manager, calls me into his office before I even have my coat off.

"Office?" It's an executive version of my workshop cubicle. Since Callum and his desk occupy most of the floor space, there's no room for a visitor chair—leaving me stood facing him like a kid caught talking in class.

As usual, he doesn't get up. 'Samantha, I've had a complaint about you.'

I'm fine, thanks, Callum. How about you? Good weekend? So, what did you want to see me about...?

'If it's Mr Davidson, I only made it clear I was on my lunch break.'

His head nods, but two reptilian eyes stay locked on mine. 'Samantha, I shouldn't have to tell you this, but professional people are *never* off duty. Also, individuals like Mr Davidson are our bread and butter. Did you know attracting a new customer costs ten times more than retaining an existing one?'

Callum goes on a lot of management courses. He thinks Head Office is grooming him for great things, but the rest of us suspect they're

13

brainwashing him. My lips twitch—keeping Callum's conditioning topped up probably only costs a tenth of the expense involved in programming a replacement from scratch.

'Callum, Mr Davidson's an old moan. He'll have found somebody else to bother by this time tomorrow. I'm sorry, but outside Cosmo-Spex my life's my own—Mr Davidson had no right to cross that boundary.'

There. I'm pretty pleased with that, considering it was off the cuff. Maybe I should have been a barrister...

He's swinging his chair through forty-five-degree arcs—an irritated cat does that with its tail. Pointy ears and a tail would suit Callum, especially with a pitchfork thrown in... Anyway, he may not like being challenged, but can't argue with what I said.

'Samantha—'

The way those syllables clacked together worries me—so does that sickly smile.

'—the professional bodies have made it plain our responsibilities extend to conduct outside the workplace. I'm disturbed you don't seem to appreciate the issue here, and I'm afraid you leave me no choice but to put a formal warning in your file. Now—' he speaks over my strangled protest '—it's not all bad news. Head office is running a course next month called "Communication with Customers" and I've signed you up. They'll send details by email—I think it's just what you need.'

He swings back to his desk. 'That'll be all, Samantha.'

I'M IN A DAZE OF DISBELIEF FOR THE REST OF THAT afternoon.

A warning?

How fair is that?

Okay, maybe I shouldn't have snapped at Mr Davidson, but really... I've been here five years, never had a single complaint (until now), and Callum didn't even ask for my side of the story. He'd made his mind up already.

I'm sick of this company's hypocrisy. They're all "patient first" and "people orientated" according to flashy adverts on billboards and buses, and the barrages of internal memos clogging our in-boxes. In reality, all anybody like Callum cares about is their next step up the management ladder. Giving *me* a warning gives *him* documented evidence of "strong, decisive leadership style".

He couldn't care less about Mr Davidson.

Daisy keeps trying to get me on my own. She'll be desperate to know what happened with Callum, but I'm not ready to talk about it. So I avoid her.

Most nights, we walk to the bus stop together—but I already told her about Jake dumping the shopping on me. So it won't be a surprise when she comes out of the loo to find me gone.   After how today's gone, it's inevitable Aldi's heaving. Every time I reach for something, somebody's blocking me. Take this idiot—does he really expect to uncover the meaning of life in that steak pie, or is he simply stricken with sudden, total paralysis?

The tills, of course, are mobbed. (The ones that are actually open.) I've been queueing for nearly ten minutes when a tannoy announces: '*We are now opening till number 7.*'

My head oscillates faster than a Wimbledon spectator's while I try to work out which way "Till Number 7" is. Probably the same direction everyone's rushing... I hurl my trolley into the scrum—and end up in an even longer queue.

When I step off the bus thirty minutes later, I'm totally frazzled.

For a moment, I stand stock-still. Two oversized shopping bags do their best to drag my shoulders from their sockets as I gaze down a canyon of four-storey tenements and start listing the reasons this doesn't feel like home. After a while, I'm forced to abandon the effort—before I get mistaken for a homeless person.

Just before the outside door to my building, I nearly step in a pet's ablutions—aptly deposited under a wall-mounted sign detailing the penalties for not picking up after your dog.

As a rule, on stairs, I make liberal use of handrails. After six years, and wearing trousers, I don't think anybody would twig my disability from

16

watching me walk on the flat. Stairs are different—
they're still tricky. With both hands otherwise
occupied, getting up to my first-floor flat takes
forever.

By the top step, Jake has appeared in my
mind's eye. Boiling oil also features prominently,
along with various blunt instruments. For a while,
I've been wondering more and more about his
contribution to our domestic situation—or lack of it.

I've just done the shopping. (Paying by credit
card, because I gave Jake my cash on the
understanding *he* was going to Aldi.)

Despite being home all day, every day, Jake
still hasn't figured out how the hoover or washing
machine works, or where things like irons plug in.
Which is ironic, considering my slobby boyfriend
generates ninety percent of the raw product for all
those.

*Far from helping with household chores, he's
the biggest one*

My front door opens onto a long hallway
ending at the kitchen and, stepping inside, I'm
greeted by raucous cheers. They get louder as I near
the living room. At the open doorway, I stop dead—
my jaw plunges into freefall when I see Jake,
sprawled out on the sofa and watching football with
a can of beer in his hand. He barely looks 'round,
despite the crash of two shopping bags hitting the
floor.

Lucky I didn't buy any eggs
'Hey, doll. All good?'

17

'I thought you were busy helping Andy with...
stuff?'

'That was ages ago...'

Simultaneous with the verbal brakes slamming on, his eyes cross so far they're looking at each other. Jake's obviously realised his excuse for not doing the shopping just fell apart.

'Jake, I've had a rotten day, after which I could have done without a bout of jungle warfare in Aldi. But don't worry, I totally understand—if *you'd* gone shopping, it might have meant missing the kickoff.'

Here it comes—his "little boy lost" look. From nowhere, Daisy's voice screams inside my head.

"*He's taking you for a mug*"

Then I hear the blare of theme music. "*Match of the Day*". Not from the telly, though—it's Jake's phone, sitting on a sideboard by the door. I didn't intend reading his message, but when a screen full of words draws your eye, you can't *help* but scan them.

Had SUCH a gooood time today R X

I snatch the phone and read it properly. Who the hell is "*R*"?

Jake hasn't got many friends. There's Andy (also unemployed). A bunch of other losers from the pub, but none of their names start with "R"—Jake doesn't speak to his family, and obviously has no work acquaintances.

Nope, I can't think of anybody with the initial "R".

18

'Who's "R"?'

His head snaps 'round. 'Who?'

'Whoever it was you had "SUCH a gooood time" with today.' Tapping the screen, I add: 'With a "kiss" at the end.'

'Oh, that's—em—Richard. Why're you looking at my phone, Sam?'

'You've never mentioned a "Richard", and this message doesn't feel like "men-speak". Do all your mates send you "kisses"?'

He spreads his arms. 'It's meant to be funny.'

It's "funny", all right. Something EXTREMELY funny about this. The obvious conclusion is one that's never entered my head until now. (Does that say more about me than it does him?)

'Are you playing away, Jake?'

'No.'

That was a pretty emphatic denial, preceded by not a shred of hesitation. He sits up straight, the picture of indignation, and locks his gaze with mine.

Also, his eyelids twitch—which makes me think he's lying.

'Sam, I know you find your work stressful, but taking it out on me isn't fair.'

Now you're cruisin'...

'Jake, it's bad enough you're too lazy to get a job—compounded by the fact I'm always short of cash because you spend it all—but then to discover...'

My voice falters, but I make myself finish. 'This is unbelievable. This is plain... insulting.'

19

'Calm down, Sam.'

In one illuminating instant, everything lights up in a technicoloured blaze. I'm almost glad I've caught him out because, truth be told, I want the excuse. I've been building up to this for a while without even realising it.

Holding his eye, refusing to flinch, I snap: 'Get your things, and get out.'

'Now, wait a minute...'

He wheedles, he pleads, he's nearly convincing as he explains how innocent the phone message is. I don't care any more—I just want him gone.

'But where will I go?'

'Not my problem.'

The message penetrates. He disappears, and I hear rummaging from the bedroom. Five minutes later, he emerges with a couple of carrier bags (travels light, does our Jake) and slams the front door behind him.

That's when I remember I didn't get his key.

So I dash after him, flying down the stairs in his wake (as much as a woman with a below-the-knee prosthetic can "fly") but Jake must have gone like a fireman down a pole because I don't even glimpse him. I step onto the street and peer both ways, but it's empty.

After storming back upstairs (at least I'm able to use the banister this time) my first thought is to get Daisy on the phone. I need a curry, lots of wine, and a friend.

And I need them now.

D<small>AISY LEANS PAST AND GRABS THE BOTTLE OF</small>
Beaujolais. Somehow, it's ended up nestled between
two cushions at my end of the sofa. Her breath
almost fries me. 'Daisy, how can you eat curry that
hot?'

'That korma crap you had isn't curry.' (She's
slurring—are we on the second bottle already?)
'Anyway, doesn't it feel better having "Jake on the
take" out of your life? You should have booted him
weeks ago.'

I flap a hand and wonder when my fingers got
so heavy. 'You don't just switch off a relationship. I
am glad Jake's gone, but I still miss him... I think?
Maybe I'm worried about being single again...'

'Single's fun,' Daisy burbles. 'I love being
single—oh boy, did you ever do the right thing when
you turned Jake down last week.'

Cringing inside, I nod my agreement. Was it
only a week ago I came home to a pile of Chinese
takeaway cartons, a bottle of cheap plonk, and Jake's
inept marriage proposal?

"It makes sense" seemed to be the thrust of his
argument. Other women get wooed with quotes from
Byron, or Shelley—I got Del Boy. It's been preying
on me since. Talk about out of synch? I'm ready to
chuck him, and he's planning wedding bells?

Daisy does her mind-reading trick and smashes into my muse. As usual, her advice is concise. 'Stop thinking about Jake.'

She watches me until I nod. 'Now, what're you going to do about Callum and his stupid warning?'

'Not much I can do.'

'He was bang out of order—you need to see a lawyer. I bet you could sue Cosmo-Spex for unfair something or other.'

I slump back on the sofa. 'Lawyers cost money, Dais'—and if I know Callum, he'll have checked with H.R. first. No, I'll have to grin and bear it—as usual.'

'By the way, old man Davidson was brazen enough to come in again, but you were on your break—so I adjusted his glasses for him.'

I reach down to grab the bottle she just deposited at her feet, and top up my own glass while replaying that last in my head. 'Daisy, you don't know how to adjust glasses.'

'That's true.'

Her grin is sheer evil, making me giggle. 'You shouldn't have done that—he'll complain about you, next.'

She shrugs. 'If he thought his ear was sore before... listen, I've had a new idea. What if you sell this dump and get a loan, then buy something bigger and turn it into a guest house? I can see us with a chain of five-star hotels, and...'

I can't help myself—I screech with laughter. *The worrying thing is, she's serious*

'Daisy, put a sock in it. My life needs a chance to settle before I plunge it back into turmoil.'

'We could, though. What about that aunt of yours—Aunt Claire? She owns a hotel. Maybe she could give us a masterclass.'

Sadness stabs me in the chest. Aunt Claire—I feel guilty for not mentioning this sooner, but it's not like Daisy even met her. 'Aunt Claire passed away while you were on holiday in Minorca.'

'What?'

One hand flies to her mouth, wine glass tipping precariously in the other. 'Oh, Sam. I'm so sorry. Why didn't you tell me?'

I press my lips together. 'I didn't *not* tell you—you weren't here. Yesterday was the first time I'd seen you since... it just never came up. Until now.'

She puts her glass down and wraps my hand in both hers. 'Was it expected?'

'That's the weird thing. It was very *un*expected—when I last saw Aunt Claire she was full of vim, even planning a foreign holiday for the off-season. When I jokingly asked who she was going with, I got told to "mind your own business".'

Daisy's eyes widen. 'You think she'd found a boyfriend?'

'Oh, Aunt Claire's had plenty of boyfriends, and getting older wasn't slowing her down any. Unfortunately, she was better at running a hotel than picking men, which is why they all came with sell-by dates. Never seemed to put her off, though.'

'Did you find out...?'

23

'No, there were no grieving suitors at the funeral, so I assume it fizzled out before...' I feel tears well, and Daisy's grip tightens.

'You were close, weren't you?'

I nod. 'She used to have me for a week every summer when I was a kid—that's apart from all the family visits. I loved going to her hotel. It's an old country house with huge, sprawling grounds—my favourite game was pretending to be an explorer, mapping out a lost continent on spiral notebooks. But since I grew up—' Daisy gets a well-deserved poke in the ribs for that '—we were lucky to get together once a year. Last time was at Easter—and you know what happened then.'

Daisy's expression darkens. 'You met *him.*'

That was why I didn't push for more details of Aunt Claire's latest romance. My own hormones were distracting me. For a moment, my feelings about Jake soften. 'Jake was really upset by the news. He said she'd been like a second mother to him.'

Daisy's got *that* look. 'Just out of interest—what did your Aunt Claire say when she found out about you and Jake?'

Something akin to guilt bites me. 'She never knew about us. When we got together in Cairncroft, Jake was worried she wouldn't approve—so we kept it under the radar. Then, after he turned up in Edinburgh... well, I didn't want to tell her over the phone.'

24

Back at Easter, Jake was a live-in handyman at Aunt Claire's hotel. It sounds corny, but when our eyes met...

Working outside had bronzed his skin. He had muscles rippling under his T-shirt (instead of the saggy paunch that sprouted after he discovered my sofa). His sense of humour was sharp, and feisty, and he made me feel... special.

Somehow, within a few weeks of our meeting, he'd moved to Edinburgh—and into my flat. He even got a new job in the Asda warehouse, not that it lasted long...

I don't want to think about Jake—I ABSOLUTELY am not missing him

Daisy lets go my hand to retrieve her wine glass. 'So, what did she die of?'

'The GP thinks a heart attack.'

'Thinks? Didn't they do a post-mortem?'

'Daisy, I know you never miss an episode of CSI, but we're talking rural Aberdeenshire here—not Las Vegas. There were no suspicious circumstances, so the procurator fiscal wasn't involved.'

'Did she leave you anything?'

Should have seen that coming—I love Daisy, but she'd cross the M1 to pick up a penny. 'I don't know—it isn't something I've thought about.'

Her brow furrows. 'What other family does she have, besides you?'

'Stop it, will you?'

Actually, she's right. Now Daisy's raised the question, I'm wondering why *I* haven't. Claire was my dad's big sister, but dad isn't here any longer, and I can't bring to mind any other living relatives—*are* there any?

When I tell Daisy, her eyes light up. 'Maybe she's left you her hotel?'

'Don't be ridiculous.'

'Well, who else *could* she have left it to?'

I take a sizeable glug of wine, thinking furiously.

But I don't have an answer to that...

3

I've got a head like wet spaghetti, thanks to finishing that last bottle of wine—but it isn't why my cornflakes are turning to mush beside a mug of cold tea.

A fancy-headed letter is lying open in front of me on the kitchen table—I'm reading it for the third time.

It's from Aunt Claire's solicitors.

Our discussion last night replays in my head. The postman delivered this life-changing epistle ten minutes ago and, despite a lot of legal-speak, I think it's saying Aunt Claire *has* left her hotel to me.

I don't believe it.

Well, I have to believe it, because it's there in black and white, but it hasn't sunk in. Aunt Claire's hotel isn't some little B&B—it has fifteen guest rooms and stands on acres of land. The property alone must be worth a fortune.

I'm rich

My sluggish mind wonders why I never saw this coming. I'm Aunt Claire's only close relative, so of course her hotel would come to me. Maybe because I haven't seen so much of her in recent years, I just assumed...

My finger feels more like a sausage as I tap the solicitor's number into my phone. It's only eight o'clock, so there's probably no one there yet...

'Dougall and MacLachlan. How can I help you?'

I almost drop the phone. 'Oh, hello. Yes—em, this is Samantha Chessington. I got a letter from you this morning—my late aunt was Claire Chessington.'

'Miss Chessington. Good of you to respond so promptly.'

The voice is cheerier than it should be at this hour. Quite proper, too, despite a distinctive Aberdeen twang. He takes an audible slurp of something. (Maybe I should ask what—it seems to work.) 'I'm Robert MacLachlan. Unfortunately, we missed one another at the funeral...'

Aunt Claire appointed her solicitors as executors, and they organised the funeral on her behalf—in strict accordance with her instructions. I smile inside, remembering shocked faces as Rod Stewart demanded to know whether "ya think I'm sexy" and Abba paid exuberant tributes to an unnamed "dancing queen". Aunt Claire was a child of the seventies who never really grew up.

'... now, when would it be convenient for you to come and see us?'

The letter asked me to make an appointment so my inheritance can be "explained in more detail". Both Mr MacLachlan's office and the hotel are in Cairncroft, a village about thirty miles west of Aberdeen. If I hire a car (I'm still comfortable driving automatics) it's a six hour round trip. My next day off is Friday, only a couple of days away...

'I don't suppose you could fit me in this afternoon?'

What? Did I say that? What about work?

'That would be splendid, Miss Chessington. Would two o'clock suit?'

'Perfect.'

I'm hearing my words as though they're coming from someone else. 'So, your office at two?'

'You'll find us on Main Street—above the tearoom. Look forward to meeting you, Miss Chessington.'

My expensive iPhone clatters to the table while I struggle to catch up with whoever made those arrangements. Callum is NOT going to be amused when I call in sick today.

A giddy wave of euphoria engulfs me.

Who cares?

I own a big hotel—so I'm able to quit my job at Cosmo-Spex. Callum can take "*communication with customers*" and stuff it where the sun don't shine.

Shuddering at the unfortunate imagery that evoked, I remember Daisy. I can't wait to tell her about this. *Daisy* won't have a hangover this morning. She never does—she's annoying that way.

In fact, I'll call her right now. She was talking about us buying a guesthouse last night—it seems like forever we've been plotting to start a business and get out of Cosmo-Spex. I don't want to do this on my own—Daisy HAS to come with me. Not just to the solicitor—I'm going to ask her to be part of my new life. We'll run the hotel together.

For a moment, I feel guilty, realising this newfound ebullience stems from Aunt Claire's untimely demise. Then the same reasoning I agonised through after my parents' deaths kicks in. Aunt Claire would want me to be happy with her legacy.

Picking up my phone, I scroll through the contacts to Daisy. Waiting for her to answer, I imagine Callum's reaction when he gets two "no show" calls in a row.

He'll be apoplectic.

I THINK DAISY'S MORE EXCITED THAN I AM.

'Fifteen rooms? You'll be raking it in. So will I, of course.' She punches at the windscreen, her hand stopping millimetres before impact.

I've already told Daisy I'll pay her a big whack more than she gets at Cosmo-Spex—along with a share of the profits—for being my "personal assistant". I'm excited beyond belief, especially since she accepted my offer. This is a dream come true, but knowing nothing about running a hotel I'll need all the help I can get.

'So, *give*—is it a stainless steel and glass sort of place? Or more oak panels and tapestries?'

Daisy seems to think we're going to a flagship Marriott. 'It might want some modernising. At

Easter, I got the impression Aunt Claire had let things slip—and according to Jake, trying to keep up with maintenance was running him ragged. Mind you, Jake thinks that about emptying the dishwasher...'

My eyes flick to the rear mirror, but it's still empty. Cairncroft is *way* out in the wilds of Aberdeenshire.

Daisy echoes my next thought. 'Where does the hotel get its custom?'

'Good point—Cairncroft isn't exactly Blackpool. I expect there'll be regular local trade in the bar, but beyond that...'

'Corporate retreats, maybe?' Daisy says, as though she knows what she's talking about.

Then her expression changes. 'Hey, you don't think Cosmo-Spex is one of their customers, for those managerial shindigs Callum's always away at?'

The thought makes me shudder. 'I hope not. How was he, by the way—Callum—when you rang in sick?'

'Like he was about to come through the phone at me.'

She puts on a pompous "Callum-voice". 'HOW CAN I RUN THIS PRACTICE EFFICIENTLY WITH NO STAFF?'

'Yeah, I got the same "understanding attitude" when *I* phoned him.'

'D'you think he thought it was because of yesterday?'

31

'Oh, yes. He came right out and asked if I was "sulking", but I told him I was too ill to talk any more and hung up.'

'Was that wise—hanging up on him? I mean, you've only spoken to this MacLachlan guy on the phone. What if it's some kind of mistake?'

'How could it be? Look, we're almost there.' This is the first time Daisy's visited Cairncroft—I don't think she's been out of Edinburgh more than a handful of times. (Not counting foreign holidays with her fellow-party-animal flatmates.) Glancing sideways, I see she's agog—and find myself trying to imagine what it must be like seeing the stone-built cottages, against a backdrop of field and forestland, through fresh eyes. From the little she's revealed about her childhood, I don't think trips to the countryside—or *anywhere* "child-friendly"—featured heavily on the agenda.

Closer to the centre we pass a modest "new-build" development—*that's wasn't here last time*—then I'm parking on Main Street, outside the solicitor's office. 'This is Cairncroft's answer to Princes Street,' I announce, watching Daisy peer through the Fiesta's windows at a cluster of small shops—including a butcher, a baker, the Co-op (of course), and a quaint little tearoom. Mr MacLachlan's premises are over "The Cuppa Tea", and Daisy's looking longingly at cakes displayed in their window. I check my watch. 'We haven't time—it's almost two. Those roadworks at Perth put us behind.'

She agrees reluctantly, and we enter through a door beside the tearoom and climb a bare-stone staircase. Without making a show of it, Daisy lets me use the banister side.

At the top, we go through a glass door into Mr MacLachlan's long, rectangular waiting area. Two battered but comfy-looking armchairs flank a stripped pine table covered with old golf magazines.

'Busy place,' Daisy mutters, and I elbow her as a petite, grey-haired lady in a tweed suit appears from nowhere. There must be some sort of silent buzzer on the door.

'You'll be Miss Chessington,' she coos, then looks confused as she realises there's two of us.

'That's me. This is my friend, Daisy.'

'I'm Miss Dobie, Mr MacLachlan's secretary. He's all ready for you—just through here.'

The door she ushers us through is almost invisible, having been painted an identical drab brown to the walls. Mr MacLachlan's office is even bigger than his waiting area, but most of the space is taken up by a massive partners' desk. From piles of cardboard wallets strewn on top, I deduce two things.

One—they haven't yet heard of computers in Cairncroft.

Two—the local solicitor isn't exactly starved for business. (Which I find reassuring after Daisy's question earlier—let's hope the hotel is just as busy.)

'Miss Chessington.' Mr MacLachlan pulls himself out of a captain's chair (finished to match the desk) and skirts his cluttered worksurface with practiced ease, ash-coloured eyes locked on mine, hand outstretched. His grip is firm without mashing my fingers, and I realise he's older than I surmised from his voice on the phone. Much older, in fact.

His round, cheery face and twinkling smile chase away any apprehension. In his brown suit (covered in creases) and striped tie, he reminds me of a kindly schoolteacher.

When his hand releases mine and offers itself to Daisy, all his attention refocuses on her. 'And you are...?'

Daisy identifies herself, and I wonder—how did he know *I* was *me*? Miss Dobie must have given him a signal—jerking my head around I discover she's gone. I didn't even hear the door close. Unlikely as it sounds, I could believe that woman's had ninja training. Mr M (Daisy's rechristened him, as is her wont, and a raft of chuckles imply he's pleased with his new moniker) returns to the business side of his desk and motions us into visitor chairs opposite. I remember him now from the funeral.

'First, my condolences. I knew your aunt for a great many years—she was a fine, fine woman.'

'Thank you. We used to be close, but in recent years it's been harder finding time to visit.'

'Forgive me but, as I say, Claire and I go way back—was there something she hadn't told me? About her health, I mean. I met her on the street just a day before… and she looked her usual hale and hearty self.'

'Not that I know of, but I haven't seen her since Easter. She didn't mention anything on the phone, either—and we spoke, oh, two or three weeks before she…'

Funny, this taboo on completing a sentence acknowledging someone's death—do we worry saying the word makes it real? Do we think, when we avoid naming the fact, it somehow raises the possibility of a misunderstanding?

He nods ponderously, eyelids at half-mast. 'I'm sure Claire would have confided in you if she had medical worries. She told me all about her niece, the optician in Edinburgh. I know she was worried your career choice hadn't lived up to expectations, and even contemplated offering you an alternative position at the hotel.'

Hand over mouth, I wait for that to sink in. 'I had no idea. She never said anything.'

Mr M swivels to gaze through a window behind and his voice floats back—musing, now. 'Things being what they were, I imagine she didn't want to risk pulling you out of a secure job.'

'What things?'

He rotates again, slowly, completing a 360 degree spin. 'The hotel's profits have fallen in recent years. Claire was getting older, the world more competitive—frankly, the Cairncroft Hotel is no longer a going concern.'

A dead weight plummets in my stomach. I sense movement from Daisy, then her hand on mine. 'I... we... planned to take over running the hotel.'

'Ah.'

His eyes bore into me, like he's searching for something. Then he smiles. 'Well, maybe you still can. First, though, there's the outstanding debt to be settled—that's around eighty thousand pounds. Next, you'd need to work out how to bring the hotel back into profit—which will commit you to more expense. Looking over the last few years' accounts, I can't see finance being readily available.'

Daisy, of course, is undeterred. 'Surely Sam could get a mortgage on the property?'

Mr M's gaze flickers to Daisy, and his eyes soften. 'There's more to mortgages than collateral,' he says, sounding sad. 'At the very least, regular interest payments are required, and any lender would require assurance of Samantha's ability to pay those. The hotel's accounts would not provide that assurance.'

My voice shakes. 'What's the alternative— could I sell?'

Those grey eyes turn back on me—is that disappointment I see there? 'You could, but no one would want it as a going concern—because, frankly, it isn't. As a property for redevelopment, I would think—after repaying the outstanding debt—it should bring somewhere in the region of half a million pounds.'

Half a million... oh, wow. I AM rich

I *could* sell my flat. That would generate enough capital to pay off our debt and leave a healthy chunk for putting the hotel on its feet. But I'm scared—I've no experience of business, and batting these colossal figures around feels surreal. A wave of dizziness engulfs me. 'This is so much to take in, Mr MacLachlan. I need to think about it.'

'Of course. In any case, nothing can be decided without approval of the co-owner.'

'Co-owner?'

'I'm so sorry. We hadn't got to the specific terms of your aunt's will, had we? Claire left seventy-five percent of the hotel to you—and twenty-five percent to someone else.'

4

'So who's Logan Brown?'
We're back in the car, still reeling from Mr.
M's bombshells. He said Miss Dobie would
ring ahead and get us cleared for a look around the
hotel, but first we need to make sense of all this. 'I've
never met Logan properly. Somebody pointed him
out at the funeral and mentioned he found—the
body—so obviously I wanted to talk to him, but he
avoided us. I also got the impression Jake doesn't
like him, although he wouldn't say why.'
'If Jake doesn't like him, that's all the
recommendation I need.'
I choose to ignore that. 'Aunt Claire told me a
bit about him at Easter—including the fact she was
training him up to be her under-manager. Seems he
came straight from school to work in the hotel. Poor
guy lost his mother a few years back—after that, he
lived with his stepfather and sister until a year ago,
then the stepfather died when their house went on
fire.'
Daisy goggles before having the decency to
look ashamed. 'Aw. Rough.'
'Luckily, Logan and his sister weren't there
when the fire started, but it left them orphaned and
homeless. That's when Aunt Claire stepped in. She
upgraded Logan's job to live-in and put him on the
management track—said it was all getting too much

for her, and she believed he had the makings of a manager...'

Did she give Logan the job she was thinking of offering me?

'... and she gave the sister a live-in position, too. Trudy, her name was—she didn't stay long, though. Moved on to Aberdeen.'

'But why leave him a share in the hotel? He's not even a relative.'

I shrug, wondering the same thing. 'You know, as this gets more complicated, the prospect of selling up sounds better and better. Seventy-five percent of half a mill is enough to give us the pick of just about any business we fancy.'

Daisy's face turns impish. 'You could start your own optician with that sort of money.'

She laughs as I hold up crossed arms, like they do in vampire movies. 'Anything but that. No, seriously—why give ourselves the grief of trying to rescue a dying duck when we could buy—I don't know—what about an office cleaning franchise?'

Her face goes from imp to grump. 'Bit boring—but I take your point. Let's look at the hotel first, then decide.' She swivels from side to side, eyes shining... 'I *do* like this place. There's something very peaceful about it.'

'It's gorgeous.' Is that passion in my voice? Or was I just making myself heard over the ignition catching? 'All those childhood holidays at the hotel left me with tons of wonderful memories. Out here, the pace of life is SO relaxed compared to

Edinburgh. The people are different, too—they're more real, somehow.

Daisy sighs, watching the view change as we turn onto a single-track road studded with passing places and, at irregular intervals, ancient but quaint cottages. 'Cairncroft sounds like the best of both worlds. Country living, but with Aberdeen less than an hour away.'

She sits up suddenly. 'Sam, if you decide to keep the hotel—don't worry about wages for me. I'll be happy with bed and board, and some pocket money, until we get the place up and running.' Then she grins. 'Although, after we turn it into a cash factory, I might want to renegotiate.'

I'm so excited about the sudden metamorphosis my life has taken, and just as glad not to be going into this alone. Another thought sneaks into my head, one that makes me cringe. If Mr M's letter had come a few days earlier, it would be Jake sitting where Daisy is. (Daisy would still be in the back seat, of course.)

And yet—as I think it through further—Jake's predictable drooling reaction to the news of my inheritance would surely have shaken me into seeing the real him. Suddenly, I feel very foolish—why didn't I recognise sooner what he's really like?

'It's massive.'

Daisy's eyes are saucering at the rectangular, three-storey stone building coming into view. Not quite Downton Abbey, but definitely a distant relative.

'Sam, watch out.'

A quick flick of the wheel gets us past a huge pothole with our axle still intact—the Sea of Tranquillity probably has a smoother surface than this. Biting down on a surge of disappointment, I try to remember. Was the road this bad at Easter? Maybe one of Jake's handyman jobs was keeping these potholes filled with sand, or gravel, or *something* to make them less like an IED-scarred track in Afghanistan—and as far as I know, after he left Aunt Claire didn't replace him.

Whatever—it's *not* a good first impression for potential guests.

There are parking bays laid out in front, although the white lines are so faded it's hard to see them. Having my choice, I park in a space adjoining the main entrance. Daisy digs at my shoulder, and I follow her gaze to a young man in a suit watching us. 'Is that Logan Brown?'

I take a deep breath, let it out slowly. Then I release my seat belt. 'I think so.'

Throwing open the door I heave myself out, and my co-inheritor walks towards us.

'M... MISS CHESSINGTON?'

I only caught glimpses of Logan Brown at the funeral, so didn't know what to expect—but it wasn't

41

this. Almost makes me wonder if Aunt Claire was going senile when she wrote her will.

At least my threatened panic attack subsides as it becomes apparent Logan isn't the smooth-talking Callum-clone I feared. He *looks* the part in his grey-wool suit, complete with waistcoat. But from there—it all goes downhill.

Logan's gait suggests he thinks his legs are shorter than they are, while those arms could generate power on a wind farm. Even when he comes to a halt, bits of him keep moving.

The only sluggish element is his mouth. He reminds me of a goldfish, with ponderous syllables taking the place of air bubbles.

THIS is Claire's management protégé?

I nod, not sure how to answer. Daisy bounces up beside me and squints at Logan's name badge—she's never stuck for words. 'Hi, I'm Daisy. So you're Logan? How's tricks? We've been wondering about you.'

A look of panic crosses Logan's face, but Daisy thwarts his backward retreat mid-step when she seizes his hand and pumps it. 'H... hello. N... nice to meet you.'

Daisy gives him his hand back and he offers it to me. 'A... and you, Miss Chessington. Sh... shall I show you around?'

'That'd be great,' Daisy answers for me. Logan turns abruptly and moonwalks towards the entrance.

Daisy's giving me the eye but I ignore her and chase after Logan, catching up with him on the other side of a door that looks like it came secondhand from Barlinnie.

Which is when my heart sinks faster than the Titanic...

Trying not to jump to conclusions, I take a second look.

At a reception desk running along the wall on one side, opposite an archway which I remember leads to the residents lounge, restaurant, and public bar; and a lift shaft closing off the far-right corner.

The entire area's carpeted, and features oak-panelled walls.

Sounds okay? Except—that carpet looks like it just arrived special-delivery from a car boot sale. The panelling's lost its varnish, along with some of its panels—there's grimy brickwork keeking defiantly through the gaps. As for the lighting, *it's* reminiscent of Jonathan Harker's first visit to Castle Dracula— and the air has a chemical smell (by the way).

Daisy gawks at me. 'You were here three months ago—you never said it looked like this.'

It didn't

'Hm... it was always old-fashioned, but I don't...'

Logan stops chewing the inside of his cheek for a moment. 'We had a problem with woodworm down here. Fixed now, but it was a big job and we were just starting the cleanup when... em, when

43

Claire... you know? Since then, everything's ground to a halt.'

Daisy swivels to Logan, eyes wide, and in an accusing tone says: 'You've stopped stuttering.'

It's not the first time I've admired her subtlety Logan glares back, then his face breaks into a huge smile. Suddenly, he looks normal—good, even. 'I... I only stutter when I'm nervous—usually when I meet new people. As I get to know them, it settles down.'

Daisy shoots me a glance full of disbelief. 'And you work in a hotel—front-of-house?'

Logan coughs. 'Yes, when you put it like that... any... anyway, it's not nearly so bad as it was. Come on, I'll give you the grand tour.'

I feel a nudge, and Daisy whispers: 'How well does he need to know us before the funny walk stops?'

We follow Logan through the residents lounge. He shows us the public bar and restaurant, then backtracks through reception. As we finish our ground floor tour in the snooker room (a relic of grander times?) his "funny walk" disappears. Poor beggar must have been even more terrified than I was.

Daisy's features freeze a little more at every doorway. I'm familiar with it all, but she's seeing everything for the first time. I have to admit, though—I didn't remember *quite* this degree of shabbiness. Of course, I was looking through different eyes before.

44

It needs redecorating and re-carpeting throughout—at a bare minimum—and from the look of those switches and sockets, possibly rewiring as well. Recalling what Logan said about woodworm in reception, I wonder if they checked the whole building? Could there be dry rot behind that flock wallpaper? What state's the roof in...?

On the second floor, I'm pleasantly surprised— the guest rooms have been (recently) redecorated in a bright, rag-roll effect and re-carpeted with a mass-produced nylon material which, while "crunchy" underfoot, is nonetheless quite plush—in an airport sort of way. A few more homely touches wouldn't go amiss but, on the whole—not bad.

By unspoken mutual consent, we return to reception via a naked stone stairway rather than risk another dice with death in the creaky, shaky old lift. I don't want to think how much *it* would cost to replace.

Daisy discreetly takes my arm and supports me on the uneven steps. I notice Logan glance over, but he says nothing. Did Aunt Claire tell him about my leg?

Staff quarters are on the third floor, I remember—the space is split half-and-half between a corridor of tiny bedrooms and Aunt Claire's flat. I wonder why Logan didn't take us up there?

Probably because he'd feel intrusive going into Aunt Claire's flat

The kitchen's our final stop, where we meet Chef Maggie. I can't argue with Daisy's summation of its (lack of) equipment. 'This is primitive—there's not even a dishwasher.'

Maggie tuts. 'Now dear, we have all the basics.'

'But do any of them work?'

'Aye, everything works fine, and has done for the last ten years—that's how long I've been here.'

Maggie's about fifty, sharp faced with a sharper nose—she's wearing a dark smock and her hair is a silver starburst, all of which imparts a "witchy" look. She insists on reciting her culinary repertoire and, to my relief, does it without cackling. 'Steak and ale pie, battered haddock, chicken Maryland with all the trimmings...'

Daisy doesn't have to say it out loud—we're both thinking the same thing.

None of that lot's going to get us a Michelin star

It turns out Maggie's also Logan's aunt—which makes me wonder how much she influenced Aunt Claire when Logan found himself homeless. Quite natural if Maggie wanted to help her nephew, of course, though I'm still puzzled about my aunt elevating Logan to management level.

Yet, as I get more used to him, I sense a quiet intelligence under that gormless exterior. His stutter's all but vanished, and the "Thunderbirds puppet" walk has given way to "Kermit on a good day".

Maggie shows us a cupboard filled with produce from the hotel's own market garden, and Daisy pounces on a collection of little glass vials containing different coloured powders, set on a shelf by themselves. She holds one up to the light, squinting at tiny granules inside.

'Ah, them's my remedies.'

'M... Maggie's a naturopath as well as a chef,' Logan explains. 'She harvests all sorts of natural medicines from wild plants in the grounds—Claire swore that was why she hadn't needed a doctor for years...' He freezes, catching up with his words, and silence ensues until Maggie closes the cupboard and offers us tea and biscuits.

It's nice of her, but I'm conscious of the time. Logan and I will need a private chat before we leave. 'No thanks, Maggie.'

Logan's still studying his feet, and I'm replaying Mr M's observations in my mind. 'Did Aunt Claire say anything to you about being unwell, Logan? I'm trying to get my head around her passing so suddenly.'

'N... no. Quite the opposite. She was full of energy right up to the end.'

That's pretty much what Mr M said. Thinking back to the funeral, I remember it's what *everyone* said—they all seemed shocked by the abruptness of Aunt Claire's demise. 'It was you who found her, wasn't it? What happened, exactly?'

He obviously cared for Aunt Claire—sadness emanates from his words. 'The day before, she was right as rain. That night, she asked me up to her flat for a chat. We were looking at lots of ideas to bring in new business—anyway, I left around eleven.'

When she didn't appear next morning...' he looks down, clears his throat '... I went to check on her. Sh... she'd died in her sleep.'

'So she was fine when you left her the night before?'

'Absolutely—more than fine. She was excited, raring to get started on what we were calling "operation phoenix". I've never seen her look more alive...'

His voice trails off, and I give him a moment. Then—'Mr MacLachlan said the GP suspected a heart attack.'

Logan snorts. 'The GP just wanted to put a label on it. He didn't have a clue—never does. Anything worse than a cold he refers to the proper doctors in Aberdeen.'

'Does it matter?' Maggie puts in, quietly. 'The poor woman's gone now. How would it help knowing the details of what took her?'

She's looking at me, hard—probably suggesting I stop upsetting her nephew. Maybe she has a point, but I'm becoming curious about the circumstances surrounding Aunt Claire's death. Something just doesn't gel.

I got the feeling Mr M was of similar mind.

Maggie, though, seems determined to steer us onto safer ground. 'Are you sure you wouldn't like some tea? I've got fresh-baked scones.'

'Actually, I could murder a *proper* drink,' Daisy announces, looking hopefully at Logan and making Maggie tut.

Logan's trying hard to suppress a grin. 'Shall I show you the bar again?'

Daisy loops her arm through his. 'Lead on, Macduff.' A sufficient proportion of the residents lounge is partitioned off for alcoholic consumption to suggest local trade contributes significantly to turnover. Good thing this is the only drinking hole in Cairncroft because, given an alternative, I couldn't see anyone patronising this dank cavern.

There's nobody serving—it's probably not even open at this time of day—so Logan does the honours. Daisy nods encouragement as he assembles her gin and tonic with a practised air.

I can only have orange juice since I'm driving, and Logan's either teetotal or conscious of being on duty because he pours himself a ginger beer. After hiking myself onto a rickety wooden stool beside Daisy, I raise my glass to Logan. (He seems content to remain on his side of the bar.) 'Cheers, partner.'

His face flushes crimson. 'You know about that? T... to be honest, I'm overwhelmed. I didn't expect Claire to leave me anything, far less a share of the hotel.'

From being terrified of meeting him, I'm positively warming to this man. 'She must have been very fond of you. What do you think we should do, Logan? Keep the place—or sell up?'

Logan's head snaps up and ginger beer sprinkles over the mahogany surface between us. 'Sell the hotel? Is that what you're planning?'

49

He grabs a napkin and dabs, first at the spill, then his mouth. 'I never thought of that. I suppose I assumed we would...'

His reaction sends a wave of guilt through me. 'Logan, you *do* know the hotel's in debt? It couldn't carry on without a big injection of cash—did Mr MacLachlan explain all that?'

Logan nods, still fiddling with the napkin. 'He did, but... couldn't we get a loan?'

Shaking my head, I set him straight. 'No chance—not with turnover as it is.'

'Oh.'

A long silence follows. I'm not sure how to break it, but I may have to—should I fake a coughing fit?

Logan beats me to it. 'Y... yes, I understand. W... well, I suppose we'll have to s... sell, then.'

Is that a tear in the corner of his eye?

The parallels between Logan's and my situation are spooky. A tragic accident turned both our lives upside down. Aunt Claire rescued Logan when he found himself homeless after the fire—now she's giving me a second chance, too.

My life is changing for the better, but—if we sell—at the expense of Logan's. The hotel obviously means a *lot* to him.

I'm conscious of Daisy beside me—I should discuss this with her, first. There's so much to think about before we jump in and plough all my capital into a failing business.

Then I look back at Logan, who's developed a sudden fascination with the bottom of his glass. He's also swiping surreptitiously at his eyes. 'You want to hold on to the hotel? Well—me too. I've decided to sell my flat in Edinburgh—that should raise enough capital to get us started. What d'you say we take a shot at putting this place on the map?'

In sharp contrast to his earlier non-existent coordination, Logan rounds the bar in a blur (are ninjas endemic to Cairncroft?) and grabs me in a bearhug. 'That's fantastic,' he breathes in my ear. 'For a moment, I thought...'

He steps back, hands sliding off my shoulders. 'You won't regret this. I've got loads of ideas for drumming up business.'

He blinks, hard. 'A... actually, a lot of them were Claire's...'

Daisy's staring at me. Her eyebrows have vanished under her fringe. I shrug—I shouldn't have done that without consulting her. 'You okay with this, Dais'?'

In answer, she jumps off her stool and pulls us into a three-way hug. 'Brill,' she chirps. 'This is *so* exciting. We're gonna turn this place into the best hotel in Scotland.'

An annoying little voice at the back of my head points out: "You haven't seen the accounts yet."

I take no notice—because I *know* we're doing the right thing.

Aren't we...?

51

5

'**D**o we *have* to work out our notice at Cosmo-Spex?'

Hunched forward, neither accustomed to nor enjoying night driving, I'm tired and grumpy. We got stuck in another queue at Perth, and this is my seventh hour behind the wheel.

Could she not be quiet for these last few minutes?

'Daisy. I have to sell my flat, and Mr M has legal stuff to tie up—we can't do anything until then. And you know what Callum's like—if we don't stick to the terms of our contracts, he'll throw a wobbly. Anyway, an extra month's wages won't go amiss.'

That sounded a little schoolmarm-ish, so (in a silly voice) I add: 'Lean times ahead, lass.'

'Humpff.' She slams back in the seat and folds her arms tight—bet she drove her parents crazy on Xmas eve.

I get it, though. Our last month's wages from Cosmo-Spex are chump change set against the financial mess we're parachuting into, and I'm raring to go every bit as much as Daisy. But I want a *clean* break—which means avoiding any dispute with Callum.

When we arrive at Daisy's flat she explodes from the car, desperate to tell her flatmates everything that's happened. Driving off, I wallow in a sudden, blissful silence.

Then my eyelids turn to lead, and I realise it was only Daisy's chatter keeping me awake.

In a stupendous stroke of luck, I find space to park on my own street. Although they stop charging after six, I'll need to be sharp tomorrow morning before council stormtroopers plaster extortion demands all over the hired Fiesta's windscreen.

I'm so drained I forget about the dog poo, and almost end up putting my face in it after a frantic, mid-step adjustment. The already throbbing juncture where my leg turns to plastic erupts in a screaming fit.

Keys—not that pocket, must be the other—no, back to the first pocket.

Through the outer door, keep hold until it closes—as per "PLEASE DO NOT BANG DOOR" scrawled on a sheet of Amazon packaging taped to the wall—then, onto the final trial, a common staircase which currently looks more like Everest's north face. Although my exhaustion's mainly mental, both legs (especially what remains of the left one) dispute that with every ascending step. It'll be heaven to plonk my bottom on the sofa and unstrap this prosthetic.

Finally—I've reached the landing. Leaning on the banister with one hand while its fellow fumbles for keys, my eyes drift up—and what I see turns me to stone.

My front door is ajar.

NOT ONLY IS THE DOOR AJAR—A SPINDLE OF LIGHT shows along its open edge. I couldn't have left any lights on—it was full daylight when I locked up this morning.

Either somebody's *been* in there, or... somebody *is* in there.

My mind races through options—so fast, I have to go back for a second look. The visceral reaction is to "flee", but a stubborn side of me says "don't run—get reinforcements". I could bang on my neighbour's door, but if there *is* a murderous thug waiting, he'll hear—and who knows what he'd do then? Besides, old Mrs Montague won't be much help unless she brains the burglar with her Zimmer.

I glance down, trying to remember if there're any musclebound warriors in the downstairs flats.

No, no, no—I need the professionals. Holding tight to the banister I start down, backwards so I can watch my door (even though I'm acutely aware a mis-step could result in a broken neck), while my free hand chases a phone determined to evade capture. Trying to separate it from keys and tissues and credit card wallet reminds me I must get a bigger bag.

Back on the pavement, I desperately thumb buttons.

HOW is it possible to misdial 999?

Finally, a capable, confident voice cuts through the aura of panic bleeding from my every pore.

'Emergency. Which service do you require?'

'Police. There's somebody in my flat. Well, there might not be, they could have gone before I got here, but the door's open and there's a light on...'

'Calm down, dear.'

She's obviously unimpressed by the magnitude of my crisis—of course, to her this is just another pair of specs to adjust. 'What's your name, and address?'

I blurt the details so fast I probably sound like Donald Duck on nitrogen. My new friend makes me repeat it all.

Then, the words I've been longing to hear. 'Officers are on their way.'

Sagging with relief, I realise she's still talking. '... where are you now?'

'I'm on the pavement outside.'

'Cross the road and wait in a doorway—I'll stay on the line until—*beeeep.*'

Oh, no. The battery died. My first thought is to add "new phone" underneath "bigger shoulder bag" on my mental shopping list, then a gurgling giggle suggests to some still-functioning part of my brain I'm in shock.

Too bloody right I am

The operator's advice echoes in my head. Translated into "clearspeak", it went: *'Get away*

from there before a drug-crazed skinhead comes piling out the door with an axe in his hand.'
Good advice. I need to take it.
Now.
Except, before I can move, said door crashes open. Suddenly, I'm face to face with—not an *axe-wielding* maniac—no, this is a *knife-wielding* maniac.

He's dressed in cliche black—black top, black jeans—and his haircut's more crewcut than skinhead, but those details barely register because my attention's focused on the knife. It's huge, something a butcher would use, and he's holding it with the handle against his shoulder so it points straight at my chest. He's staring, mouth half-open—he looks more scared than I am?

No, don't think so

Everything stops, as if the projector's stalled during what I wish was just a movie. It's not only my surroundings, *I'm* frozen too—every muscle in my body feels like it belongs to someone else. The "whump-whump" of blood thudding through my veins is all I can hear.

My mouth opens wide even though I don't remember issuing the instruction. I feel my vocal cords brace even as a voice that isn't mine booms: 'GET OFF OF HER.'

The knife-man squints over my shoulder, then spins and sprints away.

I sag with relief, the palm of my hand landing on somebody's window sill. The rubbery thuds of fleeing trainers grow fainter, and a sob bubbles in my throat as their owner turns a corner and disappears.

I feel hands settle on my shoulders—they whirl me around. Suddenly, I'm looking into the face of my heroic rescuer.

Jake???

'Sam... sweetheart, are you alright?'

Sweetheart?

'I DON'T BELIEVE THIS.'

`The way Daisy's regarding me suggests I've grown an extra head. 'You *can't* be giving Jake-on-the-take another chance.'

'Stop calling him that. He may have saved my life.'

'What was he doing there, anyway?'

My head's swimming—I'm lucky if I got two hours sleep. After dicing with death on top of everything else that's happened, I've just spent the morning on auto-pilot..

The usual buzz of conversation here in Maisie's feels disembodied—as though I'm hearing it through headphones. Ever since arriving at work I've been experiencing a most peculiar sensation of looking down from a floating vantage point near the ceiling.

Daisy drums her fingertips on the tabletop while I try to organise an answer. 'He came to pick up the rest of his stuff.'

'At that time of night?'

'He'd just come out of the pub... look, if he hadn't appeared when he did, I might not be here.'

'That's not a good reason to get back with him.'

An exasperated "Arrgh" blows out of my mouth and I dip my head. 'I'm not "back with him"— I didn't feel safe last night and was really grateful when he offered to sleep on the sofa.'

'Beats a shop doorway, I suppose.'

I ignore that. 'Then, this morning, we got talking—he insists the text was just a silly prank from one of his stupid mates, and he says seeing me in danger brought home how much he cares about me...'

I wait, but she lets her expression say it all. '... and, well, he's promised to make an effort, and last night he reminded me of the Jake I met three months ago, so...'

'You do realise he's only after your inheritance?'

'Don't be ridiculous—he doesn't even know about that. I agreed to let him come back on a trial basis, and laid down strict parameters. Until I decide otherwise, he sleeps on the sofa—plus, I've made it clear finding work isn't negotiable. Actually, I was thinking about that... we're going to need a handyman at the hotel, and Jake *is* experienced...'

58

'You have *got* to be kidding? You want to take him with us, to the hotel, and give him a job? Seriously, Sam—would you even consider employing somebody with his work record if you were meeting them for the first time?'

I didn't expect her to understand, but the fact is—if Jake hadn't arrived when he did, I could have been in real trouble.

The police agreed—they said it's not unknown for cornered burglars to lash out. And I can't let Jake find a job here in Edinburgh (I believed him when he promised to try) and then announce I'm off to Aberdeenshire. I'll *have* to tell him about the hotel sooner rather than later.

When I mentioned the potholes to Logan yesterday, he confirmed Aunt Claire didn't look for another handyman after Jake left. Probably because money was so tight...

Letting Jake have his old job back is a way to properly express my gratitude for last night. Plus, it'll give us time to think about where we want to take our relationship—or not. I don't intend rushing into anything, whatever Daisy thinks—if Jake accepts the job (along with his own room in the live-in corridor) it means a much-needed breathing space for both of us.

And if it doesn't work out at least he'll be in a better position to find something else, because (unlike Asda) I'll write him a reference. (It *was* understandable, after he told the foreman to "stick your job".)

59

'Are you sure the burglar didn't take anything?'

'Not that I could see. The police think he heard me before he got started filling his swag bag. He must have thought I'd gone, then panicked and made a run for it.'

'What about your door? How bad is the damage?'

'Actually, there isn't any—we think he picked the lock. Which reminds me—I need to organise getting a better one fitted.'

She's stopped listening. 'Sam, I've been thinking about what Mr M said about your aunt. I can't get it out of my head. Do you think there could be, well—anything *suspicious* about her death?'

Although I gape, this shouldn't surprise me. Daisy has an overactive imagination, and binge-watching crime shows on Netflix doesn't help.

'I mean, look.'

She taps a crimson nail on the first finger of its fellow hand. 'One—cause of death was never determined.'

On to the second finger. 'Two—everybody says your aunt was hale and hearty before she keeled over.'

(Daisy's never met a taboo she couldn't shatter without a shred of remorse.)

'Three—'

Silence, then: '—well, one and two are enough, aren't they?'

'Yes, okay, on the face of it, maybe... but I didn't see anything to suggest a Mafia presence in Cairncroft, Dais'. Did you?'

Her mouth opens, but I beat her to it. 'I agree, alright? In principle. Not because I think a hit man took her out, though. What I'm worried about is something non-malicious that might still be a threat. Say there was a gas leak—or the water's contaminated.'

Daisy sighs and lowers her head. 'I suppose that's possible,' she mutters.

'As soon as we take over, I'll look into it—get things like gas pipes checked, and also have a word with the GP who pronounced death.'

I can see Daisy wants to say more, but our lunch hour's nearly up, so I drain the dregs of my tea and stand. Daisy catches my eye and jerks her head as the bell over Maisie's door tinkles. 'This is all we need,' she growls, as I drop back in my chair and follow her gaze.

Old Mr Davidson's headed straight this way.

'This is your fault,' I hiss. 'You shouldn't have mucked about with his glasses.'

She sticks out her tongue. 'We've handed in our notice. Just let him try...'

Both our cups jangle in their saucers when a carrier bag lands between us. Mr Davidson leans forward, and a whiff of garlic edged with Steradent makes my stomach heave. Suddenly, I feel incredibly fragile—then he bares his teeth, and I actually consider slipping under the table. But when I take a second look...

Could that be a smile?

'I heard yis was moving on,' he says, not unpleasantly, looking from me to Daisy, then back again.

News travels fast—we only told Callum this morning

'Anyway—' he prods at the carrier bag, making it rustle '—awra best.'

He turns and walks out of the shop—leaving us both with mouths like the Mersey tunnel. Slowly, as though it might bite, I pull the bag towards me and squint inside.

'What is it?' Daisy whispers.

Her expression changes to sheer disbelief as I hold up a bottle of prosecco in one hand and a box of Quality Street in the other.

Then she sniffs, wetly, and murmurs: 'Poor old sod.'

My head buzzes. I'm used to ingratitude, but not so much appreciation. Especially from such an unlikely source—and could the timing *be* more ironic?

Slapping my brow to try and dislodge those pesky bumblebees, I force a short laugh. 'Maybe he isn't so bad after all?'

Daisy shrugs as I drop both gifts in the carrier bag and stand. 'Right, c'mon—we'd better go find out what Callum wants.'

'Wait a minute.' She's waving a small, flowery card with something written on the back. 'This fell off the box of sweets.'

After squinting at the spidery writing, she breaks into a delighted grin and holds it where I can see.

Best wishes to both of you, but thanks especially to the wee, tough looking girl. My ear hasn't hurt at all since you fixed my glasses.

6

Callum was "out" doing something terribly important this morning, so Daisy and I took the chance to write our resignations on company time and sent them off by email. Just before we left for lunch, both our in-boxes pinged.

See me, 2pm sharp – Callum

'Maybe he isn't holding us to the whole month's notice?' Daisy suggests while we're taking off our coats.

I wonder what made her think of that. 'Dream on. Callum doesn't do favours for anyone—except himself.'

Callum's never taken to Daisy, nor she to him (though *nobody* takes to Callum) and he wasn't my favourite person even before the debacle on Tuesday. I'm assuming he just wants to make sure every "i" and "t" has the correct appendage, but a flicker of unease reminds me things are seldom straightforward where Callum's concerned.

He's waiting for us, sitting there like the overgrown toad he is. Daisy does her usual parody of looking around for a seat while Callum pretends to be oblivious. 'I want to discuss your resignations— specifically, the notice you've given.'

Hi Callum—yes, we had a pleasant lunch, how about yourself? Oh, that's good. Now, what was it you wanted...?

Hmm—Daisy guessed it would be that. Except, my guess is he wants longer. 'Our understanding is we're required to give you a month's notice—which we did.'

He scratches his nose and studies the ceiling. 'Does that mean—if you could—you would prefer to leave sooner rather than later?'

Daisy looks at me and grins.

Does she know something I don't?

'W... well.' *Oops—I did a Logan* 'Now you mention it, there's nothing to keep us here.'

Callum holds out his arms, palms up. Something catches my eye, but I need a second look to figure out what it was. Ah. Third finger left—a pale indent where his wedding ring used to be.

Daisy nudges me—she sees it, too.

'It's up to you, of course, but I've no objection to your leaving sooner—at the end of this week even, if that suits you better?'

'Tomorrow?' Daisy yaps, beaming, and Callum hastily rotates his right hand to the "traffic-stop" position.

'I was thinking more Saturday...' he mutters, swinging to his desk and running a finger down the rota. 'Ah... okay. It's your week for Saturday off. Both of you. Alright then, you can leave tomorrow. Is that what you want?'

I want to know what the catch is

'Callum, our contracts make a big thing of giving four weeks' notice—sure, now the decision's made, we *would* rather just go, but we're kind of counting on our last paycheques, too.'

He's shaking his head. 'It so happens a dispensing trainee in the Wester Hailes branch has passed her exams and needs a qualified position. Wester Hailes already started another student, so Annabel's just dead weight now. That means she could take over here on Monday, and since it's advantageous to Cosmo-Spex, we'll make up your final pay to the full notice period.'

Wow

'What about me?' Daisy asks.

Callum glares at her. 'H.R. will arrange for a temp. That'll be a massive improvement while we're waiting for someone permanent.'

He really, really doesn't like Daisy

I force a smile. 'No, Callum. What Daisy means is—does she get the same deal? Obviously, if not, there's no incentive for me to...'

'Yes, same terms for both of you.'

Babies have come out easier than those words. What's going on?

Daisy pipes up. 'Sounds fine to me. What about you, Sam?'

I'm scared to say anything in case, somehow, I blow this. So I just nod.

'Splendid. Well, good luck with whatever you're doing.'

He swings around, leafing through a pile of correspondence and leaving us with a view of his back—it's obvious we're dismissed. I'm in a daze as I follow Daisy to the front shop. She stops at her desk, turns, and punches the air with both hands. Then her mouth forms an "O" and she grabs my wrist. 'Um... about little things like eating if our severance pay runs out before we take over the hotel?'

'Don't worry, I'll feed you—I've got some savings stashed away. Not much, but they'll support us until my flat sells.'

'Great. This is perfect, Sam—we'll have time to study the hotel business, and plan.'

She's right—we'll only get one crack at this. If the hotel doesn't start making money before my funds run out, I'll be flogging it to a developer—so extra prep-time is invaluable.

There's something she still hasn't told me, though. 'You didn't seem very surprised in there?'

That cackle made me think of Maggie, the chef. 'You saw his ring finger...'

'Yeah—I wondered about that.'

She leans closer, whispering now. 'Callum's wife chucked him out when she found out about his floozie—who just happens to be Annabel from Wester Hailes.'

My jaw drops and I grab both sides of my face. 'The new dispenser?'

'Yep. That's probably where he was this morning. Everybody knows, except you of course—

you never catch any of the gossip. Good thing you've got me keeping you in the loop.'

'Been nice if you'd put me in the loop *before* we saw Callum.'

She does an "Aw, shucks" with her hands. 'Didn't want to get your hopes up—it was only a theory then. Hey, do you think Callum did a time and motion study? Must take him, what? Half an hour to Wester Hailes if you factor in traffic? Plus, our cleaning cupboard's bigger.'

'You're terrible.' She winces when I jab her with a finger. Still, she's right. Everybody's happy—even Callum—and we get to jump straight into our new venture.

Of course, now I *have* to tell Jake about the hotel.

Like tonight.

ON BALANCE, THIS IS GOOD
I think...

I arrived home, teeth clenched, ready to drop the news of my inheritance on Jake—not to mention his new job (including the accommodation arrangements) in Cairncroft.

Part of me's worried about seeing pound signs appear in his eye sockets. I'm still hoping I've misjudged him, but at least I don't have to make a snap assessment of his motives if he accepts. Living apart at the hotel will give both of us an opportunity to re-assess our relationship.

I won't weaken. Despite his heroic intervention last night, Jake stays at arms' length for now—honestly, hero or not, he's lucky to be getting a second chance.

But tonight, I found him waiting patiently for me to get home—and he looked like the Jake who followed me to Edinburgh. Silk shirt, chinos, face shaved as close as his head, even a waft of the cologne I gave him for his birthday (actually, it was more than a waft, but you get away with going heavy on Versace)—faced with that, my resolve wavered.

Then I noticed (while he told me about the special meal he'd booked at Carlo's—our favourite Italian restaurant) he was fiddling with a button on his shirt and looking everywhere but my eyes, which made me wonder—*what's he up to?*

My first instinct was to turn him down—I want to talk, not go on a date, and guess who'll be footing the bill if we *do* go? Then I realised how much easier our "talk" might be under the calming influence of public scrutiny.

So, here we are—surrounded by candles in bottles on red-checked tablecloths. Jake wanted to order a taxi, but unemployed opticians waiting for their inheritance to come through are acutely aware of the benefits inherent in walking. Carlo's *is* only ten-minutes from the flat, after all. Hidden away in a back street, it's one of those "secret places" everybody knows and loves.

'How's your starter?'

'Delicious. How's yours?'

His reply's a clone of mine, and the volley continues along similar lines. Will we spend the entire meal pretending to discuss it?

I know what's on *my* mind, but Jake's distracted too, which makes me wonder what *he's* gearing up to. Perhaps he's found a job already?

(It's so embarrassing when the waiter has to thump your back because you choked on a clam...)

Alright, more realistically—maybe that text I saw wasn't a prank, and he's about to confess a fling. If that's the case, he's as motivated as me to drop his bombshell in a public place—hence this uncharacteristic surprise treat. (Which I'm paying for, remember.)

We get through the main course without incident. Then dissect our dessert options in painful detail.

Our server dashes off before we change our minds (again), and Jake launches into a boring dialogue about an upcoming darts tournament at the pub.

I've still not tried to bring up Cairncroft. If Jake *is* leading up to something, I want to hear it first before committing myself to any kind of ongoing relationship with him.

The waiter returns with a dish of multi-coloured ice creams and sets it down in front of me. There's a sparkler fizzing in the raspberry ripple.

I ordered cannoli

A screech, like fingernails dragging down glass, has me spinning to see who's torturing the cat. Instead of a moggy in its death throes, a guy dressed as an opera singer with a violin tucked under his chin is moving into position behind my chair. Then the table shudders—it's Jake, using it for support as he gets to his knees. I can't hear him over the murdered chords of "Love me tender", but a small, square velvet box sitting on his upturned palm says it all.

I *should* feel a surge of excitement. But all that's surging is bile, at the back of my throat.

The idiot's proposing? Again?

The violin stops as suddenly as it started, leaving behind a deafening silence. Jake coughs, and speaks in a voice that sounds practiced. 'Sam, nearly losing you brought it home how much I love you. I know I've made mistakes, but I'm going to try harder from now on. So... Samantha Chessington. Will you marry me?'

At least this time he's put some effort into it, but—

No

Absolutely not...

I can't say that, can I? I'm trapped.

My skin goes clammy as I glance around—everyone in the restaurant is watching. All the other

71

diners are waiting with half-open (mercifully empty) mouths for me to say... "Yes".

That's what you're supposed to say. I wonder how many women this foxy male tactic has forced into loveless marriages? Dressed up as a declaration of love, in reality it's blatant coercion.   But am I strong enough to resist societal conditioning and disappoint all these people (strangers) who've interrupted their meals to hear my answer? It would be much easier to say "yes".

I almost do...

Until I remember how I've trudged through the sludge-end of existence for six years. Dragged myself out of bed every workday morning, counted out the minutes until I could dive back under the sheets some sixteen hours later. Now I'm on the verge of a different life where I won't have to kowtow to anybody. A life *I* can shape, rather than the other way 'round. The sort of life I had before...

I *want* to wake up every day raring to go.

I *won't* swap one hamster wheel for another.

Deep breath, Sam...

'Jake, this is a lovely gesture, and I really appreciate it—but I can't sign a lifetime contract without making some pretence of thinking it over first.'

That was diplomatic—wasn't it?

Sweeping an eye over our spellbound spectators, I swallow hard—then force myself to continue. 'I'm going to take a rain cheque—I'm *not* saying "no".'

That last was more an appeal to our audience, whose stricken faces suggest they're about to demand a refund on their front-stall tickets. Face burning, I push out the final words. 'I'm just *not* saying yes.'

My would-be fiance's expression turns blank as he crams the box back in his pocket. Our violinist shuffles his feet until Jake glares and flicks a hand. The poor man slips away—quiet as whichever undertaker sold him that suit. Meantime, the other customers rediscover their pasta and attack it with apparent relish while Jake slouches to his seat and starts playing with the cutlery.

'I'm sorry, Sam. I only meant to...'

Reaching across, I grab his free hand—the one *not* twirling a spoon. 'It was a lovely thought, Jake, but... it's not the right time. Do you understand?'

He nods, looking anywhere but me. Mutters: 'D'you want to go?'

I nod back. 'Yes, I think we should. Tell you what, let's pick up a bottle of vino on the way home. I need to talk to you about something... something else.'

'Okay. Um... Sam?'

What now?

His face scrunches. 'Can you sub me for the bill?'

Neither of us said much on the walk back. I nipped into the corner shop for a bottle of wine, and the first thing we did was open it—next on the agenda is my rejection of his proposal. *Which reminds me—where did he find the cash for that ring?*

'It was obvious you thought I wasn't being romantic enough last week, so I put a lot of effort in this time. I'm just trying to make things right between us, Sam.'

'Jake, you don't get married to "make things right". I'm not even sure I want to carry on seeing you. There's still the matter of that text—from your "gooood time" friend, "R".'

He leans forward in an attempt to bridge the chasm between chair and sofa. 'I told you, that was Richard being silly. It was just a prank.'

'Uhuh.'

I've been thinking about his "prank" story. 'So how could Richard be sure I would see that text? What was the point of his so-called "prank" otherwise? And why haven't I heard his name before?'

He shakes his head, following up with a swipe of both arms. 'Richard only moved here recently—he's an old pal of Andy's. And it wasn't that sort of prank. You remember I was helping Andy with moving stuff? Well, Richard was there too, and we were fooling around—when Richard and me carried a bed upstairs, Andy was joking about us not taking too long in the bedroom. C'mon, Sam—you know what it's like when lads get together. Richard started all this "was it good for you?" stuff, and that text was him hammering the joke into the ground.'

It's believable. I *have* seen them carrying on—they're worse than kindergarten kids. Trouble is, I've also seen Jake's no slouch when it comes to lying—I've caught him out before. Not with anything so important, but...

So I slap a mental "not proven" on that one and move on to Aunt Claire's surprise legacy, and my offer of employment.

The wine bottle's level drops abruptly, but he takes the news better than I expected. 'You're okay about going back to Cairncroft, to your old job, then?'

'Sure—but I don't understand why we have to live apart. C'mon, Sam. If you didn't love me, why would you be asking me to go?'

Because you saved my bacon last night. Because I'm soft...

'Jake—I still have feelings for you, but—overall, you haven't exactly shown me your best side lately. Let me have a little space while I get used to my new life, and we'll see what happens.'

His hand's half-way to the wine bottle before he remembers it's empty and slumps back in his chair. 'Whatever you say, Sam. I'm happy to take it at your pace...'

Then his lip quivers—either he's genuine, or a Bafta nominee on the sly. '... I can't imagine not being with you.'

Time for a change of subject—and there's something I want to ask him. 'When you were working at Cairncroft before, did my Aunt Claire seem alright? Health-wise, I mean.'

Silence. Jake looks constipated—but he always looks that way when he's thinking. Then he sits up straight. 'She sprained her ankle a while back...'

I huff impatiently. 'Anything else—chest pains, for example?'

He yawns widely, not bothering to cover his mouth 'Naw—not that I can remember. Sam, I'm knackered, and you've got your last day at work tomorrow.'

Oops—I'm sitting on his sofa

I get up so fast I nearly fall over. Sometimes I forget about that damn leg.

Jake jumps up too and rushes to steady me. 'You alright, Sam? Um—' he points at the bit of me that isn't '—want me to help you take it off?'

The prosthetic killed my love life for years. Not because of a potential lover's reaction, no... rather, I was scared to find out.

When we got serious, I was terrified about telling Jake I was disabled and disfigured. I almost bailed because of that.

Jake's a crass, insensitive lout, but he guessed what was bothering me and said he knew about the prosthetic—and insisted it didn't bother him. The first night we spent together, he helped me unstrap it—and acted as though being with a part-mannequin was nothing out of the ordinary.

Which was when I finally began to heal.

So now I owe him on two counts—and somehow, I need to filter out the gratitude and see if what's left is enough to make a relationship work. Until I do...

'Thanks, Jake, but I'll manage.'

He steps back. I hate that I'm hurting him, but still hobble through the door as fast as my increasingly achey stump allows. 'Goodnight.'

A quiet 'Goodnight, Sam' follows me down the hall.

A LITTLE LATER, LYING IN BED WITH MY MIND CHURNING, I remember the conversation with Daisy in Maisie's.

I know I slagged Daisy off when she started talking about post-mortems, but now I wish they *had* done one. Everyone keeps telling me how well Aunt Claire looked, and yet she died so suddenly?

Like I said earlier, what if it *wasn't* natural— but still accidental? Can a GP tell a gas leak from a heart attack? Could the hotel have lead in its water pipes, or asbestos particles in the air? It's an old, neglected building. The woodworm's proof enough of that—who knows what else is going on inside those walls?

I've felt in my gut things weren't adding up, ever since I got the news. It's such a relief having something tangible to work with.

As soon as we take over, I'll call in whichever professionals are needed to find out what caused Aunt Claire's death. Let's hope nobody else comes a cropper in the meantime.

My final thought, before sleep claims me, is: *Where DID he get the money for that ring?*

WHEN I ARRIVE AT COSMO-SPEX NEXT MORNING—*LAST day in this dump*—there's a note propped against the frame heater in my workshop cubicle.

Samantha - come and see me straight away. Callum.

I knew the quick-release deal was too good to be true. He obviously changed his mind.

Beggar

Daisy arrived just behind me. She'll still be swapping her hoodie for a white jacket—mandatory for all Cosmo-Spex drones (sorry, employees)—so I detour to the staff room. We should see Callum together.

But when I tell her, she gives me a blank look. 'I didn't get a note.'

Hm... maybe a dispenser in one of the other branches has gone off sick, and Callum wants me to cover? I wouldn't put it past him, but he can whistle for that. A deal's a deal—after today, I never want to see another pair of specs in my life.

With Daisy's advice echoing in my head ("don't take any crap"), I tap my nails on Callum's door. A moment later, the man himself opens it—something so unexpected, I gape.

'Samantha. Thank you for coming.'

He ushers me inside and perches on the corner of his desk. It's when he kicks his chair in my direction and says 'Have a seat' that I realise aliens have abducted the real Callum.

He clears his throat, sounding like a blocked drain. 'Last day, eh? I suppose you must have mixed feelings.'

I don't know *what* I'm feeling right now. Oh, yes—I do. Gratitude to the aliens.

'Anyway, according to the grapevine you're off up North, so I expect you'll be selling your flat?'

What's that got to do with you?

'Yeah—I'm listing it with an agent next week.'

He strokes his chin and examines the ceiling tiles. 'It's shocking, the commission those agents take. Can be as much as four percent, and your flat's worth—what—a hundred and forty?'

At least one-fifty—what's going on here?
His hand crawls its way to the nape of his neck, and his attention floats floorwards. 'That's over five thousand pounds in commission—marketing fees will add another thousand.'

His head lifts. Then he smiles—a positively frightening sight. My gratitude was misplaced—this is an *evil* alien. 'Imagine if you could save some of that money.'

He pokes a finger through the dramatic pause. 'Because you could.'

I feel it's only polite to hand him the "How?" he's waiting for.

'It just so happens I am in the market for a, um, pied-à-terre. If you sell to me, the only costs you'll incur will be legal fees and a home report—about a thousand all told. So, by buying your flat, I'll save you two thousand pounds.'

He wants to buy my flat?
Wait a sec. I scratch my head, trying to crunch those figures. Arithmetic has never been a strong point (as my old maths teacher would attest), but even I can see Callum's workings don't work out. 'That's not right, Callum. Your top-end estimate of selling costs came to over six thousand. Why am I only *two* thousand better off?'

He taps his nose, drawing my attention to a perfect cuticle. I've heard the rumours about weekly manicures... 'Reciprocity, Samantha.'

He nods, pleased with himself, then dives back into the silence. 'I'd expect some small kickback for saving you a fortune in fees.'

I see

There's a delinquent delight in ensconcing myself in Callum's chair and crossing my ankles. So often I've stood rigid in here while he plays silly power games, but finally the upper hand is mine. Because I've got something he wants—although he's right, it takes two to tango.

But I won't let him lead... 'I'm definitely interested, Callum. Now I'm going to tell you how I see it—I want a quick sale, and you need somewhere to stay in a hurry.'

His eyes flash—doesn't he know the gossips have declared open season on his love life? 'So, yes— in principle, I'm in. But since we're both getting what we want, wouldn't it be fairer to go fifty-fifty on the saving in costs? While we're at it, let's pare those costs down to averages rather than extremes.'

He's squirming, sending a shiver of delight through me. Holding his eyes, I ruin his day. 'If you offer me valuation less two thousand, the flat's yours. Take it or leave it.'

At which point, the alien goes home—and Alpha Centauri sends Callum back.

He tries intimidation, then he cajoles, and all the while he lies—he uses every trick he can think of, but I'm immoveable.

I'm not his subordinate any longer. Much as I want the deal, I'd sooner go through an agent than let Callum fleece me.

He caves.

When I close the door on my red-faced ex-boss and skip across to Daisy's desk, she narrows her eyes. 'Sam, you've just come out of Callum's office and—you're smiling?'

When I tell her what happened, she jumps up and grabs my elbows. 'We thought it would take months to get the cash out of your flat. This means...'

Matching her grin, I nod. 'As soon as the legal stuff's done, we can get on with sorting the hotel out. Something puzzles me, though. Obviously, Callum's wife isn't in a hurry to let him back in, but what I don't understand is why he doesn't move in with Annabel.'

Daisy winks—a slow, lecherous one. 'You've never met *young* Annabel, have you? She lives with her parents. I don't think...'

'You're kidding? Callum's a cradle snatcher?'

She tuts and shakes her head. 'Who'd have thought it? Callum—yeeugh. Just thinking about it makes me squirm. Annabel must have a screw loose.'

Talking of which

Over Daisy's shoulder two customers, presumably waiting for me to fix their glasses, are trying to catch my eye. 'I'd better go.'

'Hey, Sam.'

I turn back impatiently. 'What?'

82

She holds up a post-it. 'Mr M's looking for you—he said it was urgent.'

I grab it and sprint past the customers, ignoring their newly acquired befuddled expressions, already howking out my phone. In the staffroom I jab the "call" button. I don't need the number Daisy jotted down—Mr M is in my contacts.

As soon as we're connected, I'm down the phone at him. 'What's wrong?'

'Hello, dear.' Miss Dobie's dulcet tones float from the handset. 'I'll put you through to him...'

'Good morning, Samantha. How are you?'

'What's wrong?' I repeat. I should have remembered the universe has this nasty habit of constantly correcting itself.

'Wrong? Nothing's wrong—sorry if I alarmed you. I just wanted to let you know the legal work is progressing faster than I expected—I'll be handing over the hotel keys in two weeks' time. Of course, you can't do much until funds from your flat come available...'

The handset drops to my side and Mr M's rich tones vibrate against my thigh. Callum said he can bully the solicitors into completing our deal in—two weeks.

In two weeks, Daisy and I (and Logan) can begin rescuing the Cairncroft Hotel.

'YES.'

FOUR DAYS LATER, A FORMAL OFFER ARRIVES FROM Callum's solicitors—for five thousand below valuation. The double-crossing weasel is trying to cheat me out of three thousand pounds.

I don't know whether to laugh or cry.

What I do is accept the offer.

FLOOR PLAN OF THE GROUND FLOOR, CAIRNCROFT HOTEL

(AS IT LOOKED WHEN SAM AND DAISY TOOK OVER)

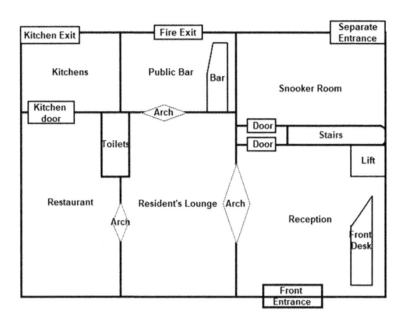

Part 2

ONE

Two weeks later, with Aberdeen's railway station at our backs, Daisy and I make our way across to the Station Hotel where Logan's arranged for us to be collected.

Daisy plonks her suitcase on the ground and sighs. 'I hope he can stop—it isn't much of a drop off point.'

She's right—comprising a narrow swathe hacked into the pavement, the "drop off point" (or in our case, "pickup point") looks barely big enough to accommodate a Mini—despite being currently occupied by a Merc. (Well, strictly speaking, only two of its wheels are actually "occupying".) 'He'll just have to circle until another space opens up,' she adds, then her eyes become slits. 'Is that him?'

I follow her finger, and stiffen. 'I hope not.'

Graham Biscombe, the hotel gardener, is supposed to be collecting us, and it looks like he's brought his company vehicle. Headed this way, indicator flashing, is an ancient, flat-bedded truck that can't possibly have an MOT certificate.

The rust bucket clanks to a stop, creating an effective roadblock, and its driver waves—oblivious to a double-decker bus slamming on its brakes. With the effortless grace of someone thirty years younger, a grizzled, cloth-capped man jumps out. He tosses our cases on the flatbed beside six bags of compost and a petrol-powered strimmer. 'You'll be our new owners?' he calls, then leaps after the luggage. A moment later he's strapping it down with elastic cords anchored to the truck's body.

Daisy shakes her head vigorously. 'We're just waiting for the bus. Who're you?'

Graham jerks upright and a bungee strap flies off Daisy's cabin-approved travel bag. Hiding my smile, I slap her arm. 'Take no notice—she thinks she's funny. I assume you're Graham?'

He touches one finger to the nub of his cap. 'That's me. You'd be Miss Chessington, then? And...?'

Words fail him, which doesn't surprise me. To celebrate her liberation from Cosmo-Spex (and their dress code), Daisy had the hairdresser convert her straw-toned bob into a mass of icy blonde spikes— then paint blue streaks through it. She's also chosen to travel in a shiny black outfit bringing "Sandy" from "Grease" to mind. Sticking both hands in the pockets of my navy M&S jacket, I shrug. 'This is Daisy.'

Graham grins. He finishes securing our cases, then springs down and throws open the passenger-side door. With a mock bow, he shouts over blaring horns. 'Yer carriage awaits, ladies.'

Graham's truck stands higher than it looks and by the time Daisy's manhandled me onto its bench-style seat the bus driver's going bananas. Graham seems unconcerned. He holds up his palm towards a line of honking vehicles (as though to say: "What?") and gets behind the wheel.

'City folk have no patience,' he mumbles, attempting to start his truck. It catches on the sixth attempt and he drives off, followed by a lengthy procession of still hooting traffic. 'Train busy?' he asks, seemingly oblivious to the yelled death threats.

IT'S NEARLY THREE O'CLOCK—THE JOURNEY LOOKS LIKE taking ninety minutes, which is thirty more than it should. A wisp of smoke rising from somewhere under the bonnet says we'll be lucky to get there at all.

Since leaving Aberdeen's city limits, vistas of grass and trees on every side have held Daisy mesmerised—she's probably wondering who planted them, and where the birds escaped from. I try to imagine my own childhood without the thrill of regular countryside forays—especially my annual holiday with Aunt Claire—and can't.

I'm sat in the centre—Daisy and Graham are pressed hard against me. 'Do you live in the hotel, Graham?'

'Nay, lass. Me and ma wife have a wee cottage just down the way.'

'You do a wonderful job with the grounds. They're always full of colour.'

He screws up his face. 'I try—but it's all show. I spend most of my time trying to hide the wild bits. Them grounds could be a real feature, but they need money spent and more than me to maintain them.'

If you're hinting, Graham, take a ticket

'How long have you worked at the hotel?' Daisy asks.

'Getting on ten years now, ever since we moved down from Fraserburgh.'

'You must have known Sam's aunt well.'

He sits up straighter, and his lips tighten. Daisy doesn't notice because she's back trying to figure out this "countryside" thing.

'I suppose,' is all he says, and I wonder—could Graham have been Aunt Claire's latest conquest?

Surely not? Married men were never her forte—there again, she was very "seventies" in her outlook. None of my business, but if they *were* close Graham might know something. 'Everyone's puzzled by her sudden death,' I try. 'Did she mention having health problems?'

'No, but I heard it was a heart attack.'

'So the GP says, but I'm told that was more guesswork than professional opinion.'

89

Graham makes a rasping sound at the back of his throat. 'Aye, probably. Tom Frame relies on guesswork—that, and the specialists in Aberdeen.'

'Logan said the same. Is Doctor Frame really that bad?'

Graham turns his head and spits through the open window. 'Total quack, everybody knows it. If it can't be fixed wi' twa aspirin, it's beyond him. Mind you, Tom's that ancient he probably had to buy a box o' leeches for his first doctor's bag. He's driven most folks away to the surgery in Donstable.'

'So why did Aunt Claire still use him?'

'She didn't, lass. He was just the nearest thing resembling a doctor that day—his cottage is even closer to the hotel than mine. He lives with his granddaughter, Rebecca—she's the hotel housekeeper.'

'So Rebecca fetched him when...?'

'Nah, Rebecca weren't there that morning. T'were Maggie, the cook, that went running to get Tom.'

Rebecca's a new name—she must have been off when Logan gave us the grand tour. 'What's she like—Rebecca?'

He grins—toothily. 'Oh—better to form your own impression of Rebecca. You'll see what I mean when you meet her.'

We're turning into the hotel driveway and Graham crashes over the potholes with a gay abandon that makes my teeth clatter and has Daisy squealing in annoyance. 'We need to do something about those. Graham, do you think filling them with gravel would work?'

'Aye, up to a point—that used to be one of your Jake's jobs before he left.'

'Jake'll be here tomorrow. I'll get him straight on it.'

Graham stops the truck outside the main door. 'Thought Jake'd be with you today,' he comments, nose twitching.

'He had things to do,' I reply, looking away.

The truth's none of Graham's business—I'm still keeping Jake at arm's length and that, combined with the explosive effect he has on Daisy, is why I drummed up reasons for travelling separately. Jake's assignment to deliver my keys to Callum's solicitor is a pretty lame excuse, granted, but the meters have to be read, too... although I thought Jake would blow a gasket when Pickfords arrived to take the furniture away yesterday. Daisy gave me a couch for the night, and I'm *assuming* Andy offered his to Jake... Being fair, Jake accepted it all with good grace. He really does want to patch things up between us.

Question is, do I?

'Jake knows he's wasting his time,' Graham muses, making me wonder where a gardener learnt to read minds until he elucidates: 'filling them potholes with gravel—it's only a stopgap. You'll need to get the tarmackers in.'

He rubs his nose. 'Cost a bit, that will.'

Tell me about it

91

Daisy gets out first. I join her, gazing at our new home, while Graham fetches the luggage down.

Once, this was a magnificent building. Now, my eye's drawn to every patch of missing pointing (well, not *all* of them—that'd take all day) and again I wonder when the roof was last checked.

Those potholes might be the least of our worries

Reception doesn't look so bad today—maybe someone gave the exposed brickwork a scrub? I realise I'm staring at the receptionist. She's wearing a top that...

Put it this way—I *think* she's wearing a top.

When she comes out to greet us, Graham gives me a sly wink. 'Meet Rebecca—Rebecca Perkins.'

'Hi. I'm Sam, this is Daisy.'

Rebecca shakes my outstretched hand while Graham staggers off—somehow, he's got all four suitcases under his arms. Rebecca's attractive in a coarse sort of way—about my height with blonde hair that complements her baby blue eyes, but despite a thick layer of gloss her lips are thin and she seems to stare a lot.

She says her piece slowly and deliberately. 'Logan sends his apologies for not being here to welcome you.'

I wonder why she's manning the reception desk? 'Um... I thought you were the housekeeper. Is the receptionist off sick?'

Rebecca looks at me the way my old maths teacher used to. 'We don't have a receptionist.'

'Oh.'

I glance at Daisy, who rolls her eyes, then turn back to Rebecca. 'So—how does that work?'

Now, her expression reminds me of the same maths teacher after he saw my exam results. 'We only man the desk when a guest's due. Any other time, they ring the bell and whoever hears comes through. By the way, I'm officially a chambermaid. The other stuff, ordering supplies and organising laundry, I just sort of fell into all that. Didn't get a pay rise, though.' She scowls.

I think about that, trying to understand. 'So who cleans the rooms?'

'I do.'

'What? You clean the rooms yourself—*and* do the admin?'

She shrugs. 'We don't get many guests—it isn't so hard. Oh...' like she's just remembered '... I double as waitress, too—now, *that* I get paid extra for.'

An ominous grinding reminds me of Graham's truck. Daisy'll ruin her teeth if she keeps that up.

She's right, though—this sounds worse than we imagined. Mind you, we were forewarned—the trading accounts Mr M sent were dire.

Swivelling to point into the residents lounge, I'm almost afraid to ask. 'Do you look after the bar, too?'

'No, of course not.' She pats my arm, sniggers.

I wasn't joking. But I am relieved, since the bar is our main source of income

'No, Logan does the bar.'

OK—so no bar staff, either

Rebecca indicates the same direction I did. 'Maggie and I laid out some sannies and coffee— thought you might need refreshing after your journey.'

'Why, thank you, Rebecca.' We've taken several steps before I realise Rebecca isn't moving.

'I'll leave you to it,' she clarifies.

'Please, join us for a coffee at least,' I plead. I want to talk to her about her grandfather.

She shoots a glance at the reception desk. 'Okay, he can ring the bell if I'm not back.'

She leads us through to the bar where a massive platter of sandwiches covered with clingfilm, a generous plate of biscuits, and a huge coffee flask with a push-button pump are laid out ready.

'I'm really glad you're here,' Rebecca says. 'It's been crazy since... you know?'

'Since my Aunt Claire's passing? Of course, that must have left you short staffed.'

She nods, hard. 'Like I said, Logan does the bar—so he doesn't start until lunchtime. I used to do the same, because I'm needed for waitressing most nights. Your aunt covered the mornings. After she... you know... Logan and me started taking turns to come in early.'

She puffs. 'I'm knackered.'

And looks it, too

'You can leave mornings to us now. Starting tomorrow.'

Rebecca makes a show of sagging, grins a glassy grin.

'So, the guests you're expecting—is it a big party?' I ask, pumping coffee into a cup while Daisy sets about peeling clingfilm.

'Not really—just one of the regulars. A salesman.'

'Do we get a lot of commercial business?' Hope blossoms. That's something we might exploit.

'Nope.'

The blossoms wither, and I take a sip from my now-filled cup. Then another.

Needed that—even if it is Nescafé

Daisy beats me to the punch. 'Graham says you live with your grandfather.'

'Uhuh—our cottage is just before you turn into the hotel drive. Grampa's an old sweetie.'

Is he any good at his job, though?

'Rebecca, Graham also mentioned it was your grampa who came the morning my aunt died.'

Rebecca's cup goes down on the bar with a clink, freeing a hand to cover her eyes. 'What a terrible day that was. I wasn't here, but Grampa told me all about it. Logan found her. Then Maggie ran around to the cottage for Grampa, but there was nothing he could do. Grampa said she'd been dead for hours.'

'A heart attack?' Daisy asks.

Rebecca nods. 'That's what Grampa said.'

95

'Rebecca,' I ask, trying to frame this inoffensively. 'Did he say *why* he thought it was a heart attack? I mean, there's no history I'm aware of, and...'

'... and you've heard the gossip about Grampa,' she cuts in, face hardening. 'They take one look and judge him by his age, but just because he's getting on doesn't make him any less a doctor. He's still sharp as a pin, and if Grampa says it was her heart, that's what it was.'

'I'm sure he is. I used to be an optician and we get some training in physiology, so when Logan told us your grampa diagnosed heart failure I was interested to know what the signs were.'

It felt like I phrased that rather well, but Rebecca's body language stiffens further. 'Sorry, I'm clueless about that stuff.'

Her lips clench. 'I was glad that was my day off—suppose it had been me who found her?' She puts a hand across her mouth. 'I've never seen a corpse.'

Something flickers in her eyes. 'Unlike Logan.'

'What—you mean his stepfather? After the fire?'

Her lips curl. 'Yes, the fire. The one that happened when Logan's sister says he was with her in Aberdeen.'

She looks over her shoulder, then leans closer. 'Except, I saw Logan cycling for all he was worth away from their cottage—around the time of the fire.

And everyone knows there was no love lost between him and his stepfather.'

Daisy bumps me in her effort to get nearer. 'Did you tell the police?'

'No—none of my business, and I've got to work with Logan.'

She looks at her feet, brows furrowed, then turns abruptly. 'That sounds like the guest arriving... Excuse me.'

I nudge Daisy. 'Did you hear anything?'

'Nope. I think she realised her mouth was running away with itself.'

I'm shaking. 'Daisy, our new partner could be—a murderer.'

Daisy's eyes gleam and she abandons her sandwich. 'Which means—you do see what this means?'

I shake my head, and she smacks my arm. 'Your aunt dies suddenly and Logan, who may have killed before, inherits a share of her hotel. What does that say to you?'

'You don't think...'

'Logan's aunt—Maggie—makes powders out of wild flowers. There're loads of poisonous plants. Sam, Logan had motive, means, and as the last person to see her alive—opportunity.'

I'm having trouble getting my head around what she's saying—but I can't argue with her logic, either. Sweet, bumbling Logan—*could* he be a killer? *Well—if we believe Rebecca, then he could*

'What are we going to do?' Squeezing those words through a dry throat was painful. Before Daisy can answer, a floorboard squeaks and we turn, expecting to see Rebecca back.

'S... Sam—Daisy. G... great to have you here.'

It's Logan.

TWO

Finally, we escape and beat a hasty retreat to the owner's flat—where I throw closed my new front door and collapse against it. '*That* was excruciating.'

Daisy giggles. 'You're a terrible actor, Sam. He kept looking at you.'

I make straight for the kitchen, explaining: 'I need another coffee after that.'

Daisy pulls a stool from under the breakfast bar and perches opposite me. 'Not for me—I'm Nescafaed up to the eyeballs. Sam, I *knew* there was something off about your aunt's death—and *him*.'

'Don't jump to conclusions, Dais'. We've only got Rebecca's word for it. What if Rebecca's an old girlfriend and Logan dumped her...'

It wasn't THAT funny

'... or she might have it in for him because he's her boss. Maybe Logan can be over-strict with...'

Okay—I can't see "strict" and "Logan" going together, either

'... wait a minute. You're laughing at the idea of Logan being strict while suggesting he's a serial killer?'

Daisy's laugh freezes mid-chortle. 'We-ell—when you put it like that—'

'Plus, all Rebecca said was she saw him cycling away after the fire started. There could be an innocent explanation... where're you going?'

She doesn't answer, so I finish making my drink and follow her to the sitting room. She's got her phone out, chewing her upper lip as she prods and swipes at the screen.

'What're you doing?'

'I'm looking for news reports about the fire at Logan's cottage...'

She jerks her head around. 'Sam, it says here the Fire Inspector thought it was arson.'

A wave of dizziness makes me sway, and I sink onto the sofa.

Daisy keeps talking, her fingers working faster. 'Now, here... someone's "helping the police with their inquiries"'—swipe, swipe—'a couple of days later, a fire investigator discovers the blaze was started with paraffin, but further on still a police spokesman says they "have no suspects at this time". I bet that was Logan they were grilling, before he sprung his alibi on them.'

'Well, the alibi obviously checked out...'

Daisy snorts. 'According to Rebecca, his sister gave him that alibi. I wonder how much he coined in from the stepfather's will? Must have been enough to give him a taste, since he worked the same scam with your aunt—including doing away with her, same as his stepfather.'

Sitting up straight, I thrust both hands out. 'Whoa. You've got him tried and convicted already—

all based on a snide comment from somebody we don't even know?'

Daisy jumps up and starts pacing. 'I suppose you're right. We can't just ignore it, though—can we?'

'No, we can't.'

My mind's reeling as I try to stay objective and plan a sensible route forward. 'Alright, but I've instructed safety checks on the hotel—which need doing anyway. If the surveyor eliminates an accidental cause of death, we'll take a closer look at Logan.'

Daisy counts on her fingers. 'Talk to Rebecca again—find out more about Logan's alibi—I still haven't heard a good reason for your aunt leaving him a share of the hotel. Didn't she say in her will?'

I'm shaking my head. 'No. The will was quite "perfunctory"—that's Mr M's word, not mine.'

Daisy stops beside a lacquered secretaire. 'This isn't yours, is it?'

'No, it was Aunt Claire's.'

I stand and spread my arms at the room. 'Anyway, what d'you think? Whoever told the movers where to put everything—probably Logan—did a grand job. I couldn't have done better.'

'Mm.' Daisy's got Aunt Claire's secretaire open and she's fiddling with a row of miniature drawers in the writing compartment. 'Or maybe the movers did it off their own bat—I can't see Logan having much idea about interior design. Hey—what happened to the stuff your aunt kept in this?'

'Mr M took all her papers so he could administrate the estate. Daisy, why are you doing that?' Now she's removing the little drawers, one by one.

'This is the sort of place your aunt would stash things—important things. I'm just wondering if she hid anything at the back of these drawers...'

She breaks off, and I move closer to peer over her shoulder. 'What's that?'

She turns, face unreadable as she hands me two identical photos. They're square shaped, with a broad bottom margin—old fashioned Polaroids, I realise—haven't seen any of those in yonks. After looking at them, I have to sit down again. 'That's Aunt Claire,' I manage, tapping one of the pictures.

Daisy sits on the sofa beside me and squints. 'I thought so.' She points. 'And *that's* Graham Biscombe...'

'Coming out of a hotel—it looks like the same one Graham collected us from earlier.'

Daisy nods. 'The Station Hotel—in Aberdeen. And he's got his arm around her. Sam, this isn't a staff performance evaluation—at least, I hope not.'

She gets a poke in the side for that. Then, for some reason, I turn the photos over—something you do without thinking. We both gasp at the scribbled messages on their backs.

One says:

What would his wife think if she saw this?

and the other is:

Let me know when you decide. L

'DECIDE WHAT?'

It might be nearly August, but that doesn't mean squat here in Scotland. Nevertheless, although all Daisy and I care about is getting out for a breather to let settle the implications implicit in those photos, a tingling touch from today's unaccustomed late-afternoon sun is a pleasant bonus. 'How should I know, Dais'?'

She glares, and I fold. 'Alright, it looks like a blackmail demand. As though whoever wrote it was threatening to tell Graham's wife about...'

'... their affair,' Daisy finishes, putting a smug slant on the words. 'I told you something fishy was going on. D'you think that's how he got Claire to write him into her will?'

'We don't know Logan was behind it,' I snap. 'It could have been anyone—you're jumping to conclusions.'

'It's signed "L".'

'Lawrence, Lee, Leonard...'

'They were Polaroids—technology from the dark ages. That sounds like Logan to me. We need a sample of his handwriting. That'll settle it.'

'Fine, we'll get one—somehow. Let's give him the benefit of the doubt 'til then, eh?'

Daisy nods, but I see she's already made her mind up. There *is* something puzzling me. 'Did you think the writing on those photos was identical? I'm not sure it was.'

'It has to be—he must have used different pens, is all.'

I'm still not convinced. I might have argued the point, but another thought distracts me. 'Where is everybody? This place is like a mausoleum. So far, we've met Logan, Maggie, Graham, and Rebecca. A hotel this size needs a bigger staff than that.'

'I don't think there is anyone else—apart from two part-time cleaners we haven't run into yet. According to those accounts Mr M sent, and excluding Jake and the cleaners, your aunt was only paying four wages—this place is in more trouble than we thought.'

We came out through a back door opening directly from the snooker room. Since passing a pair of bright green rubbish hoppers, only a stretch of rough grass sequined with brightly coloured wild flowers separates us from the single-storey brick structure I'm steering for. Daisy kicks at flattened vegetation on the path. Then stoops, grabs a stalk, and sticks it in the corner of her mouth. 'Ee by gum, lass,' she intones, making a funny face.

'I think you'll find that dialect's more Yorkshire than the North of Scotland.'

'I like it here,' she says simply, and my heart goes out to the city-reared child who was deprived of open countryside. 'We've got to make this work, Sam.'

'We will,' I say, with a confidence I don't feel.

We're getting nearer the old outbuildings and I crane my neck, then point to the bit I'm interested in. 'See that paved area? These were stables way back, and that was the courtyard where they groomed their horses. Except, I'm seeing it as an all-weather tennis court.'

With a shriek, she takes off at a sprint. 'Daisy,' I scream. 'Stop.'

She whirls, then waits until I stumble alongside. I grab her arm and point with my other hand. We both peer at a circular brick wall rising to waist height midway between us and the stables. It's about four feet in diameter, camouflaged by bushes and weeds.

'What's that?'

'An old well. Been dry for years, but it goes down at least twenty feet—and has no cover on it. Getting that closed off is a priority, before there's an accident—like some idiot running headlong at it and falling in.'

'I'd have seen it,' she protests. Then: 'Why didn't Claire get it made safe?'

I roll my eyes. 'She kept saying she would—but there was always something more important. I've asked the surveyor to include it in his costings.'

We stroll past, giving the well a wide berth. When we reach the courtyard Daisy stops and rotates slowly, causing her trainers to squeak on the stone pavers. 'Looks big enough—renting out tennis racquets won't bring in much money, though.'

She watches curiously as I let a grin spread over my face. 'I was thinking more along the lines of giving pro-lessons. I've still got contacts—and I'm a qualified coach. At one time, I saw it as a way out of Cosmo-Spex, but...' I complete the sentence in my head '... *inertia set in.*'

Back then, still in emotional turmoil, I was digging my heels (heel) in, desperate to keep a connection with my previous life. Nothing ever came of the coaching course I took, though—until now.

'Wow—that's a great idea.' Her voice softens. 'I know how much you miss the tennis. I could see this becoming a nice little earner, too. Only thing... can you... with...' She shoots a glance at my left leg.

'I'll teach people in pairs, so I don't actually have to play. Although, I've still got one whopper of a serve to show them.' I can't resist demonstrating, in slow motion—and even the mime sets my blood racing.

Daisy links her arm through one of mine, and we meander on. 'You know,' she murmurs, eyes shifting from side to side. 'Once there's some money coming in, we could take this idea further. Depends what the surveyor says, but these buildings look sound to me. Can you imagine a nice little leisure centre in there? A gym—maybe a shop, cafe even? Then a pool built on...'

'Don't get carried away,' I chide, laughing.

But I see it, too

'How about a peek inside?' Daisy pleads.

'No, it might not be safe. The surveyor's coming on Thursday to check the main building from top to bottom—I'll send him over here, too.' Pins and needles jangle in my stomach as I remember. 'You wouldn't believe how much he's costing.'

Yanking our joined arms, I turn us back the way we came. 'Once we've got the health club,' I tease, 'you could run it. That's right up your street.'

'Oh, you bet. I could also do judo and fitness classes while you're teaching the next Navratilova— hey, do you get a cut if they make it big?'

'No, don't be daft.'

We walk in silence for a moment. 'Anyway, back to reality—there might be enough left in the kitty for a tennis school if we compromise on a plain old cement court to start with. I just hope this surveyor doesn't find a lot of expensive faults in the hotel itself.'

'Will he check for gas leaks, or do you need the gas board for that?'

'Mm. It turns out the hotel's all electric. But the surveyor says he'll rule out lead pipes, asbestos, anything that could be a danger. '

107

'Good. What about those pot-holes? Are you getting them fixed?'

'Jake can keep filling them with gravel meantime, but I will get a quote for re-surfacing— again, depends what everything else costs. Assuming the surveyor doesn't recommend demolition, the ambience generally needs a major upgrade—which reminds me, d'you think you could organise some quotes from decorators and carpet fitters?'

'I'll start on it first thing.'

We're back at the plastic rubbish hoppers, and the door we came out of is just ahead.

It won't open.

Daisy thumps her fist on peeling wood. 'It must be a fire door.'

We've no choice but to follow a gravel path right around the building—and as usual, when we enter through the front door, reception is unmanned. Daisy tuts, then says 'That's going to be a hard one.'

'What is?'

She rests an elbow on the desk. 'Well, it's a chicken and egg thing. We need more staff— receptionist, maids, everything really—to cope with these hordes of punters we plan on reeling in. But we can't pay for more staff without more punters.'

Thinking about it makes my head hurt. 'Yeah. The timing will have to be right or we'll be paying our new recruits money we haven't got to sit around and read their Kindles.'

'P... pleasant stroll, ladies?'

108

The last person I want to see walks in. (Well, when I say "walks"—his legs are propelling him in a forward direction, put it that way.) 'Lovely, thanks... Logan.'

He lowers his voice. 'I've been encouraging our guest...' he draws air-quotes with his fingers '... to air out his expense account in the bar.'

'You get a lot of local trade through there, don't you?' His eyebrows rise before I add: 'We've been having a look through the accounts.'

'Ah. Yes, you're right, although...'

He bites his lip, and Daisy says: 'What?'

'Well, if our main objective's getting more people to stay here, I'm not sure we can afford to keep the locals. They're a rough bunch—Claire went through agonies of indecision over this. They *have* kept us afloat—but they chase away a lot of guests.'

Daisy pouts. 'Chase guests away—how?'

'By being loud... and drinking too much. It isn't exactly a family atmosphere when the bar's open.'

Oh, brother

'We'll pop in later and take a look.' It doesn't sound like the most peaceful way to spend our first evening, but this needs checking out—fast.

Daisy pulls a notebook and pen from her pocket and slaps them on the counter. 'Logan, could you write me down some names of local decorators and carpet fitters so I can get quotes organised? Don't worry about phone numbers, I'll find them on the internet.'

109

'S... sure.'

He writes steadily for a minute. 'I've put the ones I think are best first. These are all in Donstable, but that's the nearest to local you'll get.'

'Cheers, Logan.'

Daisy pockets the notebook in her "Sandy" trousers, which are so tight I still see its rectangular outline—including the spiral. Logan turns towards the bar. 'I... I'd better...'

We both wave as he goes back to his travelling salesman (looking from the rear as though he's negotiating a minefield), and I heave a sigh. Daisy's already crossing to the lift. She mutters: 'We need to get used to this thing. There's no chance it's getting replaced in the foreseeable.'

She's right—costs are piling up at an alarming rate and since I'll be forever having to go from one floor to another, there's also no way I can use the stairs exclusively without crippling myself. So I follow her into the gloomy cage and cringe as what feels increasingly like a moving coffin begins its ascent to a cacophony of squealing gears. I notice the sly grin on Daisy's face, and ask: 'What're you looking so pleased about?'

She pulls out her notebook (with some difficulty). 'Got a sample of his handwriting, didn't I? Now we can find out for sure if it was him wrote on the back of those photos.'

THREE

This will be our first taste of Maggie's cooking. Depressingly, besides us, there's only one diner in the restaurant tonight—Logan's travelling salesman, who waves with such enthusiasm the chair tilts dangerously. Looks like Logan was successful in syphoning his expense account into our till, earlier.

Daisy casts her eyes around, expression souring. 'Reminds me of a school dinner hall.'

'It isn't that bad. Brighten up the decor, bit of mood lighting—it could be lovely.'

'Mm. LOTS of mood lighting, and have the decorators rip everything out and start again...'

Rebecca sidles up, resplendent in black one-piece and white apron. She looks like an escapee from a low-budget porn movie—and she's empty-handed. 'Where's the menu, Rebecca?'

Rebecca laughs. 'There isn't one—it's a set menu. Beer battered haddock with chips, melon starter, and the sweet's home-made ice cream.' She brings out her order pad and waits, pencil poised.

Daisy looks flabbergasted, but with only two tables in use I see Maggie's point. And appreciate her sense of frugality.

Daisy points at Rebecca's pad. 'So, what do you need that for if it's a set menu?'

Rebecca sniffs. 'Not everyone wants a starter, and you've still to order drinks.'

'Wine list?' I put in hopefully, and Rebecca giggles. 'You can have red *or* white,' she suggests.

Oh dear

'Red for me.'

'Same here, and we'll take all three courses,' Daisy adds.

Bringing out my own notebook, I add "wine cellar" to a growing list.

Daisy shuffles 'round to read my note, then gives me a thumbs up. 'Of course, we also need a choice of proper food to go with it. Do you think we should check out ready-meals? I bet catering wholesalers do a high-end version.'

'Give Maggie a chance, Daisy. From a management standpoint, she's spot on keeping to a set menu—given there's hardly anyone here. If she'd prepped for à la carte, the restaurant would be making an even bigger loss tonight.'

Daisy's elbows land on the table, and she scowls. Probably still thinking about before, when we compared Logan's handwriting with the cryptic messages. I can almost hear her brain clicking away behind those fiery eyes. 'They've both got the same angle of slant,' she insists, returning to a discussion we've already had and pretending to know what she's talking about.

'You're not a whatever-they-call-a-handwriting expert. There were similarities, yes, but it's

112

impossible to say for sure both were written by the same person.'

We thought matching handwriting samples would be simple—until we tried. Some bits matched, others didn't. Also, I'm still not convinced the writing on both photos was anywhere near identical. Experimentally, I copied out both notes on separate pieces of paper—and even Daisy had to admit she couldn't say, one hundred percent, *they* matched.

'Think of your signature, Daisy. Mine's never the same twice—is yours?'

'But signatures prove that cheques are legit', and legal documents rely on them.'

'Yes, and if there's a dispute, I've no doubt a handwriting expert can confirm whether a signature's genuine or not. We're not experts.'

Her face sets. 'Then we need one—an expert. I'll find somebody on the internet and send them photos of our samples.'

She looks a lot happier, and I have to admit that's not a bad idea. 'Alright, so long as it doesn't cost too much.'

Rebecca arrives with our starters, and we both gape at exquisitely carved melon seashells sprinkled with fine blue and beige dust. My nostrils twitch at a fresh ocean tang. Rebecca trots off wearing a smirk (which covers more of her than that dress) as I pick up my fork and spear a shell, hold it under my nose, then pop it in my mouth.

A myriad of tantalisingly elusive flavours erupt around the ice-cold melon while melting sprinkles crackle on my tongue. The "whole" screams "*it's party time*" at my palate.

'This is bloody good.' There's an aura of bliss settling over Daisy as she chews.

I'm still trying to identify what kind of magical spice has scooped the essence of melon into a vat of fireworks. 'What *is* that... whatever she's put on it?'

'Dunno,' Daisy says, forking more into her mouth. 'Don't care—it's brill.'

Rebecca clears our empty plates and returns a moment later. The new plates each contain a slab of battered haddock sitting next to a measly helping of peas, the two surrounded by a scattering of chips. Our disappointment must show, because she whispers 'Just try it' before skipping away.

Daisy cuts a piece of fish and shoves it offhandedly between her lips. Then she sits stock still, chewing, and stares at her plate.

That bad?

Feeling downcast, I stab a chip and lift it to my mouth. A moment later, I put the fork down and look at Daisy. 'How can a chip taste that good?'

'This batter's incredible—it's Guinness on a fish.'

Maggie's even done something to the peas, infusing them with spicy zings and zests that make my eyes water.

We eat silently, dumbstruck. When we finish, Daisy sits back with a sigh. 'What d'you think, Sam?'

'I think...'

114

I grin at her and, for the first time today, a wave of optimism rushes over me. '... I can't wait to try her home-made ice cream.'

THE ICE CREAM DOESN'T DISAPPOINT. AS WE STAND TO leave, Rebecca returns for the pudding dishes. 'Well—did you enjoy it?'

'Enjoy it? That was incredible. I've never tasted anything so... exquisite.'

Rebecca picks up the empty bowls, then puts them down again. She's enjoying the reflected glory. 'Maggie's a superb cook, but it's her special herbs that make the difference. She adds them to everything.'

What sort of herbs produce flavours like that? I repeat the thought out loud.

'I'm calling them herbs, but she uses all sorts— leaves, petals, roots, you name it. She won't tell me where she learnt all that stuff, but boy does it work.'

She smirks. 'But you know that now.'

Rebecca bustles off, and on the way out we pass our dining companion. He doesn't look up—too busy shovelling ice cream at his face. His expression is beatific.

We exit into the residents lounge by passing under an archway. Opposite, at the far end, is another—which leads to reception. The third, on the rear wall, is where we're going next—the public bar. But first, a pause to catch our breath.

To our delight, the heavily upholstered armchairs scattered about the lounge turn out to be incredibly comfortable.

'Sam, that was amazing.'

'You know what? I don't think we need a new chef after all.'

Daisy's knees are pumping. 'Can't you see the Michelin stars? Showers of them.'

Her excitement's infectious. 'I'll be happy with some great reviews on TripAdvisor—anyone who experiences flavours like that *has* to rave about them. Especially when we get a full à la carte and separate wine list sorted. All we need is for people to try it.'

Daisy glances at the bar entrance, and her smile fades. The blare of a televised football match is shattering what would be a relaxed atmosphere through here—it sends me whirling back to the night Jake's pal sent him that silly text. Another flurry of catcalls and piercing whistles confirms what Logan said about the bar regulars. 'Right, let's take a gander at our biggest income stream.'

Daisy's lip curls. 'And our biggest hurdle to attracting family business.'

Grimly, we approach the bar. Even from this side of the archway we can see blue light from the telly flickering on every surface. Something vaguely "Amsterdam" about that...

Drawing closer, the noise increases exponentially. Slipping inside, we pause. Stood like statues, nobody's noticed us yet.

About twenty customers sit agog at tables and on barstools, twice that number of eyes glued to a television mounted high on the wall. They're all men, clad in varying degrees of shabbiness. Hair varies from none to shaggy, and that's just their chins. Most of them are middle-aged, with only a smattering of youths and OAPs.

On-screen, somebody's goalie leaps for the ball and bats it clear. Our customers protest, and the floor vibrates.

'That went over the line.'

'Where are ye, ref?'

'Get it, y'idjit. Ahhh. Y' wally...'

They're a rough bunch, but I'm not sure there's any harm in them. This isn't a gang of skinheads out for trouble. More like farm workers and shop staff making the most of what's essentially Cairncroft's only source of night-time entertainment.

I came in here looking for a way to get rid of them. Maybe that's the wrong approach...

On impulse, I march over to the telly and yank out its plug. The screen dies, and every eye turns to me.

They don't look friendly.

I caught Daisy unawares, but now she springs alongside and takes up what I recognise as a judo-ready stance. She whispers from the corner of her mouth: 'Are you out of your mind?'

117

Possibly

With both hands in the air, palms facing forwards, I try to keep my voice steady. 'Sorry to interrupt, but I'm the new owner and I'd like to tell you about my plans. By the way, I hope you'll all have a "how do you do" drink with me—Logan will do the honours. Order whatever you like.'

I think Logan's about to duck under the bar— either that, or he's reaching for a rifle, Wild West style.

'There's a catch,' I scream, as they all swivel to their bemused barman. 'You have to wait until I'm finished. Then you get your... *two*... free drinks.'

They look a lot friendlier after nixing tonight's profits

I thrust an arm at the silent telly. 'What do you do when there isn't a match on? Watch Coronation Street? Wouldn't you rather play darts, or shoot some pool—maybe even have a wee flutter on the fruit machines?'

I'm making this up as I go along but, to my amazement, it's all coming together. 'You know the big snooker room?'

A massive bloke with a white beard Santa would be proud to call his own yells: 'Not really—we aren't allowed in there wi' the nobs.' A muttered wave of support erupts around him.

'Well, you're more important to me than whoever uses the snooker room. I've decided to move this bar—*your* bar—through there, because it's bigger. The snooker table's going in a skip to make room for a dartboard, pool table, a one-armed bandit—we'll have regular pub quizzes, in fact I'll get you a quiz machine too—and there'll be bar snacks available, and... um... dominoes?' *Quit while you're ahead, Sam* 'What d'you think, guys?'

There's a murmur as they consult, and for a moment I'm sure it's all gone wrong. Then Santa shouts 'Sounds good to me,' and the rest follow on with 'when's it happening' and 'can we have a footie table?'

I point at the hairy jersey. 'Footie table—great idea. I'll add that to the list. As for "when?"—as soon as possible. I'll keep you posted.'

My nerves overtake me, and I practically run out of the bar.

Okay, hobble

To my amazement, a cheer breaks out behind me.

Daisy catches up at the lift. 'Sam, you're a star. The snooker room has its own back door, so they won't be coming in here at all.'

'Yep—we'll only allow public access to the new bar through what'll be its own entrance—and we can soundproof the room if we have to.'

'Genius. And the snooker room's big enough for all those toys you promised them.'

She claps my shoulder. 'Do we need to spend quite that much on bribes, though?'

'Daisy, they're the only ones giving us money just now—and think about it, most of the stuff I mentioned, like slot machines and pub food, will

generate extra income. It'll all pay for itself—
eventually.'

She looks at me the way a puppy would, and I
feel a thrill ripple through my chest.

I can do this

I'm good at it

Logan dashes up as the lift arrives, somehow
reminding me of the March Hare. Daisy gives him
an incredulous look. 'You can't leave that lot on their
own—they'll drink us dry.'

'R... Rebecca's taken over for a m... minute,' he
wheezes. 'N... nice speech, g... great ideas.'

Every time I see Logan, I grow more sceptical
about Rebecca's cliping. I couldn't imagine him
killing a fly, never mind his stepfather—or Aunt
Claire. Yet if killers looked like killers, there'd be no
unsolved murders.

'Thanks, Logan. It was all a bit spur of the
moment...'

'O... only thing,' he interrupts. 'The snooker
club in Donstable meets here twice a week. They pay
a fair whack to rent the room, and there's usually
about eight of them come through for dinner
afterwards. Th... they hold parties here, too—
Christmas, regular social evenings...'

My joints turn wooden as I swing to Daisy,
who's still staring at Logan. It takes two nudges to
get her attention.

'Daisy, nip back to the bar and fetch a bottle of
vodka. I'll see you upstairs...'

WHEN DAISY WALKS INTO THE FLAT WITH A LITRE BOTTLE tucked under her arm, I'm taking a call. (Not on my mobile—this came through on the hotel extension.)

'Would you excuse me one moment,' I say sweetly, and make a swiping motion at Daisy to hurry her over.

'It's the snooker club,' I mouth—and point at the handset.

Daisy slaps her free hand over her eyes, and I return to my call.

'Sorry about that, Mr Entwhistle. Now, you were saying?—

No, I definitely did *not* refer to the snooker club as a "waste of space". He's winding you up—no, listen, I didn't know there was this... rivalry... between your club and those bar guys. If I had, I would have spoken to you first—

Absolutely not. In reality, it's more you I'm doing it for. The snooker club's custom is so valuable I've decided to upgrade you to a new room more in keeping with your status. The current one is far too big—you must get lost in it. Also, you're cut off back there—you deserve to be in the swing of things. It'll give you easier access to refreshments, for example—

121

What? But...—

No, I mean, yes, of course we'll be buying you a better snooker table—

Yes, naturally I'll want to consult with you on the best model. Oh, really? Well, the baize is so important—I agree, good solid stuff, oak. Yes, that sounds—

How much? Really, that's what they cost? No, of course it isn't a problem. I agree, we need to meet up—

Yes, lunch is a good idea. I'll ring you—

Oh... yes, of course you'll be our guest at lunch—

And the committee? How many are we talking—

That many? Goodness. No, that's fine. I'll look forward to it—

Goodnight, Mr Entwhistle.'

I drop the handset into its cradle. Then point a shaking finger at the bottle still lodged under Daisy's arm. 'Get that open while I fetch some glasses.'
    My mind's swimming and my stump's throbbing as I stagger through to the kitchen, grab

122

two glasses, and return with them. Daisy has the bottle uncapped and pours us both healthy measures. I knock mine back in a oner and slam my glass on the coffee table. 'Again.'

She giggles, gives me a refill. 'Have I got this right, Sam? One of those toe-rags downstairs got straight on the phone to that snooker club and started crowing—told them they were being ousted—and you've just smoothed it over by promising an upgraded snooker room complete with top of the range table and a free lunch for this Entwhistle character and his hangers-on.'

'Right in one,' I croak, half-way through my second shot. Daisy tops up her own glass and takes a gulp while I wait anxiously for her reaction.

'You did good, Sam. I'm proud of you—that's what I call thinking on your feet.'

She sips this time, then: 'Have we got enough cash for all that?'

My lips tighten. 'We'll find it—even if it means shelving the tennis school. It's my own fault—I should have prepared properly before shooting my mouth off. Studied those accounts, talked to the staff—Daisy, I should have *known* about the snooker club.'

She pats my shoulder. 'Chin up, Sam. You've worked a blinder—hey, maybe we should put some one-armed bandits in the new snooker room, too.'

I have to laugh with her. I'm glad she doesn't think I'm the fool I feel. 'Mr Entwhistle didn't sound the Vegas type—Daisy, let's get drunk. You can sleep here.'

'But my room's only across the passage.'

'I know, but… this thing with Logan? I'd rather not be by myself tonight. Hey, maybe you should just move in—we could be flatmates. It seems daft you sleeping in a staff bedroom.'

'What about Jake?'

'He's got his own room…'

Oh, I see what she means. Jake, no doubt, expects to move in here, too—when we "sort things out". He wouldn't be chuffed if Daisy beat him to it—and there's no way those two could be flatmates. Think Joe Biden sharing a flat with Vladimir Putin…

The vodka's taking hold—suddenly, Jake doesn't seem all that important.

Surprisingly, Daisy scowls when I share that. 'Sam, you know how I feel about your so-called boyfriend, but you shouldn't use me as an excuse.'

'I'm not…'

'Yes, you are. If you're going to tell Jake he should sling his hook, do it properly—don't make namby-pamby excuses like "Oh, Daisy's here now".'

She's right. I'm looking for an easy way out. I think—trouble is, my thinking's getting hazier with every refill. Is this the third? 'You'll stay tonight, though?' I plead.

'Course I will,' she says immediately—and pours me another drink.

FOUR

My head still feels like a mealy pudding next day when the surveyor, Mr Kerritson, calls my mobile—am I free? He's ready to give the verbal report.

It's four o'clock, and I've only been up a few hours. Luckily, Daisy was around when Mr Kerritson arrived—*she* was up with the birds (despite the fact she drank more than I did last night) and outside doing Tai Chi when he rolled up on (apparently) a motorbike fit to send your average Hells Angel into paroxysms of envy.

I suggest we meet in the restaurant and when I arrive, Mr Kerritson's busy making a display of plans and photographs on one of the tables.

He looks up through blue-rimmed spectacles complete with side-shields. They sit slightly crooked under an orange hardhat that tries (and fails) to cover a shock of jet-black hair that, taken together with the bandanna beard, makes me think of Hagrid.

'Please,' I beg, already regretting the late breakfast I inflicted on my still-delicate digestive system. 'Give me it straight—don't beat about the bush. Do we need bulldozers and wrecking balls?'

He smiles—is that good? Or maybe he's trying to soften the blow? 'For a building this age, showing an obvious lack of maintenance in recent years, you're actually in decent shape.'

125

He raises a forefinger, holds it vertical. 'But... there *are* some issues. Nothing too horrible, I promise.'

I slump in the nearest chair. 'What are they? The "issues".'

'Well, for a start, the roof needs work...'

I've dreaded hearing those words

'... you'll need some pointing doing outside, and there's more woodworm in the attic. On the plus side, your electrics are sound—I know the fittings look ancient, but that's because they are. Easily replaced with jazzier styles as part of your refurbishing—where was I? Oh yes, and the plumbing's all fine. So's the lift—well, it's safe, that's the best I can say about *it*. The roof, pointing, and woodworm—they're the priorities, but I've also got a long list of niggly little jobs that can't wait—shall I take you through them?'

I swing my head from one side to the other— slowly, because my brain and skull are still playing at dodgem cars. 'Let's jump to the nitty gritty. How much will it cost to put right? In total.'

He stares at all his neatly arranged papers and photos, then sighs. 'Okay, bottom line? You're looking in the region of twenty-five grand—that includes my fee.'

Oh, wow. I was expecting... a LOT more

Suddenly, the world looks less jaded. Steeling myself, I pose the second question that's kept me awake. 'You remember I asked you to check specifically for safety hazards? Did you find *anything* that could have caused my aunt's death?'

'Absolutely nothing.' He didn't hesitate for a nanosecond, speaking with the unshakeable authority of someone with more letters than Royal Mail after his name. Is this good news or bad?

If there'd been lead in the water, or electricity loitering around looking for someplace to go, I'd have a tangible explanation for Aunt Claire's unexpected demise. Something I could fix—and an end to speculation. 'Alright, what now?'

He lowers himself into the seat opposite. 'If you want, I'll factor the work for you. That would add another ten percent, but I know the best people to use and they know me—and quote accordingly, which goes a long way to offsetting my fee.'

I don't really have any choice, not having a scooby where to begin—I'm the sort of person who makes builders rub their hands with glee. 'You've sold me. When can you start?'

He looks at his watch. 'Right now. I'll make a few calls before I leave, to get the ball rolling. Is it alright if I stay in here for another half hour?'

Dinner's not 'til seven thirty, so I assure him that's fine. Turning away, I remember. 'Oh—did you have time to look at the stable block?'

'I did—no problems there. All you have to do is sweep out the dust and it'll be ready to use. Pouring a tennis court won't break the bank either—I'll get you a quote for that. Tell you what, though, the old well is dangerous. It *has* to be made safe—that's a lawsuit waiting to happen.'

Sugar—I hadn't thought of that. I was just worried about anyone getting hurt. 'Did you include capping it in your quote?'

He grins. 'Sure did. Hey, I nearly forgot.'

He feels in his pocket, brings out a black mobile phone, and hands it over. 'I found this in the stable block—it'd slipped through a gap in the floorboards. You see how grimy it is—obviously been there a while. Just a "pay as you go", but somebody might want it back.'

Who could have lost a mobile phone in the stable block? Nobody goes there, and it's kept locked. I press the "on" button—nothing happens. 'The battery's dead—I'll charge it up and try to figure out who's it is. Thanks, Mr Kerritson.'

'Davy,' he says, shaking my hand—and I'm surprised how soft his feels. 'Call me Davy.'

WALKING BACK THROUGH THE RESIDENTS LOUNGE, I come to a sudden halt. Jake's standing in reception, a suitcase at his feet, talking to someone—I can't see who. I wasn't expecting him until later, but he must have caught an earlier train.

A frisson of excitement catches me unawares. It could be association—seeing him here, where we met.

Or, maybe I've been too hard on him—despite putting on a few pounds, Jake's a good-looking guy and (when he's not in the pub) a brilliant listener. Suddenly, I miss those intimate evenings and all-round sense of togetherness that were our first weeks. We talked for hours about anything and everything.

Then I remember it was me doing most of the talking—brilliant listener he might be, but Jake gives away so little I know practically nothing about his past life.

Forcing my legs into action, I carry on through the archway and immediately see who he's with—it's Logan. I can't make out what they're saying, but Jake's tone is hostile. Logan looks pale, eyes fluttering like the wings of a trapped moth.

Then Jake spots me and throws his arms wide. 'Samantha—babe.'

I wish he wouldn't call me that

Logan turns abruptly and scuttles off, disappearing through the stairway door. It also leads to the snooker room, but today's not a club day and I can't picture Logan balanced on one foot, sinking coloured balls.

Maybe he's just headed anywhere Jake isn't...

Fending off Jake's clumsy grab, I remember where we are and rein in (some of) my annoyance. 'What was that all about?'

Jake glances over his shoulder. 'Logan's a prick. Never liked me, and he's narked 'cos I'm back. Don't worry, though—I set him straight.'

'You set him straight?' I repeat, separating the words.

'Yeah—let him know he's not my boss any more. Not now *we're...*'

Daisy's told me I bounce between two extremes—either I'm a walkover, or bursting out of my shirt like "The Hulk" used to do.

I can feel my blouse getting tighter. 'Now that we're *what*? Hasn't it penetrated your thick skull that *we* are on a pretty shaky wicket? Jake, I'm trying to rescue a failing business, and what I *don't* need is you fighting with my under-manager.'

He backs off a step, mouth open to deliver words that sensibly decide to stay where they are. Then he grins his trademark grin, the one that reminds everyone he's a nice guy. 'Sorry, Sam, but I know him better than you. Logan's a little Hitler, and now that I don't answer to him any more...'

When I hold up a hand, Jake flinches. A quick glance confirms my skin hasn't turned green—yet. 'You DO answer to him, Jake. You're the handyman—he's your boss. Try not to forget it. Rebecca will give you the key to your room—I'll see you later.'

An image of Jake's slack mouth and bulging eyes stays with me while the lift doors close. Then I let myself slump against cool metal and start trying to work out what just happened. The lift's doing its

130

usual "one step forward, two back" routine and right now I'm grateful to have thinking time.

Why am I sticking up for Logan, who may well have blackmailed and murdered my aunt? Was it an excuse to lay down ground rules to Jake? Or am I getting carried away with my new role as boss of this place and (*shudder*) becoming a female version of Callum?

When the doors open up again, I've calmed down. Daisy's favourite mantra rings in my head.

"*Don't think, do*"

Right at this moment, I've got more to worry about than Jake.

SAFELY BACK IN MY FLAT, I STRAIGHTAWAY PLUG IN THE phone Mr... *Davy...* found. My charger doesn't fit, but Daisy's does, and she won't mind me using it—if she does, she shouldn't have left it lying about.

Then I plonk my laptop on Aunt Claire's secretaire and open the cardboard folder Davy gave me. He's thorough, no doubt about that—even this scribbled summary reads like a post-mortem, littered with technical terms I'm having to google.

Post-mortem—I flop back in my chair, plunged yet again into the mystery of Aunt Claire's death. If only the procurator had ordered a PM, we'd know why a seemingly healthy woman died in her sleep. I still can't believe Logan had anything to do with it. I've only known him a few weeks, but he's the last person I'd suspect of being a criminal—especially a murderer. He's just too... nice.

There *has* to be another explanation for those photos and the notes on their backs.

Shaking myself, I finish digesting Davy's jottings and start allocating what's left of our meagre operating capital.

I'm almost finished when the door bursts open and Daisy makes a typically dramatic entrance. '*Sam.* I got an answer from the handwriting people.'

'That was quick.' My pulse quickens. 'What did they say?'

She closes the door first, then turns to face me and her voice drops. 'The samples are too small to be... definitive. Our handwriting expert says there's a seventy percent probability they match.'

'Seventy percent. Hmm—I'd call thirty percent reasonable doubt.'

'I know—I wasn't expecting "probabilities". I thought he'd just say "yes" or "no".'

'Did he give an opinion on whether it was the same person who wrote the notes on both photos?'

'I didn't ask—he charges by the sample and, with you narking about the cost, it didn't seem worth paying extra to confirm something that's already obvious.'

It is?

'Which photo did you send him? The "what would his wife think" or the "let me know when you decide"?'

She scratches her head. 'Can't remember—does it matter?'

'S'pose not, seeing as how the opinion isn't exactly conclusive. How much *did* it cost to find out he didn't know?'

If looks could kill, I'd be talking to Aunt Claire now

'Not much. Why are you grinning?'

I've just noticed what she's wearing. A denim trouser and waistcoat combination has superseded yesterday's "Grease" outfit, and that red neckerchief under the neck of her billowy white shirt lends a "Wild West" slant—if she had a pair of six-guns strapped to her waist, I wouldn't fancy Buffalo Bill's chances against "Deranged Daisy". Although, I do think the hair would be more at home on an Apache warrior...

'Nothing.'

Daisy "humph"s, then moves behind me and scans Davy's notes over my shoulder. 'Oh, has the surveyor finished? What's his verdict?'

She exhales like I did at the bottom line. 'Beauty,' she croons, then looks thoughtful. 'Actually, he is—easy on the eye, I mean. Can't you just feel that hair scrunching between your fingers...?'

'Don't talk to me about men,' I protest, and fill her in on my encounter with Jake.

133

'I wonder what that was about—him and Logan? You said before they aren't buddies. I'll have a nosey around—see what I can find out. Anyway, what're you doing now?'

'A business plan, and I want to bounce it off you.'

'Go ahead.'

She throws herself on the sofa, and I turn my eyes screen-ward. 'Alright, so after paying Davy—I mean Mr Kerritson...'

'Oooh—*Davy.*'

'Shut up. After paying—the surveyor—including what it costs to fix the faults he found, and after clearing our inherited debt, we've still got nearly twenty-four thousand pounds left from selling my flat.'

She whistles. 'We can do a lot with...'

'If we repair the potholes properly, refit both bar and snooker room—and buy a new, top of the range snooker table—'

'How much is that, anyway?'

'You don't want to know. I'm also budgeting for another bar in the residents lounge to keep guests and locals separate. After all that, plus a very budget-conscious redecoration and re-carpeting, and if we bring the kitchen equipment up to a semi-modern standard—and ditch the tennis school for now—it leaves us a balance of... minus fourteen thousand pounds.'

'And that's without marketing?' she wails. 'We're dead in the water before we start.'

'No, we aren't. I gave Mr M a ring and he thinks, now the debt's cleared, our bank would front an overdraft up to twenty thousand—maybe more. It still doesn't leave a lot for marketing, though.'

She relaxes a little. 'But we can throw our profits at marketing. How much are we making?'

'Um... well, assuming you and I don't take any wages until things improve, and Logan's in a position to do the same, then our monthly profit's somewhere around fifty pounds.'

'What?'

Her face disappears into her hands. 'How's that possible? With bar takings, and the snooker club...'

'Daisy, it costs over *ten grand* a month just to keep this place open.'

Being Daisy, her despair's fleeting. 'At least we're not trading at a loss.'

If her glass was empty, Daisy would get excited about the volume of air still swilling around inside it. She does have a point, though... 'You're right, Dais'. We don't need to generate tons of money straight off—my savings will feed us for a few months yet. And until we can afford a proper marketing campaign, there're loads of ways to start putting the word out...'

'Facebook' she screams, and I cringe.

'I'll leave social media to you. There'll be enough cash for some modest advertising, and we could try and tout conference business from companies in Aberdeen...'

'What's that?'

Springing up, she zeroes in on the "lost" phone and picks it up. 'This isn't yours.'

'No, Davy found it at the stable block. I'm waiting for it to charge so I can identify the owner.'

Daisy stabs the on-button. 'It's turning on now.' She starts clicking.

'Don't go nosing into someone's phone. We only need to know...'

'I'm just looking at the messages, to see whose it is...'

She stiffens, stares at the screen. 'Sam, this is Logan's.'

'Logan's?'

I jump up as she strides over and waves the phone in my face. 'Look at this.'

It's a "sent" text.

Sis - call me back - it's urgent L

I shrug. 'What's the big deal?'

She taps a sparkly fingernail on the "details" at the bottom. 'It's the last message in his "out" folder—went out at three pm on the third of August, nearly a year ago.'

I still don't get it. 'So?'

'That's when the fire was—on the afternoon of third August. Around three pm. When, according to his alibi, Logan was supposed to be in Aberdeen—with his sister.'

FIVE

'He made a twenty-second call to his sister—Trudy—then fired off that text a minute later.'

'So *she* didn't answer and *he* left a voicemail, then backed it up with a text?'

Daisy nods. 'That's what I think. Sam, this is huge—it breaks Logan's alibi for his stepfather's death.'

'Does it, though?'

I'm thinking, hard. 'Logan could have been in Aberdeen when he sent the text, then come back here however many days later and lost his phone. Did the sister reply?'

Daisy smacks her forehead, winces. 'Never thought of that—I haven't checked his inbox.'

She taps furiously, then thrusts the handset at me. 'Trudy did reply, after ten minutes—but it doesn't tell us anything.'

What's up, Logan? T x

'And *he* definitely didn't reply to *that*?'

'Nope. Which suggests he'd already lost the phone. Probably shoved it at a pocket and missed—his text sounds agitated, suggesting he wasn't firing on all cylinders. Having tried and failed to get hold of his sister, he rushes off to deal with whatever's bothering him. Later, he discovers the phone's missing—but can't find it. If that's how it happened, Logan was here when he was supposed to be in Aberdeen. Just as Rebecca said.'

Slapping a palm against the nape of my neck, I try: 'What if Logan and Trudy got separated in Aberdeen—then found each other right after Trudy replied? That would explain why the texts stop so suddenly.'

I recognise that look—my old maths teacher is still haunting me. 'And you're also suggesting he didn't use his phone again for however long it was until he came back here and lost it?' She purses her lips. 'On the other hand, this is Logan—he won't have many mates, so it's possible...'

She thumbs the handset, staring intently, then shakes her head. 'Naw, sorry—looking at his history he makes an average of five, six calls a day, and sends the same number of texts. There's no getting away from it—Logan lost this phone around the time his stepfather died, when he was supposed to be in Aberdeen. Sam, what are we going to do? I think you *have* to involve the police.'

Every instinct recoils. 'I see how it looks—but, Logan? Logan couldn't hurt anybody—far less murder a member of his family. Some things you just know in your gut.'

But what if I'm wrong, and Logan has me fooled?

138

Daisy has no such qualms. 'You only met him a couple of weeks ago. And anyway, sociopaths are renowned for being the last people you'd suspect. That's why they're so difficult to catch.'

'Okay, okay...'

She's right, we can't sit on this. I hold out my hand for the phone. 'I'll take it into Donstable, to the police, first thing tomorrow.'

As if the thought of that isn't making me feel sick enough, there's also... 'Listen, I have to see Jake. Thinking about it, I was too hard on him when he arrived—I should clear the air.'

Mentioning friction between Jake and me cheers *her* up no end. Then she knits her brows. 'By the way, where am I sleeping tonight?'

I really can't believe Logan's a psycho, but I'm coming 'round to the idea somebody is, so I'd rather not be on my own listening to an old building make creaky noises in the dead of night. 'What about a compromise? Why don't you unpack in your own room, then bring what you need for the next few days over here? After that, we can play it by ear.'

'Okay—fine. To be honest, sleeping on my own before this is sorted gives me the heebie-jeebies.'

That, I *didn't* expect. If Lara Croft's worried, where does it leave me? But I don't let on how taken aback I am. 'Great. That's settled. If not before, I'll see you downstairs for dinner?'

Daisy nods, her eyes turning dreamy. 'I wonder what Maggie's cooking tonight.'

OUTSIDE JAKE'S DOOR, KNUCKLES RAISED AND READY, I decide to put in some genuine effort. I've been pretty "off" with him recently—yes, sometimes it was like living with a pig, but I'm hardly genteel myself. If I believe him about the pranky text, what's he done that's so terrible?

Nothing

But instead of knocking, I lower my hand. Who am I kidding? I need to get a handle on my feelings—or the sudden lack thereof—before we talk.

Then the door swings open and Jake beams out. 'Thought I heard somebody. Come in.'

His arm sweeps into the room and I follow it, trying to hide the numbness settling over me.

I *will* make that effort.

Casting my eyes around, they land on Jake's suitcase. It's lying on the floor, in a corner. The lid's up—all his things are still inside. He obviously regards this as a temporary stop not worth unpacking for. Probably intends to live out of a suitcase until he takes his rightful place in my new flat. Thinking back, I don't actually remember *agreeing* to him moving into the flat in Edinburgh...

And just like that, all my good intentions vaporise. Suddenly, I'm irritated—angry, even—at his presumption. He's a cuckoo—a parasite.

Daisy was right

Though I can't forget he probably saved my life... 'What?'

I shrug, because I didn't hear the question. 'Jake, let's get something straight. We've grown apart—or maybe it's me. Doesn't matter. We are NOT an item any more. I promised you this job, and a roof over your head—and we need a handyman anyway, especially during the renovations—but it's time you and I established some ground rules. We're friends. I'm your boss—for now at least. But that's all.'

I wait, the silence getting louder while Jake's face stretches through a variety of expressions, each signalling the moment one of those declarations hit home. Then he sinks onto the bed and dips his head. 'Whatever you say, Sam.'

I feel better for delivering that message, but what to do next? My favourite option, leaving without another word, seems unnecessarily harsh. Yet the dynamics between us are changing so fast, I don't know how to carry on a conversation with him any more. 'Did you find somewhere to stay okay, in Edinburgh?'

'Andy's couch,' he mutters.

Then his head comes up, a laboured movement that matches the effort in his voice. 'What about you—where'd you go?'

'Daisy's place—couch, like you.'

Oh, this is painful. I've just remembered— there is something I want to know

141

I glance at a chair beside the bed, then decide against it. Despite the protest rally being organised under my left knee, I'd rather keep an air of formality. 'Jake, what's going on with you and Logan?'

'Nothing.'

An automatic response, like the email acknowledgements from customer service departments. 'It's not "nothing". Why is there bad blood between you?'

He drags the back of a hand across his brow. 'I hate bothering you with this stuff, Sam...'

Translation—I'm dying to tell you

'Go on.'

'Logan and me—we fell out when I was here before. This may shock you, Sam, but Claire was having an affair with Graham the gardener.'

He looks surprised when I don't. Seeing nothing forthcoming, he carries on. 'Okay, so Logan does a private dick gig, takes photos of Claire and Graham together, then threatens he'll show them to Graham's wife unless Claire pays up. When Claire decides she's involving the police, Logan pins it on me by telling her he used his master key to search my room—and found copies of the photos.'

'Wait a minute. How do you know it was Logan blackmailing her?'

'Sam, the photos weren't mine—how else do you explain it?'

Well, I'm dead wrong about someone. Whether it's Logan or Jake is anyone's guess. 'So what happened then?'

'Claire confronted me and I denied it, but she fired me anyway. Couldn't see past her blue-eyed boy.'

'She fired you? That's not what you told me... the story I got was you'd resigned, a big romantic gesture so you could come looking for me in Edinburgh.'

He clacks his teeth together. It's loud. 'I could hardly tell you she'd sacked me...'

'Wait a minute,' I snap, remembering. 'All that stuff about "don't say anything to your aunt yet—she might not approve". Making out you thought she'd be upset I'd taken up with the handyman. That was to keep me from finding out you'd been sacked.'

He wobbles his head from side to side. 'Well, yeah—what else could I do?'

'Um—tell the truth, maybe? Trust me to believe you? You could at least have given me the option to decide for myself. Jake—you must have known it would come out eventually.'

'Of course, but I reckoned by then you'd know me better, so it wouldn't matter. Sam...'

I thrust a palm at him. 'No. Whatever it is, that's all I can take right now.'

I make for the door, and he wheedles: 'Sam.'

'What?' I stop, but don't turn.

'Is there still *any* chance for... us?'

What planet do you live on?

143

I leave without answering.

MEALS ARE PART OF THE DEAL FOR LIVE-IN STAFF—BUT they're expected to eat them in the kitchen. So at least I don't have to worry about seeing Jake in the restaurant when Daisy and I come down to dinner.

'Now I get it,' Daisy crows, as the main course arrives.

'Get what?'

'Well, it's Chicken Maryland tonight, so that starter was melon "eggs".'

'What did you think they were?'

'I dunno—rugby balls?'

Our pudding is—three guesses—ice cream, but we're not complaining. Maggie's food is magic—sheer magic. Maybe she is a witch. What's worrying me is that Daisy and I are the restaurant's sole occupants.

When Rebecca comes back for our empty dishes, I ask: 'do we not have any guests staying tonight?'

She looks embarrassed. 'I heard Logan take a booking for tomorrow.'

As she slopes off, I turn to Daisy. 'One booking every other night? We won't last long on that.'

Daisy grins. 'In a few weeks, there'll be no room for us in here and we'll be eating in the kitchen. That's a point—the kitchen isn't big enough. Where are all the new staff going to eat?'

Rebecca's ears are flapping. She stops, turns, and edges back. 'You hiring, then? Only, I know a couple of lasses in the village who're good workers.'

'Not yet,' I say firmly. 'But soon—I'll keep that in mind, Rebecca.'

She leaves, looking disappointed. 'Rebecca's just bored,' Daisy says. 'Wants young company. Hey, weren't you planning to grill her some more about seeing Logan after the fire?'

'I decided, if I'm going to the police, that's best left to them.'

Daisy nods her approval. 'Yep, you don't want to queer their pitch.'

'Actually—' I've been giving this a lot of thought, despite the sit-in Jake's staging in my head '—I had an idea. What if I phone Mr M first thing, and ask his advice? I'm hoping he might put me onto someone in the police who would—well, handle the situation with more aplomb than if I just chuck it at some desk sergeant.'

'Good thinking. Also, Mr M will make sure they don't come after us as accessories.'

'Daisy, we were still in Edinburgh when Logan's house burned down. How could we be accessories?'

'Ah, but you're delaying handing in vital evidence. That could make you an accessory.'

'Davy only gave me it this afternoon,' I protest, feeling a familiar sting of exasperation. 'And what's

145

with the "you"—don't forget, it was *you* who started tampering with that "evidence".'

A hand flies to her mouth, and I grin. 'Relax, I'll visit you in prison.'

Then, an all too brief upswing in my mood takes a dive when Daisy returns to the "subject du jour". 'So you've really finished with him this time?'

'It looks that way.'

Lifting my paper napkin, I pull off a corner. 'I think Jake was an infatuation that's run its course—I regret now offering him a job here.'

She makes a "pff" sound. 'Infatuation? He conned you, has been right from the beginning. I told you...'

'You did.'

I cock my head. Put a hand to my ear. 'Daisy, is that...?'

Daisy giggles. 'Yep, that's Jake singing along with the bar crowd. He's probably a founder member of the—I've decided to call them "The Cairncroft Cowboys". That reminds me, have you thought about toilets?'

Please tell me that outfit you're wearing doesn't mean... did she say "toilets"?

'Not recently, no...'

She puffs. 'There're no toilets in the snooker room. If we're cutting off this new public bar's access to the hotel proper, you'll have to install toilets.'

Sugar

'That never occurred to me. Oh—beggar. I haven't budgeted for it.'

A chunk of paper napkin joins its smaller predecessors.

Daisy waves her fingers, as though she's shooing a wasp. 'The overdraft'll cover it. Are you going to use Davy for the alterations as well?'

'Yep. I'll ring him tomorrow and ask for quotes, then I can do a proper projection and talk to the bank.'

'You like him, don't you?'

She waggles a finger in front of my nose, and I'm tempted to snap my teeth at it. 'He's good at his job. I'm glad to have him helping us...'

'And you're single again.' She says it in a sing-song voice.

Deciding I can't take any more of this, not right now, I stand. 'Come on, let's have that chat with Maggie.'

And try not to run into Logan

WE FIND MAGGIE SITTING ON A STOOL, BLOWING cigarette smoke out the door.

She jumps up and frisbees her fag (more or less) towards the rubbish hoppers. 'Miss Chessington—did you enjoy your dinner?' she blurts, batting at her hair.

For a chef who comes up with the sort of flavours still dancing a flamenco on my palate, I'll ignore our smoking rules. 'It was… I can't find words to do it justice, Maggie. You're a genius.'

She simpers, and Daisy gets down to business. 'Maggie, you know we're hoping the hotel will get busier soon. Could you start thinking about a bigger menu? We'll need a choice of at least three starters, four mains, and maybe five puddings.'

Daisy's theory is: after any given course, tempting diners further requires progressively more choices.

Maggie looks as though her budgie just died. (Or her black cat?) 'Oh, no—that won't work,' she cries. 'That won't work at all.'

'Why not?' I ask, wondering what I'm missing.

She starts pacing, head flung back. 'You don't know how long it takes to prepare my infusions—I can't manage more than one for each course. It isn't possible. A bigger menu would mean cooking ordinary stuff again.'

Ah. By "ordinary stuff", she means conventional recipes stripped of the zest we plan to base our food marketing on. Daisy's pacing too, now. With Maggie examining the ceiling and Daisy's eyes fixed floorwards, I'm expecting a collision any second.

After two near misses, Daisy wheels on Maggie. 'Mags, if I got a supply of ready-meals, could you do *them* as extra choices and still have time for the special stuff?'

Maggie thinks, then nods. 'Aye, that wouldnae be a problem. But… ready-meals?'

Daisy turns to me. 'They exist. I've checked. High-class ready-meals—expensive, granted, but they're only padding, so people won't be put off by a "set menu". What I thought—we could keep the ready meals the same price as now, and charge extra for Maggie's specials.'

I see where she's heading—and like it. 'So there won't be much profit on these new ready-meals. But when the word gets out about Maggie's specials, and how good they are, everybody will want *them*—and we'll make a killing?'

My choice of words catches up with me, and I cringe

Daisy nods and grins while Maggie's eyes pendulum between us. 'That's all above my head—just tell me what to do, and I'll do it.'

'We'll give it some thought and let you know,' I say firmly, turning to go, but Daisy's not finished.

'Mags—is there any hemlock or oleander growing around here?'

CSI's answer to Miss Marple is back

Maggie frowns. 'Aye, ye can find oleander down behind the old stable block, but don't go near it. That stuff's deadly.'

She goes to walk past, but Daisy heads her off. 'How hard would it be to poison somebody with it—without them knowing?'

Maggie stiffens. 'Are you suggesting...?'

I step between them. 'Maggie, Daisy's not suggesting anything. She's only asking because of your expertise in—uh—botany?'

149

'Hmpf.'

Maggie looks slightly appeased—only slightly. She draws herself straight. 'Water hemlock would work best—there's some growing down by the river. Lethal it is, but with a carroty sort of taste, so it might be easier to mix in with somebody's dinner. T'would only take a wee drop to...'

'Would it look like a heart attack?' Daisy interrupts, eyes glowing.

'Never mind *look* like one—it can *cause* a heart...' She breaks off, and her forefinger springs up. 'This is about Miss Claire, isn't it? What nonsense—nobody would have wished that poor woman harm.'

Daisy turns to me and smirks. I breathe in slowly, in, out... then take hold of Maggie's shoulders. 'Sorry, Maggie. She gets carried away. Would you mind not mentioning this to anyone?'

Maggie shakes her head. Her lips are so tight they're almost invisible. I let go of her and grab Daisy's hand. 'Thanks. We'll be in touch about the menu.'

Then I drag Nancy Drew out of the kitchen.

At least she didn't bring Logan—Maggie's nephew—into it.

In the lift, Daisy looks thoughtful. 'It wasn't her.'

Here we go

'How do you work that out?'

'Far too forthcoming—she wouldn't admit knowing so much about toxic plants if she'd used one on your aunt.'

'How did *you* know about hemlock and... whatever it was? Oh, don't tell me...'

We say it together. '*The Internet.*'

The lift stops, and Daisy bounds out. She skips, key in hand, to our door. 'C'mon, roomie. Your turn to make cocoa.'

SIX

Although I call Mr M first thing, as I said I would, I've decided this is too sensitive to discuss over the phone.

Miss Dobie puts me on hold after I ask for her soonest appointment while emphasising the urgency. A minute later, she's back. He has someone due at ten, she says, but if I'm there in the next twenty minutes, he'll make time for me.

Great—even I can walk to the village in less than that.

When I arrive, Miss Dobie takes me straight in. Mr M has a half-drunk mug of coffee at his elbow and Miss Dobie offers to make me one, too. I refuse— mainly because I don't want her interrupting at a crucial moment.

Mr M beams. 'So—how can I help today?'

Once I've told him the story, he looks less cheerful.

His chair creaks as he leans back, both arms flopping on the rests. 'I have known Logan Brown all his life—not well, mind, but I've watched the lad grow up—and he always struck me as a decent, forthright sort of fellow.'

His fingers are drumming. 'I'm glad you came to me first, Samantha. The police must, of course, be informed—but I wonder if you would consider having an informal chat with an officer from Donstable before we make this official? Just so everyone gets—the whole picture, so to speak.'

I nod, feeling relieved. It would have felt so impersonal to walk into a police station and toss Logan's future at whichever Tom, Dick or Harry was on duty. This is much better—Mr M is directing me to someone who'll look at this fairly and professionally. Hopefully, sympathetically.

'Good.' He takes a slurp of coffee and lifts the phone. 'Would you mind terribly waiting outside while I make a call? Oh, and if I can arrange it, are you free to talk this morning?'

'No problem—to both' I confirm, getting up.

In the waiting room, Miss Dobie tries again to foist coffee on me. I politely turn her down, *again*, and wish she would go away. Mr M's door is solid, but even over Miss Dobie's twittering I can hear his voice. I just can't make out what he's saying.

With a final résumé of this weekend's weather forecast, Miss Dobie vanishes at the exact moment Mr M emerges. If I were a suspicious person, I'd wonder if ensuring the privacy of her boss's telephone conversations was one of her duties.

'Samantha, Detective Sergeant Bishop from Donstable CID can meet with you in half an hour—I hope that's alright?' he adds hastily.

He must see the panic on my face. 'Do you know the bus times to Donstable?' I blurt.

He looks puzzled, then laughs. 'Relax, my dear. You don't have to go to Donstable, the DS offered to come here.'

153

'Here—to your office?'

Brilliant—Mr M will look after me

My elation vaporises when he shakes his head. 'No. We felt neutral territory was more suiting to the occasion. DS Bishop is hoping to find you in the cafe downstairs at ten.'

'Fine.' I smile, try to stretch it into something more convincing. 'That's... fine...'

And terrifying

'... thank you, Mr M.' I'm already on my way out.

'Samantha, you've got at least fifteen minutes. You can wait here if you wish.'

Mr M followed me out, and now I turn in the outer doorway. 'No, that's okay. I need a couple of things from the shop. Thanks again.'

He waves, and I let the door close behind me. I don't need anything from the shop—well, nothing I can think of offhand—but I *do* need a little time on my own, to calm down.

The thought of talking to the police—of ratting Logan out to them—has set my heart thumping.

I so hope this is all a misunderstanding.

WELL... THAT'S TWENTY-FIVE MINUTES AND COUNTING. I'm on my second pot in "The Cuppa Tea", sitting at a table by the window so I'll see the policeman coming. Leaning sideways, I scan the street both ways—for the umpteenth time. Still no sign. The only people walking this way are a teenager who doesn't look old enough to get into the pub (never mind the police force) and a woman.

I sit back and sip my cooling tea. I just want this over with. Why does the thought of talking to a policeman make me feel nervous? Guilty, even—which is ridiculous. I've done nothing wrong.

As for Daisy's stupid comment about being an accessory because I didn't hand in the phone last night—come on. The fire was a year ago.

My head jerks up as the table moves, but it's not the policeman. 'I'm sorry,' I tell the woman settling in opposite me, 'but you can't sit there. I'm waiting for someone.'

She throws down a leather wallet, and I gape at her ID behind the cellophane. 'That'd be me. You *are* Samantha Chessington, aren't you?' She reaches out and I accept her hand. Mine shakes before she grasps it. 'DS Bishop—but call me Jodie.'

'I see.' Switching to automatic pilot while I give myself a mental kicking, I babble: 'Sorry, I was expecting... that is... '

She grins. Now she's stopped inspecting me as though I was a piece of evidence I see how attractive she is. Her stiff suit can't hide a figure that probably stops more traffic in a day than her uniformed colleagues manage in a month.

'Can I get you...?' Then I see the china cup in front of her—she must have stopped at the counter.

'Okay. I don't know how much Mr M—sorry, Mr MacLachlan—told you, but...'

'Let me stop you there, Sam. Is it alright if I call you Sam?' She obviously assumes it is, because she carries straight on. 'I need to make a disclosure before we go any further.' She takes a deep breath. 'I'm Logan's girlfriend.'

My first thought is—she's kidding.

The next is—*Go, Logan*

Then it dawns on me this has just become very complicated.

'So you're not here in an official capacity?'

'No, not really. Look, I'd like to tell you about that day, the day of the fire. And what led up to it. Will you let me? Then I'll answer any questions you have, and after that—well, it'll be up to you what happens next.'

If it wasn't for Mr M's involvement, I'd get up and walk out. I don't know what's going down here, but I'd rather not be part of it.

Yet, Mr M inspires trust. I can't believe *he'd* be part of anything unsavoury. So I tell Jodie to go ahead—and she starts talking.

Maybe it's the practice she's had writing police reports, but Jodie's a masterful storyteller.

She describes it all so vividly I feel as though I'm there. Watching it happen...

156

LOGAN HAS HIS THUMB IN HIS MOUTH, WORRYING AT A loose piece of skin. He's been waiting more than an hour for his stepfather. He checks his watch—the Cairncroft Hotel bar closes in five minutes.

Which means he can expect his stepfather in ten.

Nervously glancing around the front room of the cottage he grew up in, Logan reflects (not for the first time) that it's just as well the hotel is only a few minutes' walk away. Any further and Arnold, Logan's stepfather, would never make it home from his drinking sessions.

The feelings of disbelief and disgust raging inside Logan haven't lessened—quite the opposite. He's quivered with rage since last night, ever since he spoke to his sister, Trudy.

At first, he found it hard to believe. Then he realised part of him already knew, only he'd kept that part locked away, deep inside, rather than face a horror beyond his comprehension.

Making the most of a week's leave from his job at the hotel, Logan's been away visiting a friend in Aviemore. When he returned home last night, it was to find his sister in a state.

She told him their stepfather came to her bedroom the previous evening, and though his drunken stupor worked in her favour—insofar as she

157

successfully fought him off—Trudy is terrified about next time.

She might not be so lucky next time.

Logan tells her there won't *be* a next time.

Arnold's liqueur cabinet is sacrosanct, but Logan raids it regardless and pours two brandies. It should be hours yet before Arnold arrives home.

After a second brandy, Trudy breaks down and confesses what really happened the day their mother died, three years ago. Logan has always believed she fell down the stairs—a tragic accident. He'd been away when it happened—visiting relatives in Aberdeen this time.

Trudy says she saw Arnold, in a drunken rage, push their mother from the top step. Afterwards, he cried and begged Trudy not to say anything. When begging didn't work, Arnold told the then sixteen-year-old what would happen to her if she told.

Terrified, Trudy kept her silence—until now.

Logan sleeps on the floor by her bed. In the early hours, they hear their stepfather fumble his way into the house and collapse on the sofa downstairs.

Next morning, they slip out before he wakes. Logan phones their relatives in Aberdeen and explains everything. Then he puts his sister on a train. Logan's uncle suggested going to the police, but what could *they* do? Even with Jodie backing them, it would be Trudy's word against Arnold's.

Logan's nature is that of peacekeeper rather than warrior. He doesn't relish the coming confrontation, especially with no proper plan.

But the man he's waiting for attacked his sister and murdered his mother.

The front door crashes open. Logan jerks to his feet as vibrations ripple through the old building and set a paraffin lamp dancing on its rickety table by the fireplace.

Arnold weaves into the sitting room, stops dead when he sees Logan. His face turns purple—even under two days of growth. 'What are you doing here?' he yells. 'What are *you* doing here?' he yells. 'I thought you weren't back until tonight.'

'And I thought you were a human being,' Logan croaks back, his fists balling.

Logan's stepfather is bigger than he is, taller *and* wider, with muscles hardened by years of farm labour. A sickly grin lifts Arnold's white whiskers, stretching broken veins at the side of his bulbous nose. 'She told ye, then?'

'Aye.' Logan nods. 'She did.' His throat catches. 'She told me about my mother, too.'

The older man cackles. 'What are *you* going to do about it?'

'Nothing.' Logan hears the shake in his own voice, but ploughs on. 'It's you who's going to leave— leave, and never come back.'

'You're getting above yourself, laddie. I think it's time you learnt a lesson.'

When his stepfather charges, Logan's surprised at how easy it is to sidestep the clumsy attack. He watches helplessly as the older man's momentum throws him into the table by the fireplace. Arnold

159

goes down in a mess of broken wood and the old lamp shatters, showering the drunk with glass and paraffin. The lamp's metal base bounces off the stone hearth, and a spark arcs through the air—straight at Arnold.

Then Logan's backing away from a wall of flame, his stepfather a dark shadow within it, a pitiful silhouette that flails and wails in a dance of death.

Logan's legs make their own decision and he runs from the cottage, grabs his bike, and pedals like his life depends on it. He shoots up the road and through the hotel entrance, then turns sharp right and hurtles between the edge of the front lawn and its adjoining hedge. He only dimly registers a figure half-way up the drive, turning to stare at him—from the scanty outfit it's probably Rebecca—but there's no time to dwell on that.

At the far end of the lawn, Logan wrenches the handlebars left and vanishes into undergrowth so wild it threatens to overrun the earthy track beneath his wheels. The main building passes by on his left, and soon he arrives at the old stable block.

Logan leaps from the bike and lets it fall to the ground behind him, breaking into a sprint as he gropes for his keyring. As he thought, there's a key to the stable block amongst all the others. Seconds later, he slams the door behind him.

Groping through his pockets again, he locates his phone and calls Trudy.

There's no answer—panicking, he leaves a voicemail, then follows up with a text.

Sis - call me back - it's urgent L

Logan sinks to his knees on dirty straw, puts his forehead against bare brick, and tries to think. There's only one person who can help him now. He stabs at the keys.

The screen lights up.

Calling Jodie...

SEVEN

'You can imagine the state he was in.'
Jodie's pale as a ghost. Hardly any wonder—
my heart's hammering, too.

'There's an old farm track behind the hotel—
it's just about possible to get a car down it. I told
Logan to wait for me there. Then I lead-footed it
over and picked him up. The original plan had him
joining Trudy in Aberdeen after confronting their
stepfather, so he'd already bought a train ticket—
conveniently time-stamped from before the fire. Do
you know, if things had gone pie shaped with
Arnold, I don't believe Logan intended coming back.'

'*If* things had gone pie shaped?' slips out of my
mouth.

Jodie's head sinks to the table and lodges
between her arms. 'Sorry, I didn't mean…'

She sits up, slowly. 'I just find it unnerving that
Logan nearly vanished into thin air. I'd like to think
he'd have contacted me from wherever they ended
up, but I'm under no illusions—if Logan thought
Trudy's wellbeing depended on it, I'd never have
seen him again.'

'They're close, then?'

'Trudy's a—vulnerable—sort of girl. Logan's
been her protector since primary school, but after
their mother died, she withdrew inside herself.
Grief, it was assumed—now we know better, and

Logan's had to deal with a hefty dose of guilt for not twigging sooner. He'd do anything for her—especially after the truth about their mother's death came out.'

Jodie looks away, lips retracting over pearl-white teeth, and her voice drops. 'What I wouldn't give for five minutes in an empty room with Arnold...'

She takes a deep breath, lets it out, then her eyes return to mine. 'Anyway, I'm pretty sure that if he hadn't sorted the Arnold situation, they'd be long gone.'

'But he did,' I whisper. 'Sort it, I mean.'

Jodie pulls a face. 'You know what Logan's like. He had this airy-fairy idea that calling Arnold out would have him falling to his knees—"*the game's up, I'll go quietly*"—and he'd have scarpered somewhere far away by the time they came back from Aberdeen. What happened wasn't planned or intended in any way. And anyway, it was Arnold's actions that caused the fire, not Logan's.'

'So you covered up for him?'

She cringes. 'It went against everything I believe in—well, actually it *didn't*, because I believe in Logan and I believe what he told me. It *was* an accident—but once these things go to court, there's no guarantee what happens. They do get it wrong, you know—more often than you think.'

She turns to the window. 'He never had any problems with his speech before—this stuttering

163

thing only started after the fire. Doesn't *that* tell you something?'

Daisy would be furious if I didn't ask. 'There's CCTV cameras at the railway station—why didn't they blow his "alibi"?'

'The station was busy that day—a football match in Aberdeen—so my colleagues couldn't say for sure he *wasn't* in the crowd somewhere. The investigating officers thought they were onto something when the passengers were interviewed, later, and it came out that Trudy was sitting on her own. The train was so packed, though, it meant nothing. Logan could have been standing in a corridor—as he claimed—along with too many others for the ticket inspector to remember whether he saw him or not.'

'Which neatly leads to the possibility they left the station in Aberdeen separately.'

Jodie nods. 'And with the number of lads wearing hoodies, well—Logan might have been any of them.'

She winks. 'He's never owned a hoodie, not until he bought one for coming back.'

'But what about the train he *actually* took? If the cameras picked him up getting on that...'

She's shaking her head. 'Not likely—I drove him to Aberdeen.'

Now she's waiting for me to speak. To announce my "verdict".

If I say what she wants to hear, it *will* make me an accessory. I'm not sure what *to*, exactly, but I do know it's breaking the law.

But, like her, I believe Logan's story. Poor Logan, facing down his stepfather armed only with a driving sense of self-righteousness. Arnold would have beaten Logan senseless—might even have killed him.

And let's not forget, it was Mr M who set me up with Jodie—I have a sneaky feeling he already knows all this. Jodie and Logan probably went to him for a legal opinion before deciding...

I clear my throat. Reach over and cover Jodie's hand. 'I think justice was done, don't you?'

A gasp explodes from her, then she sags. 'Thank you,' she says simply, hand rotating to grasp mine.

Logan's phone lies next to my teacup, ready to show the "policeman". I nod at it. 'Take that, will you? Get rid of it.'

I pause for a couple of quick breaths. 'Now, what's this about Logan blackmailing my Aunt Claire?'

IT'S NEARLY ONE O'CLOCK WHEN I LIMP UP THE HOTEL drive. Walking from the village only takes ten minutes, but I can't keep doing this. Yet a car's out of the question in my current circumstances—i.e. zero cash flow.

Bicycle? A thought probably inspired by Logan, who refuses to leave my mind. Cycling isn't impossible, although I can expect a few bruises while my good leg learns to synch with the prosthetic.

I wonder if you get adult tricycles?

Reception's deserted—as usual. I've seen busier tombs.

I find Daisy in the restaurant, clicking away at her laptop. The restaurant's fast turning into our daytime office.

It's not like we're in anyone's way...

'What happened?' she demands, and I give her a summary of my meeting with DS Bishop.

Her jaw drops further, and further, and somehow I overcome the impulse to make a quick, upward sweep with my hand. 'Did I do the right thing?' I end—hoping for the answer I want.

'Deffo,' she affirms, to my huge relief. 'But... what about the blackmail stuff?'

'Ah, that's another story. Jodie assured me Logan's innocent on that score too, but says it isn't her place to explain. She'll tell Logan about our chat, then I'll get together with him and hear what *he* has to say. Jodie's quite definite, though. She insists Logan had no part in Aunt Claire's death, and I believe her.'

Daisy wiggles her eyebrows. 'So, what's she like? Jodie? Big, butch, brick house of a copper, I expect. Yeah?'

I describe Jodie in some detail, shattering Daisy's preconceptions.

I think we may have to get her counselling

Gathering herself with a visible effort, Daisy plows on. 'So, if Logan didn't top your aunt, has the gorgeous Jodie given you any pointers on finding out who did? And by the way, she must need glasses.'

'Uhuh. She said we would have to get an exhumation, then a post-mortem. And she doesn't need glasses.'

Daisy ignores the rejoinder and rubs her hands together. 'Cool. How do you go about arranging an exhumation?'

'Jodie says I should talk to the GPs, both Rebecca's grampa and Aunt Claire's regular GP. If even one of them says the death was suspicious, Jodie thinks she can persuade her boss to take another look. If *he's* convinced, the police will arrange for an exhumation order—and a post-mortem.'

I'm not surprised when the lid of Daisy's laptop clacks shut. 'Let's go...' she starts, as I hold up both hands.

'No way—I've had enough for today, and we've got a hotel to run. This is Friday—GPs aren't available at the weekend, so I'll phone them and ask if they'll speak to me on Monday.'

'Can I come?'

I don't have the heart to refuse

Before the afternoon ends, Daisy's arranged for quotes from three decorators, two carpet fitters, and a tarmac company.

And they're all coming tomorrow.

The rep from Daisy's high class "ready-meals" supplier agreed to fit us into her busy schedule on Monday, and Davy phoned me five times to arrange work-slots for various tradespeople. He also agrees to factor the bar and snooker room swap-around, and books a time for himself to discuss what's involved.

When Daisy asks if I've contacted the GPs yet, I shrug. 'Our diary's still in a state of flux—everything's happening at once. Tell you what, we'll just drop into Rebecca's grampa's cottage when we have a minute—that might be the best way to approach him, especially having an "in" through Rebecca. I'll not phone the other GP in Donstable until next week, when we know better what our schedule is—and I'll have to find out about buses before we can go to see him.'

Daisy wrinkles her nose. 'Leave buses to me, I'll download the local timetable app.'

Time to shut up shop for the day. It's exciting seeing our plans take shape, but everything's overshadowed by the questions still surrounding Aunt Claire's death. I *am* relieved about not having to suspect Logan any more—but it *does* put us back at square one.

I'm more determined than ever, though—I *will* find out what really happened to Aunt Claire.

EIGHT

Saturday morning is a whirlwind of paint, paper, and carpet samples. By noon, my head's spinning. Daisy's must be, too.

No sooner have we flopped on armchairs in the residents lounge when Logan appears and holds out two coffees. 'I th… thought you might need these. How'd it g… go?'

Logan disqualified himself from participating in decor decisions, claiming to be colour blind. We assumed it was a typical male ruse, like dropping plates during the washing up. His choice of tie, however, argues otherwise. To be honest, I was glad it was just Daisy and me—although I'm satisfied Logan's no Hannibal Lecter, we've still to clear the air over this blackmail business.

'Cheers,' I breathe, reaching for a mug, surprised there's no dribbles of coffee running down it. 'Everything went fine—it helped knowing roughly what we wanted. Seeing the sample books sparked a few new ideas, though. Now we're waiting to see what the quotes look like—with our fingers crossed.'

'Wh… what colour's reception going to be?'

I don't think he cares so much as feels compelled to show interest. I point at Daisy. 'Same colour as her hair—the blue bits. With a burgundy carpet.'

Poor Logan—he nods, looking serious. 'Good choice—um, Sam? Can we have a chat later?'

Seems Logan wants the air cleared, too

'Of course. Could do it now, if you like. I'm free until two.'

He jumps back, arms flailing. 'I can't... I'm on the bar, then doing a stocktake, and...'

'That's okay, Logan. When would suit you?'

'W... what about tonight? After the bar closes? I could come up to your flat...'

Kind of late—is my first thought. The bar doesn't close until eleven.

Daisy tries to catch my eye, and I can read her mind. "*Don't put this off.*"

She's right... and so's Logan. Better we aren't interrupted during what could be a difficult discussion. 'Alright, fine. Daisy'll be there—is that okay?'

From his face, it's anything but. To his credit, he pretends it is. 'Y... yes, I suppose so. I'll see you then.'

Daisy waits until he's out of earshot. 'Jodie's spoken to him, then.'

'Looks like it. I'm terrified of what he's going to say, Daisy. If he had any hand in blackmailing my aunt, I can't go on working with him. But I can't afford to buy him out, either.'

'Don't worry about what might never happen,' she says, and winks. 'I'm sure it'll be fine.'

I hope you're right

'Anyway,' she goes on, swallowing the last of her coffee. 'If we're looking for something to do, how about knocking on old Dr Frame's door? GPs have every weekend off, so we've a good chance of catching him.'

I can't argue with that, much as I'd like to—since I'm dreading this meeting only slightly less than the one with Logan. I've no idea how to play detective, and scared of what we might find out. But I finish my own coffee and jump up, trying to look more confident than I feel. 'Let's do it.'

On our way out, we pass Jake. He's busy in reception, replacing light switches with fancier, brass-framed models. I got a shock at the cost of them, even at trade prices, but it's already apparent they add a touch of style disproportionate to their diminutive size. While I'm distracted, Jake looks around and our eyes meet.

For an instant, something makes me catch my breath. Then he smiles, albeit a sickly one, and waves—and I wonder if my imagination's getting the better of me.

As Daisy and I carefully make our way down the front steps, I try to recapture that impression. It's hard to describe what (I *thought*) I saw—it was more "feeling" than "observation"—but the words "contempt" and "fury" jump into my head before I shake them out. I refuse to dwell on that unsettling moment because I probably imagined it, and anyway, right now I feel too fragile to deal with it.

171

Sunshine abounds today, turning the lawns greener than they really are. Graham does a sterling job. Nobody would guess the grounds are a jungle further back.

Daisy's head is bobbing faster than her walk. 'So, I was looking at our social media options last night. I reckon...'

'Yes, I heard your keyboard clacking in the early hours. Look, I don't understand that stuff, so there's no point telling me details. Run the posts by me before putting them up, though. Hang on—this won't cost anything, will it?'

'Only our website, but that's pennies. Cairncroft Hotel dot com is just waiting for your credit card info before it goes live. Our Facebook page is already up, and ten people followed us on Instagram last night...'

She holds up a hand. 'Fine, I'll show you it all later. Don't worry, I've not said anything that isn't— or won't be—true.'

'Daisy...'

I know how Daisy's mouth (or in this case, fingers) sometimes runs away from her, but before I can interrogate further, she nudges me and points. 'Look, we're in luck.'

We might be—unless the old fellow weeding Dr Frame's flower beds is his gardener.

Daisy's bellow makes me jump. 'DR FRAME.'

The doctor/gardener looks up as Daisy swings open his front gate. 'Can we talk to you for a sec?'

He drops his trowel and takes what seems an age to get up. Going by his expression as he marches towards us, exertion might not be the only reason he's red-faced. 'Surgery hours are Monday to Friday,' he snaps.

I still have the smile I used on gripey Cosmo-Spex customers. 'I'm Samantha Chessington—Claire's niece—and I was hoping to have a word about her?'

Dr Frame huffs. 'Oh, I see. Well... you'd better come in.'

He points at wrought-iron chairs set around a matching bistro table, on a small patio in the centre of his smaller lawn, in case we're so deluded as to think he was inviting us indoors.

'Thank you. We won't keep you—I just wanted to ask about the morning my aunt died.'

'It was probably during the night,' he counters offhandedly and sits, as we do likewise. 'What do you want to know?'

Wrong thing to say near Daisy. 'What made you decide it was a heart attack?' Her face is innocence itself.

Dr Frame's mouth smacks shut, becoming a tight line. He speaks through it, suggesting some skill at ventriloquism. 'It was obvious.'

We wait.

So does he.

'In what way?' I try.

'She was dead,' he replies, without a flicker of irony.

Daisy leans in—Dr Frame leans back. 'Were her lips blue?'

She's learnt a lot from CSI

He shrugs. 'Didn't look that closely. No need— I mean, what else would it be?'

'So, let me get this straight.' I'm trying to hide my rising anger. 'You just... *assumed* she'd had a heart attack. Without knowing her medical history, or examining her...'

He stands, obviously intending to seem abrupt, but his arthritis spoils the effect. 'Now, see here, I won't be cross-examined by you or anyone else. When you've practised medicine as long as I have, *then* you can question my medical opinions. Not before.'

'But it wasn't an opinion—was it?' Daisy says quietly. 'Sounds more like a guess to me.'

'Get out,' he thunders. It's obvious we've overstayed our welcome. I'm half-way to the gate when I realise Daisy isn't with me. I hear her languid tones, though.

'So, what you're saying is, you signed a death certificate without...'

When I sprint over, sharp pains under my left knee make me realise I probably look like Logan from a distance. I grab her hand, and yank. Dr Frame looks like he's about to explode. 'C'mon,' I hiss, pulling her along.

'Don't come back,' thunders behind us.

'WELL,' DAISY SAYS, LOOKING UNPERTURBED. 'WHAT d'you make of that?'

'You shouldn't have pushed it...'

Then I give in. 'Yes, alright. We got what we came for—his "opinion" means squat.'

'D'you think that's an offense—declaring a cause of death because "what else could it have been?"'

I breathe out like a punctured tyre. 'Who knows? So—having established Dr Frame hasn't the foggiest how Aunt Claire died—we need to find out if her proper doctor has any ideas. Trouble is—confidentiality and all—will he tell us?'

'You're her next of kin. Surely you have a right—hey, call Mr M and ask him about it.'

'Good idea, that's what I'll do—first thing on Monday.'

We're half-way up the hotel driveway, and I've just noticed a monster truck parked at forty-five degrees in front of reception. 'Meantime—looks like the tarmacker is early.'

I'M SITTING AT RECEPTION, REGRETTING THE FACT IT'S AN ideal spot to have a quiet think, and frantically trying to do mental arithmetic. (My old maths teacher would be in stitches.)

The estimate for re-tarmacking is more than I thought—a lot more. Yet it has to be done.

It also has to be paid for.

A pound coin skids across the desk and bounces off my elbow. Looking up with a jerk, I see it's Davy—another ninja? A slow smile spreads over his face. 'Those thoughts looked like they'd cost more than a penny. Problems?'

I tell him about the tarmac estimate—it'll be helpful to hear what he thinks.

His eyes narrow. 'That's extortionate—don't pay it.'

'They're the only tarmackers in this whole area—and if I don't get it done, potential customers are going to make a U-turn at the gate and take their business elsewhere.'

He leans over and brushes my arm with his fingertips. 'Give me a few days. I might know someone...'

'Really?'

Without thinking, I grab his hand. He winces, then grins. 'You've got strong fingers.'

'I used to be an optician—adjusting spec frames makes your fingers triathlon-ready.'

'How d'you go from being an optician to running a hotel?'

I don't think it's just small talk. He looks genuinely interested. 'Long story. Fancy a coffee and I'll give you the short version?'

Then I slap a hand to my mouth. 'Sorry, you must be wanting to get done and enjoy your Saturday. I wasn't thinking...'

He leans closer, and the reception desk seems to shrink. His eyes twinkle as an already huge grin widens. 'Right now, I can't think of anything more enjoyable than the prospect of... coffee.'

Neither can I

On our way to the bar, we pass Jake. He's replacing more switches, in the residents lounge this time. He looks up, then again a moment later, and his lip curls. I look away before I see something else I don't like—I'm still grappling with that last view of Jake and his inner savage.

It being Saturday, the bar's open all day. However, the regular punters haven't arrived yet, so we have it to ourselves. Logan's eyebrows shoot up.

What? Has somebody pinned notes on our backs?

We take our coffees to the furthest table, and that's when I discover my surveyor is also a good listener. The more I tell him—the more I want to. Before long, he's had the entire story.

The accident, Cosmo-Spex, my surprise inheritance, Aunt Claire. He agrees there's something not right about the way she died and encourages me to keep investigating. Obviously, I give him the edited version—without mention of

177

Jake, or what Jodie told me yesterday. The only other minor issue I redact is my leg injury—and then he asks: 'I've noticed you limp sometimes. Is that because of the car crash?'

Panic

My leg's out of bounds on a first date. Not that this is a... but I'm not comfortable rolling out that sort of information. Trouble is, as time passes and I get closer to someone, it becomes all the harder to revisit that little detail. It would be much better if I just...

'I lost a chunk of my left leg in the accident.'

Even to my ears, that sounded like a Dalek fighting laryngitis. An icy hand squeezes my innards while I wait for Davy's reaction.

'Wow. You would never know.'

His forearms slide across the tabletop, leaving our fingers a centimetre apart. 'You must have worked incredibly hard—I'm in awe. I can't imagine how you—adapt—to something like that. But *you* have. And after all that, you end up doing—' his arm sweeps the surrounding air '—all this. Methinks you are a very special person, Samantha Chessington.'

I'm not sure what I was hoping for, but he's surpassed it. Trouble is, I don't know how to respond.

So, I revert. 'Right, well, this is the bar, soon to be a snooker room. Shall I show you the *old* snooker room now? Oh, and I need another bar in the residents lounge, for the use of guests.'

He's nodding, and although suddenly sombre, the corners of his mouth twitch. 'Let's get work out of the way,' he drawls, and I become aware of Logan, drying glasses, pretending not to notice us.

Davy's thorough, as I've come to expect— tapping walls, measuring, constantly scribbling in a notebook. Eventually, back in the bar, he snaps his notebook shut and declares: 'I've got all I need. Probably be Wednesday before you hear from me— that alright?'

'Fine.' I nod like one of those plastic dogs that used to live on rear parcel shelves. My face gets hotter. We're done here, he's ready to go, and suddenly I'm tongue-tied. "Bye" doesn't seem to cut it. Anything else feels too much.

Davy rescues me. 'I can phone with prices and so forth, or we could meet for a drink in Donstable to... discuss things?'

'I haven't got a car.'

Why'd I say THAT? It just came out...

'I'll pick you up.'

Smooth as silk

A wave of panic runs through me. 'But Daisy said you drive a motorbike...'

He cocks his head. 'I have a spare helmet.'

When nothing's forthcoming, he laughs. 'You've never been on a motorbike, have you?'

I have no idea why, but I instantly retort: 'Of course I have.'

'So we're on for Wednesday, then?'

I nod—again. I'm getting good at nodding.

He raises a hand. 'Seven thirty—Wednesday,' he clarifies, and I—yes, you guessed it.

Then, so swift I don't see it coming, his lips brush my cheek—and I'm left contemplating the back of his sweatshirt as it disappears under the archway. A sudden smash of shattering glass spins me around. Logan's behind the bar, a towel in one hand, staring at his feet. 'Whoops', he says.

FLOOR PLAN OF THE GROUND FLOOR, CAIRNCROFT HOTEL

(AFTER PROPOSED ALTERATIONS)

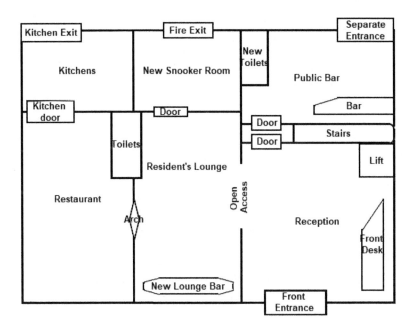

NINE

At dinner, Daisy looks worried. 'Sam. I've been thinking—we can't keep eating in the restaurant.'

I've been thinking that too—but avoiding saying it

'I suppose you're right. It's been a novelty, but two nights ago we were the only ones here—which means Rebecca got paid for an entire shift, just to serve us.'

'I'll pop into the Co-op tomorrow and do some shopping. So, what's this I hear about you and Davy going on a date?'

How'd she know about that?

Logan. It has to be. Not that it's his fault— Daisy has this superpower that would extract the latest gossip from a tailor's dummy. 'It's *not* a date. We're meeting to go over estimates for the new bar and snooker room, that's all.'

'If you say so.'

'I do.'

She smiles and starts playing with her hair. I know she's dying for me to confide in her. Thing is, I'm still trying to make sense of it myself.

Davy's nice—he's charming, thoughtful, and didn't run a mile when I mentioned the peg-leg. But—the feelings he stirred left me feeling guilty about Jake.

182

It sounds like Ross, from "Friends", when I remind myself: *"We're on a break"*. A break I don't see mending. But Jake will have different ideas—I know he's still hanging onto some forlorn hope we'll get back together. And *am* I leaping from one relationship to another without even leaving a decent interval in between?

Although, with only a single three-month relationship in six years to my name, surely nobody could label me a philanderer? (I'm not counting Davy yet—this business-meeting-come-date doesn't equate to a relationship.)

Rebecca arrives with our starters and bangs the plates in front of us. Daisy stares at her still-dancing melon balls. 'Oi—careful.'

'Sorry, I'm sure,' Rebecca snaps, and flounces off.

Daisy's halfway out of the chair before I grab her arm. 'Leave it, Dais'. She must be angry because we went to see her grampa.'

'That's no excuse... what if tonight's guest saw that? By the way, where *is* tonight's guest?'

'That was yesterday—looks like we're on our own again.'

We eat our (delicious) starters in silence, and Rebecca returns with the main course. Daisy scowls. 'Try and keep it on the plate this time, willya?'

'Shut up, Daisy. Rebecca, what's wrong? Is this about your grampa? I'm sorry if we upset him.'

'You had no right going and bothering him like that.'

183

Daisy sighs. 'We only asked him a few questions.'

Rebecca throws back her head. 'According to Grampa, you questioned his medical competence.'

I've had enough. 'Look, Rebecca. Without wanting to cause any bother, I intend finding out why my aunt died the way she did. If that upsets anyone, it's their problem. Having said that, I apologise if you think we were out of line today.'

She makes a "harrumph" sound and turns to go.

'One more thing. In future, if you have an issue, bring it to me in private. I will *not* tolerate that sort of outburst in the public areas of this hotel.'

She stiffens, and for a moment I wonder if she'll throw the empty starter plates at me. Then she says: 'Sorry, it won't happen again,' in a voice that suggests Grampa's been teaching her ventriloquism. (Unsuccessfully.)

Daisy waits until Rebecca's out of earshot. 'Whoah. Go, girl.'

'I learned a lot from Callum,' I mutter. 'Being honest, I don't really trust Rebecca. Not just because of that. Every time I talk to her, it feels like she's saying one thing and thinking something else.'

'Yeah, I get what you mean—she gives me bad vibes, too. I'll keep an eye on her.'

She hesitates. 'Did you know she used to go out with Jake?'

'What? No, I didn't. I can't imagine those two together.'

184

Would I listen to myself? I never knew what Jake was thinking, either—he and Rebecca are made for one another

'Mags told me—it was when Jake first started working here, but she doesn't think it lasted long. I reckon Mags is wary, too, going by the look on her face whenever Rebecca's name comes up.'

'Hm.' I pick up my fork and dig in. It's steak and ale pie tonight, and Maggie's magic moondust sets the pastry ablaze with crackling flavours that perfectly complement both its meat filling and an amazing Guinness gravy. 'What time is it?'

'Logan minus three hours,' she replies, chewing.

A KNOCK AT THE FLAT DOOR. DAISY CHIRRUPS: 'I'LL GET it'

She returns with Logan trudging behind—no funny walk tonight. He slumps in the nearest chair and Daisy offers: 'Coffee?'

'Thanks—I could murder one.'

'Long night?' I ask, as Daisy scoots off to the kitchen.

'Same as always,' he says in a resigned tone. 'Getting them out's the biggest problem.' He leans his head back and we wait in silence until Daisy re-appears with a tray of coffee and biscuits.

185

I take a deep breath, 'So. Jodie told you about our chat yesterday?'

Logan slurps at his coffee, then wraps the fingers of both hands around his mug and bends forward. 'Sh… she did. And thank you for… understanding. And giving her the phone.'

Daisy raises a hand. 'Didn't you look for it, when you realised you'd lost it?'

'I… I did. The stable block was where I checked first.'

I've got the answer to that. 'Davy said your phone had dropped through a crack in the floorboards. He only found it because he was… well, doing whatever it is surveyors do.'

'Th… that was puzzling me. I searched everywhere. Anyway—Jodie says I need to tell you about the blackmail incident.'

I say nothing. Daisy wriggles to the edge of her seat. She has her mug of coffee in one hand, a digestive biscuit in the other. I'm surprised she hasn't made popcorn.

'Claire received a photo showing her and Graham together, and a note threatening to send Graham's wife a copy unless Claire paid up—to the tune of a thousand pounds. She dropped the cash in a litter bin on Main Street, as instructed, then… another demand arrived a few days later. Asking for *five* thousand this time.'

'I never realised she'd actually paid anything.'

'Well, she did. That was when, at her wits' end, Claire confided in me. She didn't *have* five thousand

186

pounds, but couldn't let Graham's wife find out what was going on. Sadie would have chucked his stuff on the street and fitted new locks—she's a scary woman. I think Claire's biggest worry was Graham appearing at her door—with his suitcase.'

I bite my lip—knowing Aunt Claire, that rings true. She enjoyed her men, but wouldn't want one underfoot. 'What happened then?'

He reaches for a biscuit, changes his mind. 'I'm sorry, Sam, but my first thought was Jake. Something about him never gelled with me... so I used my master key to get into his room. I discovered copies of the photograph Claire received and destroyed them all, except one, which Claire kept as evidence. Jodie says you found it—and the original?'

I nod, a hand over my midriff. The tummy-flutters started when he mentioned Jake.

Daisy's enthralled. This is Netflix in real life.

'Claire was away that day. She wasn't due back 'til late, and I didn't want her suffering another sleepless night. So I jotted a note explaining what I'd done and suggesting we go to the police. I put both note and photo in an envelope and pushed it under her door. Scribbling on the photo was an afterthought—"let me know when you decide".'

'What did she say?' Daisy's breathless.

'Claire didn't want to involve the police in case her—thing—with Graham came out. But Jake lost his leverage when I took away the photos, so I

187

convinced her she could safely give him his marching orders...'

Daisy interrupts. 'Surely he had digital copies?'

I snigger. 'Jake? He's computer illiterate—has trouble working a calculator.'

Logan blinks. 'Yes, that was my reading of him, too. Especially since those photos were Polaroids—and that meant there weren't any negatives to worry about, either. Anyway, Claire confronted Jake and gave him the sack. That was the day before you arrived at Easter, Sam. Claire also told Jake to return her money, but he claimed to have spent it already. So then Claire demanded he come back next day and finish all the jobs outstanding—or she'd go to the police. He must have known she was bluffing, but didn't dare risk it.'

Daisy bursts out laughing. 'That's Jake all over—fronts it well, but he's a big wuss.'

I clear my throat to get Logan's attention. 'Jake told me he'd been sacked—but also claims you framed him, Logan.'

Logan looks at his feet, doesn't speak. If it was Jake, the air would be thick with denial—but Logan's not saying anything.

Maybe because *he's* got nothing on his conscience?

I take a big breath, try to hold my voice steady. 'Thing is, Jake's admitted the sacking now—which proves he lied about it before. For months. Looking back, he put an enormous amount of effort into making sure I didn't find out. That shows how devious and underhand he is. So, how can I believe *anything* he says?'

Then my temper flares. 'The nerve of that guy—waltzing in here again, like nothing happened.'

Logan shifts in his seat. 'I... I think he must have assumed nobody else knew—apart from me. Yesterday, when you interrupted us, he was telling me in no uncertain terms to keep schtum.'

He straightens. 'Until then, I assumed you already knew all this, Sam, and had forgiven him— that's why I didn't say anything before. When I told Jake he couldn't intimidate me, things turned nasty—that was when you arrived.'

My flutters have become painful cramps. I just make it to the bathroom, where tonight's "Maggie's special" performs a U-turn.

Re-entering the sitting room, clutching a glass of water, it's to an uncomfortable silence. Daisy breaks it first. 'You ok, Sam?'

'No, I'm not.'

I start pacing. 'It's all replaying in my head. Jake told me he had a week's holiday at Easter, starting the day after I met him. Then he avoided coming anywhere near the hotel. He was so convincing—I never suspected a thing. The man's a natural liar—OH. I was so stupid.'

'Y... you believe me, then?'

Stopping in front of Logan, I lean forward and grip his shoulder. 'Idiot. Of course I believe you. Deep down, I've known all along you wouldn't blackmail anyone. In fact, I'm beginning to

189

understand why Aunt Claire left you a share of the hotel.'

Pausing, I squeeze harder. 'I think you were the son she never had.'

He breathes out in a hiss. 'Th... that means a lot, Sam. Thanks.'

I spin away, and Daisy jumps up. 'Where are you going?'

Ignoring her, I flounce out of the flat, stride along to Jake's room, and rap my knuckles hard against his door—so hard, I feel them crack. When that doesn't work, I kick it (being careful to use my good leg).

The door opens partway and Jake keeks out. His hair's tousled and one hand's fisted at throat level, holding together a rumpled dressing gown. 'Sam? What's going on?'

A strange calm enfolds me. 'Get out,' I order, enunciating each word. 'Take your things and leave—now.'

His eyes pop. 'But Sam, I've got nowhere to go. I can't...'

A sense of déjà vu almost overwhelms me— suddenly, we're trapped in a remake of "Groundhog Day"? Deep breath...

'If you're not gone in ten minutes, I'm calling the police. I'll show them the photo, have Logan speak to them, and they can take it from there. Your choice.'

I whirl, stifling a groan when the prosthetic doesn't keep up. Ignoring a hot sensation like broken glass scraping raw flesh, I march back along the corridor and slam my door.

Ten minutes later, Jake's gone.

TEN

Next day, I sleep late. Probably something to do with being up half the night.

Throwing on a robe, I go through to the kitchen. Food's the last thing I want, but my stomach's gurgling. Accepting it knows better than me, I force down some dry toast. There's no sign of Daisy, although I hear movement from the spare room.

A desperate need for coffee's what really brought me in here. Perched on a stool, arms splayed on the worktop either side of my mug, Brazil's best rewards me with the sort of revitalising aroma only caffeine can generate.

Suddenly, I crave a smoke. Which is curious, since I've never even tried a cigarette—when my teenage friends were experimenting with fags and booze, I was too busy hitting a tennis ball for four hours every day.

Endorphins were my drug of choice.

But my endorphin days are gone forever. Gradually, caffeine and alcohol have crept in to fill the void—I still draw the line at nicotine, though. Whatever my mutinous body is telling me.

Caffeine's quite magical enough. After two mugs of coffee, I'm wide awake and buzzing—and mercifully, my toast is staying down. Immediate needs satisfied, I let myself lapse into reflection on this new "Jake-less" state.

There's no going back this time.

A stab of guilt gives way to surging rage.

How could I have been so blind?

Daisy never liked Jake—and from the first moment she saw him, insisted he was up to no good.

What did he think?

The aunt's a no-go—let's try the niece?

He was obviously playing a "long game"— Daisy was bang on when she accused him of targeting my flat. If I'd fallen for either of those marriage proposals, Jake would ultimately have taken half of everything I own.

Something else pops up in my head. The thousand pounds he extorted from Aunt Claire—that explains how he was able to buy an engagement ring.

Ha! I hope he takes a massive loss flogging it

A cough from behind makes me jerk and tepid coffee splashes on the worktop. Craning around, I see Daisy looking apologetic. 'Flipping heck, Daisy. You're worse than Miss Dobie.'

'Sorry. I was trying not to scare you.'

'Nice job.'

'You okay?'

'No... yes. I will be. I was thinking about Jake— you know, I'm remembering so many things he did and said, and seeing them in a different light now.'

She grins. 'Good thing you've got Davy to console you.'

It is, isn't it?

A wave of excitement ripples through me. Davy's so easy to talk to, and there's not a trace of guile about him. After Jake, that's what I need—somebody I don't have to second guess, who doesn't have a hidden agenda.

When Daisy speaks through a giggle, I'm suddenly conscious of my cheeks burning. 'I won't ask what you're thinking—I'm just glad you look chirpier. Hey, come see what I'm doing.'

She leads me back to her room, and a familiar sense of foreboding sends that toast cartwheeling around my stomach. What's she up to?

'How about that?' She points at a wall, studded with brightly coloured "post-it" squares. It was bare yesterday.

I scratch my head. 'Hell of a complicated shopping list, if that's what it is.'

She drags me forward until her scratchy writing comes into focus.

Ah. I'm starting to understand. 'Is this CSI stuff?'

'It's an evidence board. See, every potential suspect in your aunt's murder has their own post-it...'

'We don't *know* she was murdered...'

'... and the post-its underneath list motive, means, and opportunity. The threads represent links between suspects—like Logan being Mags's nephew, and you being Claire's niece.'

'Wait a minute. What am I doing on there?'

She looks at me pityingly. 'Sam, stay objective. You inherited a major share in the hotel—that's motive.'

I don't believe this

'Okay, let's talk about opportunity. I was in Edinburgh when she died.'

'Ah, we've only got your word for that. Oh, and Jake's—see, I've linked the two of you with a blue thread.'

With a snort, I rip my post-it off the wall. 'Daisy, I'm not a suspect.'

She glares at me. '*I* know that, but we have to eliminate you properly so our case against the real perp is watertight.' She snatches my post-it and slaps it back where it was, tutting while her thumb smooths the Sellotape holding my link with Jake in place. It's the *only* thing joining us now.

'Alright—who's our chief suspect?'

'Well... there're several candidates. Take Sadie, Graham's wife—if she found out about the affair, that would be motive. Logan's still a possible, I don't care what you say—he inherited, that's motive.'

'He didn't even know about that until...'

'So *he* says. Then we've got Mags...'

'I thought you liked Maggie.'

'I do, but she has means—her encyclopaedic knowledge of plant poisons.'

Gotcha, Miss Clever-Clogs

'When we spoke to Maggie, you said she was too up front about her herbicidal expertise to be a suspect.'

195

She giggles. 'Herbicidal—I like it.'

Then she scowls. 'Yes, I did say that, but I've since realised she could be double-bluffing us. Talking of Mags, I was chatting to her yesterday and she told me Claire planned to sack Rebecca—did you know that?'

'No, I did not.'

'There you are, then—Rebecca's got motive.'

'Why was Aunt Claire going to sack her?'

'Because she's a mouthy cow—oh, and some petty cash went missing. Claire was sure Rebecca took it, but had no proof, so she asked Mags to keep an eye on her. Mags also says Rebecca's a serial offender when it comes to timekeeping and generally doing her job properly, so she was for the push anyway. By the way, we can't dismiss Graham—not if we introduce a spurned lover scenario. I checked with Mags about his alibi and he was supposed to be at home with Sadie, so they're each other's alibi, like you and Jake—that's why there's a blue thread connecting them. The other one—see, *it's* green— that means they're partners.'

I *was* feeling better, but my head's throbbing again. 'You're doing a great job, Daisy—tell you what, let's wait until we hear what Aunt Claire's GP says. If she died of natural causes, all this becomes moot. And if she didn't, the police will take over.'

'Pooh. Country coppers? I wouldn't trust *them* to manage a murder case by themselves.'

Between me and the local constabulary, shares in paracetamol are suddenly looking cheap. A piercing "beeep" is a welcome interruption—sounds like a text message

'It's been doing that all morning,' Daisy says, and follows me through to the living room where I left my phone charging.

She's right, I've got four texts waiting. I read the first. Then the second. And let out a whoop.

'What is it? Don't tell me—you've won the lottery?'

'Better,' I breathe, scrolling through the remaining messages. 'It's those tradesmen we saw yesterday—putting in their quotes. Daisy, the lowest ones are within our budget.'

She's hanging off my shoulder, scanning the screen. 'And look—the same ones say they can start tomorrow.'

'I see that. I'll message back and tell them they've got the job. Will you speak to the cleaners? They'll be getting a lot of overtime from this.'

She nods vigorously, her breath coming quicker. 'I'll catch them in the morning.'

'Oh, Daisy. Won't it be great watching this old relic turn into something special?'

'Yay.' She hops from one foot to the other. 'We should celebrate.'

'We should. We will. Let's buy a bottle of wine when we do the shopping.'

'Shopping?' She freezes. 'I forgot about that.'

'I thought you had.'

THEY MUST HAVE GOT A DR WHO FAN TO DESIGN THE Cairncroft Co-op. Its street frontage is so narrow you could walk right by, yet inside it'd take a telescope to see the back wall.

A central divider forms an inverted U-shaped shopping track that isn't wide enough for trolleys, which is why we're pulling oversized, bucket-like baskets fitted with wheels and extending handles. In the middle of a discussion regarding the merits of several ready-meals (what we fancy versus sell-by dates), somebody pokes my shoulder from behind. 'You'll be her, then?'

I swing round to a small, beak-nosed woman whose fierce manner matches her face. 'Sorry, do I know you?'

'You'll be our new lady of the manor,' she amplifies. 'My Graham works for you.'

Daisy's shoulders quiver and she slaps a hand over her mouth as I hold out one of mine. 'You must be Mrs Biscombe. Nice to meet you.'

Mrs Biscombe glares at the hand and makes no move to take it. For a horrifying moment, I worry she'll slap me.

'I'm Sadie, never mind that "Mrs" balderdash.'

'Oh, okay. I'm Sam—and this is Daisy.' I smile my special smile, but even Cosmo-Spex never threw anyone quite like this at me.

Sadie glances quickly at Daisy, then moves closer to me. 'Your aunt was a wicked woman' she tells me, in what might be described as a stage-whisper. (If the prompter was using a megaphone.) 'She was always giving my Graham the eye—not that he was interested.'

'Of course not,' I agree, discreetly kicking Daisy.

'You look too young to be bothering a mature man like my Graham,' she says, her tone musing. 'But I'll warn ye now, lady—I won't stand for him being abused again.'

'I can understand that.'

She rounds on Daisy. 'What's so funny?'

Daisy licks her lips, scans the ceiling. 'Um... just the thought of Sam and "your Graham"—having trouble getting my head 'round that one.'

Sadie nods. 'Yer right. She's no' in his class, is she? Don't know what I'm worryin' about. Still, best to be plain about these things. Could have saved a lot of bother if I'd confronted the aunt sooner than I did.'

Now she's really got my attention. Bloodhound Daisy gets in first, though. 'What happened when you "confronted" her, Sadie? Was she reasonable about it?'

Sadie licks the tip of a finger. 'Denied it—well, she would. But I made it very clear what would happen if she carried on with her nonsense.'

I can't help myself. 'And what was that, exactly? What would you have done?'

199

Sadie smiles, a thin, tight mashing of lips. 'Don't matter no more, does it?' Her voice goes down an octave. 'She'll no' bother my Graham now.'

Abruptly, she takes off towards a rack of eggs. We follow her with our eyes, mouths hanging open. Sadie plucks a box from the display and lifts its lid to check for cracked shells. Presumably there aren't any because, after a quick shufti both ways, she stiffens her index finger and stabs.

The popping sound of an egg crumpling is unmistakable.

Then Sadie disappears around the U-bend without a backward glance.

Daisy looks at me, wide-eyed. 'She must get them cheaper when there's a broken one.'

'Never mind that. Do you think she knows what was really going on between Aunt Claire and Graham? Or did she actually believe all that nonsense about Graham being sexually harassed?'

Which gets a giggle. 'Maybe she's planning on taking us to a tribunal.'

'Don't joke about things like that.'

I'm replaying Sadie's words in my head. 'Daisy. Could she have been telling me in a roundabout way that she—did—something to Aunt Claire?'

'Dunno—but she just earned herself a red post-it on my wall. She's got motive a-plenty by her own admission, although I'm not so sure about opportunity.'

'Mm. Graham has access, and inside information—she could have used him to *make* an opportunity.'

'You're right. I think we need to take a long, hard look at Sadie.'

'Let's wait until we've spoken to the other GP before you waterboard her—there still might be an explanation that doesn't involve poisons.'

I give myself a mental shake, the memory of Sadie's beady eyes making me shiver. 'Now—where were we? Oh, yes—pasta. There must be some *somewhere...*'

ELEVEN

'They've arrived. Hurry up—you need to get down here.'

Daisy sounds excited as I feel. Even yesterday's run-in with Sadie can't dampen our thrill at seeing the hotel begin its transformation. In my mind, we're about to lay the first ceremonial brick on a new foundation.

Daisy was up at dawn (of course) and she's calling me on the internal line from reception. My hair's still damp from the shower, but she's going to blow a gasket if I don't get down there.

I mean, c'mon... it's not eight yet

The need for speed (*Daisy's* need for speed) means risking life and limb in our ancient elevator instead of making my now-customary, start of day, slow but leisurely stairway descent. I emerge to find Daisy standing in the centre of reception surrounded by five hunky guys. She waves both hands when she sees me. 'Here's Sam. Sam, this is...'

Her new friends are three decorators and two carpet fitters. 'Where's your carpenter?' I demand, and the decorators' spokesperson turns to me.

He's wearing John Lennon glasses (they're completely the wrong shape for his face). 'For the panelling? He's coming tomorrow, so we'll do reception last. Thought we'd start through there.'

He inclines his head towards the residents lounge, then jumps back as I advance on him. 'You can't do anything in there until the new lounge bar's installed. I told you that on Saturday.'

'Oo... kay.' He pushes the glasses up his nose. 'Restaurant?' he tries, looking worried.

'Restaurant's okay, we're refusing bookings until all this is finished.'

Chance would be a fine thing!

'Fair 'nough, love. We'll start in there—so, when's your new bar being fitted?'

'I don't know—as soon as it can be. I told you all this...'

'Sure,' he says, flapping a hand. 'I remember now—problem is, we've got another job week after next. I need this one done and dusted by then.'

A ginger-topped man keeks around him. 'I can't start laying carpets until the painting's finished.'

John Lennon swivels. 'Course you can—we'll put covers down.'

Reaching behind my head, I grab two handfuls of hair and squeeze until my eyes water. Daisy puts a finger to each corner of her mouth and lets rip a whistle capable of giving the Flying Scotsman an inferiority complex. All five men snap to attention.

She points at the decorator. 'You—restaurant.' She shifts her aim to the carpet fitter. 'You—do anywhere *except* the restaurant.' Her head tilts at the decorators as she adds 'They'll put covers down' before Ginger can protest. Rounding back on the decorator, she asks, 'The restaurant—what're we talking, timewise?'

He scratches his scalp. 'Three days, I would think.'

Daisy purses her lips. 'Your carpenter should be done in reception by then, so go there next—how long for reception?'

'Um... Couple of days?'

'Don't suppose you work weekends?'

He shakes his head, looking like he'd rather be somewhere else.

She turns to me. 'So, we need either the residents lounge or new public bar ready for them by Monday coming.'

Then she glares at the decorator. 'If you get access to one of those next Monday, will that leave enough time to finish both of them—including the new snooker room—before you leave to start this other job?'

This time he nods. 'Assuming we can go straight from one to t'other.'

'Okay.'

She focuses back on me. 'You'd better call your... em, Davy. See if he's able to speed things up on his end.'

She giggles. 'Good thing we don't have any guests to worry about.'

Did she really say that?

So—another unplanned trip on our death-defying lift. Because I'm not phoning Davy in front of Daisy.

Having survived a ride worthy of Alton Towers, my hand trembles as I reach for the landline. After pouring so much effort into designing colour schemes and getting things moving, I see now we didn't think enough about coordinating the work. Maybe I should have asked Davy to take charge of the decorators and carpet fitters, too?

That's the *only* reason my hand's shaking, I tell myself.

Davy answers after two rings and I launch in without nicety.

'Slow down, Sam.' He speaks over me—voice unhurried, matter of fact. 'I get the picture. Look, I've got your budgeted figures for the alterations. If you trust me to stay within those, I can organise all the work today. Let your guys know the residents lounge will be ready for them by next Monday.'

'What about the new public bar?'

'Day after.'

'Whew.'

The tension leaves me like a punctured balloon. 'Oh, one more thing.' I tell him about Daisy's "toilet moment" and he laughs, trots out an add-on figure off the top of his head so I can update the overdraft estimate.

He thinks for a second. 'It'll probably put the public bar back a day. I shouldn't worry, though— your decorators will need at least two days in the residents lounge.'

'Great. Davy—before, you said it would take until Wednesday to get all this organised?'

'I did imply that, didn't I?'

He coughs and I hear a crackle when something brushes the microphone at his end, followed by a series of "glugging" sounds. Which reminds me—I've only had one coffee this morning. Cordless handsets are a wonderful invention, I reflect, making for the kitchen.

'See...' his tone's become hesitant '... I'm away in Dumfries until Wednesday.'

'Oh, Davy. I'm sorry. It's not fair of me to throw this at you while—are you already in Dumfries?'

'Yes, but don't worry—I intended arranging your stuff today. It's only a couple of phone calls—I'll make them, then call you back.'

Now I'm confused. 'So what was Wednesday all about?'

This time the silence stretches until I wonder if he's hung up. When he speaks, it's in a voice so low I strain to hear. 'Wednesday was about us having a drink together. Are you still up for that?'

'WHAT ABOUT THE BANK? WE HAVEN'T ARRANGED AN overdraft yet?'

I wasn't surprised when she reappeared just as I finished my second call—patience and Daisy are two incompatible forces. 'Davy said he'd stay inside our budget, and out of thin air he conjured up a price for putting toilets in the public bar. On that basis, I called our business manager at the bank— and he's given me an "agreement in principle".'

'Okay. I still don't understand why Davy was making us wait until Wednesday when he could arrange everything this quickly.'

'Beats me, but it's sorted now.' I tried to make that sound offhand, but her nose is twitching.

Then she snaps her fingers. 'Oh, I get it. Davy's in Dumfries—Wednesday was the first night he could tell you *in person.*'

I hand her a coffee, not daring to meet her eye. A little smile dances on her lips. Before she can say anything, I blurt: 'I'd better let the guys downstairs know.'

'No, I'll do that. You've still got Mr M to ring, remember? About the GP.'

'And gaming machines for the new public bar. I wonder how much rigmarole's involved in getting a licence, and if it's expensive. What about your coffee?'

She looks at the mug in her hand, as though it has no right being there. 'I'll take it with me. Hey, when's your lunch date with the snooker club committee?'

'Don't remind me—tomorrow. I'm dreading it.'

She gives me a "Glad it's not me" smile and turns. 'Back in ten.'

The door closes behind her.

Does she really expect me to face the snooker club alone? If so, she's got another think coming

Sitting at Aunt Claire's secretaire, coffee by one hand and landline in the other, I marvel at a sudden sense of calm. It's like the stillness hanging in the air after a rampant thunderstorm, when your ears seem to hiss with silence.

This will be the first time I've spoken with Mr M since Jodie's revelations. I wonder whether to broach it with him—then decide I'll wait to see if he does. If he doesn't—I won't.

Miss Dobie answers and immediately confirms that "of course" Mr MacLachlan is available. Have I been lucky up to now, or is the local solicitor's office *not,* in reality, the bustle of activity Mr Ms permanently cluttered desk suggests?

After explaining about our proposed barroom refurbishment, I await his response with gritted teeth. I just *know* getting this gaming licence will be a nightmare process.

'You won't need one,' he says, and I wonder if I heard right. 'Your alcohol licence already covers up to two machines. It was fortunate Claire had Logan down as licensee—applying from scratch takes forever.'

'Why did she do that?'

'Logan took to do with running the bar—I presume he still does? So it made sense. It also spared your aunt certain obligations—particularly in terms of making personal appearances.'

208

'Ah, that I can understand. Listen, Mr M. Not needing a separate license is an incredible weight off my mind, but I promised them more than two machines. Do coin-operated pool tables and quiz machines count?'

'No. They're "skill machines", which don't need a licence. There *are* restrictions on the gambling machines themselves—stake and prize limits, for example. Also, you must display mandatory notices. I would suggest contacting a hire company—they'll keep you right, and renting the machines under a profit-sharing arrangement would mean nothing to pay upfront.'

'Wow. This gets better and better. Do they do footie tables on the same basis?'

He laughs. 'You'd have to ask them. Would you like me to track down a reputable company?'

'Yes, please.'

'Alright. I'll have somebody ring you—should be later today.'

He's about to hang up, so I speak fast. 'There's something else—something personal.'

'Fire away.'

Grappling with a stubborn mental image of admirals and gunboats, I explain why we need to talk with Aunt Claire's GP and our worry about patient confidentiality getting in the way.

'You're quite correct. Confidentiality requirements continue after death. However, the executor of an estate—that's me—can apply to view the decedent's medical records. As can anyone with a claim on the estate, particularly family members—that's you.'

'Okay—so how do I go about it?'

'Your aunt was with Dr Mackenzie in Donstable, nice young chap—shall I have a word? I could probably persuade him to chat informally with you.'

'Would you?'

'Of course. Are you free today, assuming he agrees to see you?'

I think fast. 'We've got a rep coming at two—I need to be here for that. And I'm waiting for a call back about the refits...'

He interrupts. 'How's tomorrow?'

'I'm hosting a business lunch. Other than that, it's clear.'

'Hmm. Busy lady. Actually, Joe would probably be more amenable to a quick meet before his patient list begins. Can you be in Donstable for half-past eight tomorrow?'

'A.M.?'

I catch myself—needs must. 'Yes, no problem.'

'Leave that with me,' he says, making it sound like a benediction. Then hangs up.

Well—that went so much better than I could have hoped. No need to apply for a gaming licence, and one less expense to worry about.

Yesss

My only concern now is getting to see Dr Mackenzie (at the crack of dawn) without Daisy tagging along and giving him the third degree.

Still, two out of three isn't bad...

THE READY-MEALS REP IS A SNAZZILY DRESSED, BRIGHTLY painted ball of sales-energy called Kim. If Kim eats what she sells, Weight Watchers should push her products.

'They're so nutritional—look at this list of ingredients.'

'What do they taste like?' Daisy deadpans.

'Yes,' I cut in. 'That's our big worry. They've got to taste as though someone prepared them from scratch.'

Kim waggles a finger. 'I have total confidence in my product, ladies—what I'll do is leave you a bag of samples. Eat on us for the next few days—then fax me a massive order.'

'Are we able to choose which ones?' Daisy asks. I can almost see the drool forming.

After Kim departs, leaving behind a cloud of expensive perfume and eight "Gold Level" meal packs (and an order form), I say what's worrying me. 'They're awful pricey.'

Daisy puts down a boeuf Bourgogne and picks up the lobster paella. 'She's giving us ten percent off.'

'Even with that, we aren't making much.'

'We don't need to—it's just padding. As soon as we convince the guests to try a "Maggie special", they won't be interested in anything else.'

'Mm. Talking of which, we'd better show these to Maggie, seeing as how she'll be preparing them.'

Daisy laughs. 'Ten minutes in the microwave? I could do that. But you're right, it's only courtesy to keep her in the loop. Hey—have you decided which of these you're trying tonight?'

'Not yet.' Actually, I have—but I don't want to say. It's this terribly British guilt thing—I'm scared my choice is the same one Daisy wants.

Going via the restaurant involves avoiding men with paintbrushes. At the kitchen doorway I'm two steps ahead, Daisy hampered as she is by continuing to read ready-meal packs while dodging ladders. I stop so suddenly she runs into me. 'Ow. Sam, what're you doing?'

I barely hear her—I can see right into the kitchen through a wedged-open swing door and my legs (all 1½ of them) have frozen. I'm staring at Maggie's back. She's holding her broomstick in a two-handed grip, making rhythmic, pendulum-like motions, and humming something macabre.

Daisy goes up on tiptoe to peep over my shoulder, then giggles. 'D'you think she's trying to bump-start it?'

'Don't be silly.'

Maggie hears us and turns. 'Hello, ladies. Just taking care of a wee flour spill.'

I knew that

Something's puzzling me. 'Maggie, you're *always* here. Even when we're not paying you to be. Where do you live, anyway?'

Her broomstick clatters to the floor, and Maggie stoops to pick it up. 'I've got a little cottage outside the village. Not much, but it does. It's very quiet... Now, what can I do you for?'

I was watching her eyes when she said "quiet". Daisy seems oblivious—for once, GCHQ hasn't picked up the vibes. 'Wanted to show you these, Maggie.'

I empty the bag of samples on a work surface and Maggie lifts one and scans its blurb. 'Easy enough. What do they taste like?'

'Funny you should ask. The rep left these samples so we can find out. Will you take a couple and try them—then give us your professional opinion?'

'Aye—I'll do that. Ee, this looks nice.'

The lobster paella. That's the one I wanted... never mind. 'Choose two, Maggie—whichever you fancy. Have you and Daisy finalised the list of new kitchen appliances?'

Daisy nods. 'We have—no thanks to Mags.'

Maggie glares at her. 'We don't need none of that stuff.'

'Come on, Maggie,' I reason. 'You need a dishwasher—remember, we're expecting to be a lot busier soon.'

'Aye, well, maybe that's alright, but some o' them other things—mixing machines, electric grinders—waste o' money. What's wrong wi' a little elbow grease? And I'll tell ye now, I only use fresh ingredients, so it's beyond me why ye're insisting on a freezer.'

'It's for the ready-meals,' Daisy sighs. 'Let us know what you think of them.'

'Crabbit old witch,' she mutters, as soon as we're out of earshot. 'It would take a new mortar and pestle to get her excited. Where are we going?'

'I need a word with Logan,' I answer, steering her through what feels like hordes of decorators, then across the residents lounge towards Logan's domain.

The bar should be closed now, but a pair of old men are still sat nattering—and they've got unfinished drinks in front of them. Logan sees me looking, and skips out from behind the bar. (Well— "skips" is somewhat charitable for a movement that's classic John Cleese.)

'R... right, you two,' he shouts, his stammer draining all authority from the reprimand. 'Out. Now.'

The old men raise their heads and grin until Daisy steps forward and cracks her knuckles. Suddenly, the glasses stand empty as two pairs of arms thrust their way into jackets.

After they make their hurried exit, I lift my eyebrows at Logan.

He shrugs. 'I know... licencing laws.'

214

'We can't afford to lose our licence,' I emphasise, then nod at Daisy. 'You can borrow her any time you need.'

Daisy disappears behind the bar to mix herself a gin and tonic—*'I'm a resident'*—and I place a hand on Logan's arm. 'Logan, hopefully there'll be joiners starting in here tomorrow. Will you put the word 'round we're closing for probably a fortnight?'

'They're not going to like it,' he says, with a frown.

Daisy chortles. 'The Cairncroft Cowboys are getting a brand-new saloon,' she burbles. 'Trust me—they'll horse-trade one dry fortnight for the bounty a' coming.'

Logan catches my eye. 'Cairncroft Cowboys?'

I roll my eyes. 'Don't ask. Logan, I was wondering—what's the story with your Aunt Maggie? I get the impression she's lonely at home.'

His eyebrows go up. 'She told you that?'

'No, just a guess.'

'Well, it's a good one.'

He sighs, deeply. 'Aunt Maggie's lived in a cottage outside the village most of her life. Her husband died a few years back, and the place is crumbling around her. There's not enough money to put it right, you see. Roof—rot—you name it. But money aside, I don't think she has any incentive to fix it up because she's happiest here playing with her herbs.'

'Does she have friends?'

'Outside the hotel? Just her sister, but Dinah's a pharmacist—her and Herbert have their own business, so they're working all hours.'

Then my phone rings. After glancing at the screen, I mutter: 'Got to take this.'

Daisy sidles into the residents lounge a few minutes later, glass in hand. She stops and gives me a look, asks: 'What're you grinning at?'

'Nothing.' I push the phone back in my jacket pocket, succeeding on a third attempt. 'That was Davy. The joiners are all sorted and guess what? He found us a tarmacker, too—at nearly half the price that tinker quoted.'

Daisy laughs. 'Do you think he's really a tinker? Do you still get tinkers?'

'If he is one, that wide boy gives tinkers a bad name. This new guy's coming on Wednesday, so we'll need to block the driveway with "no entry" signs.'

'There's only staff using it anyway since we've no guests—I'll go 'round and let everybody with a car know.'

She thinks for a moment. 'Actually, that's only Graham. Oh, and the workmen of course... so, you were grinning fit to burst a minute ago, and I heard you say "Absolutely, can't wait". Anything you want to tell me?'

I flap my hand. 'Just telling Davy how much I'm looking forward to having those potholes fixed.'

Before she can press further, I go on the offensive. 'The Snooker club's free meal is tomorrow—and I need you there. For moral support.'

'Eeurgh—do I have to?'

She's already sidestepped every attempt to leave her out of my meeting with Dr Mackenzie. She's not coming to that and getting out of this. 'Yes. You do.'

Her face creases, then she grins. 'Sam, where are you going to hold this lunch?'

I smack my forehead—too hard. Now I'm seeing stars.

The restaurant's full of decorators. Davy just told me his joiners are starting through here, including the old public bar, first thing tomorrow. Where does that leave?

Picnic on the lawn?

If I cancel, Mr Entwhistle will blow a gasket.

Luckily, one of us is thinking straight. 'Sam, it's alright. We'll use the snooker room—the original snooker room. I'll get Logan and Graham to stash the snooker table somewhere. Mm—we can put it in the stables.'

She tuts suddenly. 'Oh, but when's the plumber coming in to fit new toilets?'

'Not until Wednesday.'

'That's all right, then.'

Ah, but...

'Those panels in reception are being fixed tomorrow—that won't look good, not to mention the noise.'

217

She makes a throwaway gesture. 'The decorators aren't starting reception until Thursday, so the carpenter can come on Wednesday instead.'

'Suppose he can't?'

She pulls a face. 'I'll find another carpenter. Now—what about getting food from the kitchen to the snooker room? Trying to manoeuvre through all those workmen is a... *recipe* for disaster.'

Her pitch rose on those last words and she waits, expectantly. Realising I'm determined not to give her the expected chuckle she scowls, but then her face lights up. 'I know—we'll serve via the back yard. Out one fire exit, in the other. It'll be fine, Sam—leave it to me. I'll sort it.'

TWELVE

M r M worked his magic, and Dr Mackenzie agreed to meet first thing. So, Tuesday morning sees me (and Daisy, of course) on an early bus to Donstable. But she's promised faithfully to behave herself.

Yeah, sure

'You didn't need to come.'

Is it too late to fight a rear-guard action?

'You don't ask the right questions, Sam.'

There's a finality in her voice that implies she won't be catching the next bus back. Before I can think of a last-ditch reason to change her mind, she nimbly switches subjects. 'You know our "chicken and egg" staffing problem? Remember—came up when Rebecca was touting her mates for jobs?'

'Ye-es.'

'I've been asking around. Sam, there're loads of people in the village happy to work on a casual basis. Stay-at-home partners, retired folk—a lot of them with experience. I reckon we could put together an on-demand workforce.'

'Nice one, Dais'.'

Another problem solved. That one's been worrying me. Yep—Daisy definitely has her uses. Her "ready meals" idea came good, too—I wouldn't have felt cheated being served last night's salmon mornay at the Savoy Grill.

219

Though it might have been cheaper there

'When we've finished with Dr Mackenzie, let's take a walk around Donstable—it's yonks since I've been there.'

'What are the shops like?'

'Donstable's not big enough for department stores, but there's an upmarket dress shop I want a look at.'

Her eyebrows dance. To my relief, she doesn't vocalise their message. I *am* after a decent outfit for Wednesday night—though I'll deny it if asked. Daisy's sense of fashion, which far outstrips mine, is a silver lining to her insistence on coming along today.

For our visit to the Donstable Medical Centre, and maybe also with our snooker club lunch in mind, she's dumped both cowboy and seventies-musical looks in favour of a classy, aqua-coloured pantsuit that matches her streaks. A silky, black polo-neck sets the jacket off perfectly. Actually... Beggar. If only we were the same size...

Alighting in the middle of Donstable, I check my watch. 'It's a five-minute walk to the surgery from here—we'll be a few minutes early.'

On the way, we pass a hairdresser. 'Pity we don't have time to get you a makeover,' Daisy says, looking straight ahead.

Grabbing at my head, bunching two fistfuls of hair, I wheel on her. 'What's wrong with my hair?'

'Nothing—just needs styling, maybe some colouring.'

She's right—I've not even thought about my hair for weeks. Inspiration strikes. 'Tell you what— we've got this stupid snooker club meal at twelve, but do you fancy coming back tomorrow? I'll book a hairdo while you have a wander around on your own, then we'll blitz the clothes shop and I'll treat you to lunch.'

'I'm game,' she says quickly.

'Talking of the snooker club and their free grub—are you sure this is going to work? Rebecca running along the back path with plates of food?'

'Yeah, I'll be helping her, and we've got plate covers so it doesn't get cold. Oh, and the carpenter was okay with switching days—seems there's another job he can go to. Stop worrying, Sam—you said yourself everything looked fine after Logan and Graham brought through tables and chairs from the restaurant.'

We're at the surgery door, leaving me no choice but to shelve my scepticism.

Inside, a receptionist who looks like Miss Dobie's (slightly) younger sister ushers us through to Dr Mackenzie. He shakes our hands in the doorway, then points at two red-plastic seats opposite his wheelie stool.

'Perfect timing,' he announces. 'You're five minutes early, and for once, so am I.' He sounds relaxed and friendly—I take to him straight away.

There's no desk between us. He sits side on to a work surface which has room for his computer, prescription pad—and little else. Daisy's eyes fix on him, her pupils dilating. Dr Mackenzie must be ten years her senior but, given opportunity, I'm sensing a mere decade wouldn't put her off. I hope she's clocked his wedding ring...

'First, my condolences on the passing of your aunt. Mr MacLachlan explained your concerns, and I'll do my best to help. He already forwarded evidence of your identity and status, together with proof of his own authority as executor, so I can be fairly open with you.'

Mr M is an absolute gem

I tell Dr Mackenzie what we know, including details of our explosive visit with Dr Frame. He rolls his eyes ceilingward. 'You must understand, it would be unethical for me to comment on the actions of another practitioner. Even if those actions were themselves *blatantly* unethical, not to mention suggestive of incompetence—I couldn't actually say that.'

His gaze flits from me to Daisy, then back. I hear Daisy take a breath and shake my head at her. 'Understood. And thank you. Is there anything in my aunt's medical history to explain her death?'

He turns, flicks a mouse, and the monitor lights up. 'I already went through her records and no, there's nothing here. She wasn't on medication, and her rare visits to the surgery paint a picture of glowing health.'

His eyes travel down the screen one last time, then he swings away. 'I have no opinion regarding her death except to say there was no obvious reason for it.'

'And you don't think it was a heart attack?' Daisy interjects—then blushes when his eyes settle on her.

That's a first

He reaches for the mouse again, scrolls down. 'I did an ECG as part of her annual check-up six months ago. She had a heart like a horse—a racehorse.'

Squeezing my own fingers until they hurt, I cross my good leg over what's left of its fellow. Then I uncross it. I have this sudden compulsion to jump up and run outside, stop half-way across the road, and scream my lungs out.

I can't ignore the facts any longer.
Somebody MURDERED my Aunt Claire

AT TEN MINUTES BEFORE NOON, DAISY AND I ARE BACK IN reception, waiting for our guests. Thinking about meeting Mr Entwhistle in person is giving me the heebie-jeebies. When Daisy brings up our discussion with Dr Mackenzie (yet again), I can't help myself.

She's done it to me often enough
'You fancied him, didn't you?'

Daisy looks at her feet and shakes her head— not the reaction I expected. Her voice is low—

musing, almost. 'He reminded me of somebody—a doctor I used to know.'

'Who? You never told me anything about going out with a doctor.'

Her lips set in a tight line. 'Ben wasn't *my* boyfriend—he was one of my mother's.'

Ah. Daisy's childhood is a period she doesn't enjoy talking about. Not so long ago, and halfway through a second bottle of wine, I found out she lost her father at an early age and Gwen, her mother, reacted by cultivating a wide social circle of male friends while single-handedly guaranteeing bumper profits for the local licensed trade. 'Is it a good memory?' I ask, not sure if I want to hear the answer.

To my relief, she nods. 'Dr Ben was great. He included me in things—talked to me like I was a real person.'

Her expression darkens. 'He wasn't around long, though—far too nice a guy for Gwen's taste.'

Daisy wouldn't go into detail about those early years, but the fact she never speaks to Gwen says it all—this is the most specific she's been. I want to pursue it, help her talk through a period I suspect involved life-changing trauma, but a hubbub outside telegraphs the untimely arrival of our lunch guests. Daisy blinks away a tear and I can almost see the shutters come down.

'Here we go.' She says it in a high-pitched voice, her expression that of a teenager next in turn for the roller-coaster—as she steps nimbly back into the practiced persona that separates who she was from who she is.

One of these days...

The snooker club committee is pouring in, en masse—I wonder if they hired a minibus?

'Miss Chessington? I'm Reginald Entwhistle.' The long-legged, longer-armed man reaches for my hand and grins ingratiatingly. I suppose his build is ideal for traversing snooker tables. The diminutive woman beside him offers a set of limp fingers and simpers wordlessly.

'Hi. I'm Sam.'

'This is my wife,' Mr Entwhistle cuts in.

'Do you play?' I ask, for something to say.

'No, she doesn't,' Mr Entwhistle answers. He says it as though the very idea is too ridiculous to contemplate.

'Is it only the men who play?' It's not that I'm particularly interested, just struggling to make conversation.

Mrs Entwhistle looks around at the mob of people still streaming in and, while Mr Entwhistle's drawing breath, decides to break her vow of silence. 'Well... not all of them. Reggie didn't think you'd mind if he brought a few friends.'

'... three, four... yep, that's four extra.' Daisy, behind me, is craning to monitor the inflow.

Swivelling, I hiss: 'Four extra? Better tell Maggie, though how she's supposed to conjure up four more meals from thin air...'

And if she does, I'll be taking a closer look at that broomstick

From the glint in Daisy's eye, she has something in mind. 'Don't worry, Sam,' she says, sotto voce. 'We won't need extra meals. What we'll do is reduce the portions and pretend it's nouvelle cuisine. You stall them while I get Rebecca to help me drag in another table. We'll bring it through the old bar's fire exit.'

Stall them? How does she expect me to stall them? Show them where the woodworm was? Or maybe: "Who wants to play *I spy*?"

As it happens, they're all so busy talking amongst themselves, all I have to do is pretend I'm not here.

When Daisy sticks her head 'round the connecting door and gives me a thumbs up, I herd them through—which turns out to be a lot harder than keeping them in reception—explaining our destination by declaring work's already under way on their new clubroom.

Mr Entwhistle's power complex shows again in his insistence that each committee member (and the hangers on) take seats he makes a show of picking out—plonking *himself* next to me.

Daisy's at my other side and keeps nudging me, her eyes practically on springs. 'I didn't know men still wore Brylcreem,' is one of her whispered comments.

At least it's useful watching their reactions to Maggie's magic food. Multiple "oohs" and "ahs" lay to rest any lingering doubt about our appraisal of her cuisine. The silence that follows, punctuated only by cutlery clinking crockery, says it all. Happily, nobody notices Rebecca and Daisy's increasingly red faces and laboured breathing as they fetch the various courses.

Finally satiated, but compounding the drain on our resources by guzzling a large brandy alongside his coffee, and encouraging his entourage to follow suit (*must* have hired a minibus) Mr Entwhistle decides it's brass tacks time. The back of his hand smacks flat on the table, fingers wiggling.

Mrs Entwhistle grabs her suitcase-sized handbag and fumbles in it, brings out a brochure, and slaps it into his waiting palm.

Daisy hisses in my ear. 'Aww—they're playing doctors and nurses.'

'Shush. What? No, not you, Mr Entwhistle.'

Mr Entwhistle smooths the brochure in front of me and points to a glossy picture. (I think it's a snooker table.) 'This,' he says, in hushed tones, 'is a "Break-Dancer".

'It looks splendid, but... on the phone, you told me something called a "Snooker-King" was what you wanted...'

He leers, and for a moment I could swear I'm looking at Kenneth Williams. 'You are correct, my dear. I did. Since then, I have researched the position in more depth and discovered "Break-Dancer" is taking over as premiere snooker table for serious clubs. There's even talk of the Scottish Open considering it for next year's tournament.'

I've just spotted the price, which made my knees go weak. (Well, one of them.) 'Why is it so much more expensive?' I say, timorously, when I should tell him he'll get a Snooker-King and like it.

He leans closer, and his eyes swim as he whispers: 'It's the baize, you see. The cloth is practically frictionless.'

I look desperately to Daisy, but she's absorbed in her phone. 'Thing is, Mr Entwhistle, the budgets are kind of allocated now, and...'

Mr Entwhistle already has a long face (goes with the limbs), but when he sucks his cheeks in, it makes him a dead ringer for Red Rum. 'I thought you wanted the prestige of retaining our presence in your establishment,' he says slowly. 'I'll be frank. I've talked with several other hotels, and the only thing keeping us here is your promise of cutting-edge facilities.'

A plump man with a van dyke looking a little the worse for wear leans past Mrs Entwhistle and slurs: 'Don't forget the food, Reggie. Them other places aren't a patch on Maggie's grub.'

"Reggie" bristles. 'Yes, thank you Herbert, but that's only relevant to the social nights. We could still hold those here, but...'

'Anyway...' a woman further down chips in (not men only, then?) '... none of the others offered to get us a new table.'

'They might—if we offer them the social night custom as well.'

His measured tones climb the decibel scale to compete with a chain reaction of protest. 'Now, see here. What's more important—the snooker, or your bellies?'

I'm gathering it's a close contest, but what the heck—it means another five hundred quid on the overdraft, but I can't risk losing our second-biggest income stream. 'Mr Entwhistle, you misunderstand. I was going to say we have just enough left over to get you a... Break-Dancer.'

He rubs his hands together, shooting derisory looks at the dissenters. 'There. I've sorted it out. That's why I'm president.'

He jumps at Daisy's touch on his arm. She leans over his shoulder and holds her phone where he can see the screen. 'Mr Entwhistle, did you know about this?'

I catch her eye. 'What is it?'

'The Break-Dancer's popular all right—it's so popular there's a twelve-month backlog on delivery.'

'That's no good,' the plump man shouts. 'Let's stick with a Snooker-King.'

Mr Entwhistle pushes Daisy's phone aside, his face turning a shade of raspberry. 'Don't be ridiculous,' he booms. 'That just proves the point. We can still use the old table while we're waiting.'

'No, you can't,' I cut in. 'I had it taken away yesterday to make room for the Snooker-King I already arranged to be delivered on Friday.'

Mr Entwhistle gapes at me. Behind him, Daisy mouths: "Liar."

She jumps clear as Mr Entwhistle springs from his seat. 'Now, listen. Everybody. I can see where the less forward-thinking amongst you might feel this changes things, so let's settle it with a show of hands. Anyone who wants to make do with a Snooker-King, raise...'

He drops back in the chair, and a weary expression settles over his equine features. He looks at me and raises his eyebrows. 'I declare the motion carried. Do you think we could have another cognac...?'

By the time our guests call it a day, they've cost us more in brandy than food. And, as I discover when we walk them out—the blighters *did* hire a minibus.

Just as well, since none of them is legal to drive.

The plump man hangs back—he and Daisy seem to have a lot in common. They're still chatting while he climbs aboard.

As the doors close, he calls: 'Bye, Daisy.'

'Bye, Herbert.'

Watching the green seventeen-seater negotiate our very own lunar landscape, Daisy and I dutifully wave goodbye. As soon as it's out of sight, I collapse on her shoulder. 'Thank goodness that's over.'

Even Daisy seems frazzled. 'They're hard work,' she agrees.

'Who's Herbert?' I ask, as we saunter back to the hotel.

To say Daisy looks smug is like saying pigs in clover are reasonably happy with their lot. 'Herbert's a pharmacist—him and his wife have a chain of shops.'

'Okay—so we know now where to take our prescriptions?'

'Sam, pharmacy's constantly changing in today's NHS. Pharmacists have to upgrade their knowledge regularly—it's compulsory.'

'You're planning a career change?'

'Every few months, Herbert arranges a weekend away for his staff to bring them up to date. But he's not happy with the place they went to last time...'

Ah... gotcha

'We don't actually *have* a conference centre yet, Daisy...'

'Pshaw. We've got tables and chairs, and we can hire a projector. Never fear, I'll sort all that.'

She taps her phone. 'Herbert gave me his email—I'm going to make him an offer he can't refuse. Will you help me with the boring stuff—like prices?'

'I think I'd better. No, well done, it's a start. Nice work.'

'His wife, Dinah, couldn't come today, but guess what—she's Maggie's sister. That was my "in".'

Now I remember. Logan mentioned Maggie's sister, Dinah the pharmacist. The fact she was too

busy to accompany Herbert today bears out what
Logan said about Maggie not seeing as much as
she'd like of her sister. 'Daisy, while you're on a roll,
see how soon we can have a Snooker-King delivered.
Oh, and any idea what to do with the old snooker
table? Do you think a scrappy would take it—and do
scrappys collect? We need to get shot before Reggie
Entwhistle finds out it's still here.'

'Scrappy?'
Her face twists in a caricature of pain. She fiddles
with her phone, then holds it up. 'I put it on eBay last
night—buyer collects.

'What? Nobody's going to want that old thing?'
'That's where you're wrong.'
She shoves the screen at my face so I can see
the latest bid, which is—*£725?*

THIRTEEN

I can't help stopping outside the hairdresser and admiring myself in their window. Daisy called it right—my hair *was* manky.

Elaine, the stylist, didn't use quite those words. She simply said it "needed a little TLC".

(Half-way through, she changed "a little" to "*quite a lot of*".)

She also sold me a carrier bag filled with fancy potions that hydrate, separate, and even un-split split ends. (I hope she put some shampoo in, too...)

Still, I am chuffed with my new image. The old me had straight, mono-black hair standing rigidly to attention on her shoulders—that woman in the window looks more like Meg Ryan.

If Meg had dark hair with blonde highlights.

Oh, and if she had my face...

Elaine waves through the glass and, red-faced, I raise a hand and walk swiftly away.

I'm not due to rendezvous with Daisy for another half-hour. There *was* a degree of subterfuge involved, when I added thirty minutes to my hair appointment, but Jodie hasn't met Daisy yet. This is going to be difficult enough without worrying about Daisy's big mouth.

When I rang Jodie yesterday, we agreed to meet in a cafe again. This time, she's first here.

Luxuriating in a richly pungent scent of roasting coffee, my nose draws me towards the barista until Jodie points exaggeratedly at our table and two lattes standing on its pink-plastic top.

'Cheers, Jodie. Hope you haven't been waiting long.'

'No, I only got here a minute before you.'

She blinks. 'Have you changed your hair?'

'Just had it done—what d'you think?'

Jodie being the first person to see my new image I'm a little anxious, but she smiles and says: 'Suits you. It's lovely. Take some looking after, though—won't it?'

Will it?

Heck—is that why Elaine shoved ten photocopied pages of closely printed text into my goody bag?

I'll worry about that tomorrow

'I wish I was as brave as you...' Jodie murmurs. Leaving me no chance to seek clarification, she changes the subject. 'So, what happened with Dr Mackenzie?'

She listens carefully while I tell her.

'Did the GPs give you anything in writing?'

'Oh—no. Well, like I told you on the phone, Dr Frame ended up chasing us off his property. I think Dr Mackenzie would go public with his opinion, but he was guarded about challenging Dr Frame directly.'

She nods and twirls a long-handled spoon around her fingers. 'I had a word with my inspector—he's not sure you have enough to warrant opening a case.'

I almost choke on my latte. 'But Aunt Claire died for no good reason...'

She holds up her other hand, waggles the index finger. 'Trouble is, we don't know that. Sam, people can have diseases their GP is unaware of—take cerebral aneurysm, for example. That's a weak patch on one of the blood vessels in your head—you could have it for fifty years with no symptoms, then *bang*. Surely it's more likely something like that killed your aunt.'

She's right. I know she is. What I don't know is why I'm equally sure she's wrong.

Maybe because I took so long to accept the notion of a sinister force at work, first investigating and discounting all the other possibilities—it's burrowed in all the deeper? In eliminating alternate scenarios, I've sort of proved a negative to myself.

Or am I being over-influenced by CSI's biggest fan?

No, neither of those—or, not *just* them. I sense it now, deep inside—a gut feeling, blocked off until Davy and Dr Mackenzie disproved the obvious alternatives and opened my mind, but burning now with an all-consuming heat. 'Jodie, I'm convinced there's something "off" about my aunt's death. I *feel* it—' clasping a hand over my heart '—in here.'

Jodie sits back with a sigh. 'I'm familiar with that feeling—but it's not enough on its own. Who do you suspect?'

Now I wish I'd brought Daisy

'Okay, we've got a chef who's into herbalism—she knows all about poisonous plants. We also have an employee my aunt was planning to sack. Then there's the jealous wife of a man Aunt Claire was having an affair with—who's behaving suspiciously.'

'And you've got Logan—his inheritance is a motive.'

I feel my cheeks burn. 'I'm glad *you* said it, but yes—obviously.'

'What about the handyman? Logan's not at all keen on him.'

'Jake? Um... you know about Jake and me?'

'Logan mentioned it—and that you've chucked him out.'

'Thing is, Jake was in Edinburgh when Aunt Claire died, so he couldn't have done anything to her.'

'Fair enough. Alright, who do you like best for it? Out of—correct me if I'm wrong—Maggie, Rebecca, and Sadie.'

I press a palm against both temples. 'None of them, to be honest.'

She tilts her head. 'Your gut again?'

I nod, feeling miserable.

'Look, Sam. You don't have to convince me about instinct—it's our most powerful sense. But you *do* have to convince my DI if you want this taken further—and what you've given me so far won't cut it.'

'I know.'

I gulp back the rest of my drink in a oner. 'Give me a few days—I'll try and come up with something else. I have a friend who's... resourceful. She may have some new ideas.'

'Daisy?' Jodie laughs. 'Logan told me about her. She sounds scary, to be honest.'

'She's not really.'

I stand, ready to go, but Jodie grabs my wrist. 'Sam, thank you... for, you know? And believing Logan about that blackmail nonsense. Listen—I want to help you, honestly I do. Get me something I can take to my DI and I'll do my best to sell it.'

'Thanks, Jodie—I appreciate that. I'll give you a ring—hopefully soon.'

I'm meeting Daisy outside the dress shop, and walking slowly gets me a few precious minutes to digest what Jodie said. I'll have to tell Daisy about our conversation, pretending I "ran into" Jodie, since "Daisy in a huff" is not something I'm up to dealing with right now.

My thoughts are in knots—Jodie made an excellent case for Aunt Claire's death being natural. It would be so easy to accept that—especially with everything else going on.

But the itch won't go away—I need to know. One way or the other.

Another worry edges in—if somebody did poison Aunt Claire, and until we find out why—the rest of us could be in danger, too.

I'VE NO SOONER SPOTTED DAISY WAITING OUTSIDE "Dressed to Kill" when my phone beeps. Unlike Edinburgh, in Donstable it's perfectly feasible to read a text, whilst out walking, without feeling like the white ball on a "Snooker-King" table.

The text's from Davy.

***Just got back – pick u up at 7.30?
Looking forward to it - take care - Davy x***

Quickly, I punch in a reply.

See you then x

After pressing "send", I experience a frisson of panic in case that sounded offhand—but I wanted the phone safely away in my bag before Daisy saw it. Normally, I tell her everything, but I'm feeling strangely protective of my budding romance. Maybe there's a touch of guilt involved, since Jake was still in the picture when I agreed to this drink. Whatever—it's best kept private until I figure out where we're going.

If anywhere.

It's just a drink, after all—means nothing. I hardly know the guy...

Daisy shrieks when she sees me. 'That's more like it,' she declares, skipping a circle around me.

'*Enormous* improvement, and not before time. Right—' she grabs my arm '—let's get you kitted out with something Jean Brodie *wouldn't* wear.'

The assistants in "Dressed to Kill" remind me of "Bond girls"—wearing the latest, skimpiest fashions, they converge on us straightaway, obviously "licenced to sell". Glancing at a couple of price tags and guessing how much commission is involved, it's easy to see why they're so keen.

Daisy brushes them off. 'We'll shout if we need you,' she growls, and they melt away. 'Can't trust salespeople's advice, Sam—they just want to flog you whatever's dearest.' She's stalking around the rails—and already has six garments draped over her arm.

A Halle Berry clone (but without the attitude) dares to hover. 'I'm afraid you're only allowed three items at a time in the changing rooms.'

Her eyes widen as she grabs for the bundle of clothes Daisy thrusts at her. 'Fine. You stand outside the curtain and hand them in to us—three at a time.'

It's lucky I'm restricted to trouser suits, or we could have been there all day. Daisy makes a lot of turbulence, but she also has a good eye. With her help, I end up choosing a pantsuit very like the one she wore yesterday, only in burnt orange. Maybe it's because I stick to starker shades at work, but warm colours make me feel softer—lighter. (When I told Daisy that, she asked if the name "Pavlov" rang a bell...)

The top Daisy insists on has a plunging neckline that falls outside my comfort zone, mainly because I'm worried what else might fall out, but like Halle Berry before I defer to my friend. Life's too short...

Back on the street, Daisy's stomach rumbles. 'Where are you taking me for lunch, then?'

I'm still staring at my credit card receipt. 'Bag of chips do you?'

SHE TALKS ME INTO A CHINESE RESTAURANT WHICH HAS A special lunch deal. Over Singapore noodles, I take the chance to raise something that's been bothering me. 'Daisy, do you think Maggie's lonely?'

'Mm?'

I lean over and snatch the chopsticks, drop them out of reach, and slide a fork between her fingers. 'Daisy, you've been trying to master chopsticks since I met you.'

She glares. 'I nearly had it then... Maggie? Lonely? Maybe—now you come to mention it. She does spend a lot of time in the hotel.'

'Exactly—I talked to Logan. Her cottage is falling apart, and it's buried away in the woods somewhere—'

Daisy yelps and throws a hand over her mouth. 'Is it made of gingerbread?'

'Be serious. Maggie's out there all on her own, living in a hovel, and she's not getting any younger. Is it any wonder she never wants to go home?'

Daisy slumps in her chair. 'You really think it's that bad? Poor Mags—I hadn't realised. But what can we do?'

'Well... I've been thinking about it. I'm going to spin a yarn about needing her on the premises because we're expanding. Then I'll ask her to move into the staff corridor.'

'Brilliant.'

She cocks her head. 'Plus, it'll cut the wage bill when we adjust her money to "all-in".'

'Daisy. That's got nothing to do with it.'

She giggles. 'Your face. Sam, I think it's a lovely idea. Mags will be much happier living with us—given that she practically already is. When are you going to tell her?'

I put my fork down. (*I* can use chopsticks, but showing Daisy up isn't worth the aggro.) 'This might sound silly, but I want to wait until we've cleared up the mystery surrounding Aunt Claire's death.'

'What, you still think...?'

'No, not for a moment—but what if I was wrong?'

She nods, slowly. 'Yep, let's play it safe. A few more weeks won't make any difference to Mags.'

I haven't told Daisy yet about my meeting with Jodie. 'While we're on the subject of Aunt Claire...'

She takes the news about Jodie's inspector and his reticence about opening an investigation with her usual stoicism. 'We'll just have to find something to change his mind, won't we? Leave it with me.'

Neither of us is in the mood for pudding, and half an hour later we're back in Cairncroft. Approaching the hotel gates, weighed down with shopping bags, we're stopped dead by cloying smells reminiscent of oily-seaweed accompanied by heavy-machinery-like bangs and crashes.

Resurfacing is obviously underway—forcing a detour onto the front lawn.

Daisy covers her ears with both hands, bags and all, as a bright-orange vehicle that closely resembles an oversized ride-on lawn mower rumbles by. Further up, men in dirty yellow jackets are sweeping aggregate into potholes. As we draw level, one stops and waves. 'Miss Chessington—hello again.'

'I don't believe it.'

Daisy looks round sharply. 'What?'

'That's...'

Dropping his brush, the man in question ambles over and pulls out a packet of cigarettes. 'Want one?'

'No. What are you doing here?'

He spreads his arms. 'You hired me to fix your drive. Well, Davy did. How? Was he not supposed to?'

'Yes, he was.'

I pause to gather my thoughts. 'What's confusing me is, last Friday, you quoted me nearly twice the price Davy says you gave him.'

242

He takes his time lighting the cigarette, blows smoke out of his nose. 'Aye, well—Davy gets a trade discount.'

'Of fifty percent?' I'm fuming. He obviously tried to rip me off.

'I could put the price back up if you want,' he drawls, with a show of helpfulness.

Daisy pulls me away. 'C'mon, Sam—you're distracting the workmen.'

'He's nothing but a chancer.'

Daisy just laughs. 'If it makes you feel any better, getting good prices is how Davy justifies his fee. You're right, though—that blighter tried to con you. But—' she adds hastily '—you weren't having any of it. Makes you the winner here, Sam.'

'S'pose so,' I admit, not feeling like a winner.

'What time's Davy picking you up?'

NOW I feel like a winner

'Seven thirty.'

'On his motorbike?'

'What's funny about that?'

She eyes me for a second. 'I'm having trouble picturing you on a bike—especially that mean-machine Davy drives. You must *really* be into this guy.'

'Going back to Jodie—what will we do? We don't have a viable suspect to give her inspector—or even know for certain there *was* foul play.'

'Sam—we can't just let it go.'

She's right—but since talking to Jodie, I'm not sure what else we *can* do. At the steps to reception,

Daisy stops and puts down her bags. She leans an elbow on the stone balustrade. 'If somebody poisoned Claire, they did it after she went up to the flat. Whoever it was couldn't risk administering the poison before—someone might have seen she was sick and called an ambulance. *If* it wasn't Logan—' she holds up a hand, and I close my mouth '—it happened after he came back down. So—who had access to the flat after— when did Logan say he left?'

'Ten.'

'After ten.'

She thinks for a moment before carrying on—it's plain the question was rhetorical. 'The bar doesn't shut until eleven. Rebecca must have taken over while Logan was talking to Claire. So *she* was here, and as housekeeper, or maid, or whatever it is she does, has a key to the flat. Like we were saying earlier, Mags is always around—be easy for her to take a wee treat up to Claire. Hot chocolate or something.'

'Sadie didn't have access,' I offer, trying to see Daisy's post-its in my mind. 'Well, we don't think she did. Is there anyone else?'

'I reckon it's Mags or Rebecca,' she breathes. 'And my money's on Rebecca. We have to figure out exactly how she did it—reconstruct the crime—then find a way of proving it.'

'How do we do that?'

'The important bit—proving it—follows naturally when we know how it was done. I'll work on reconstruction scenarios while you're out tonight, then we'll take it from there.'

She picks up her bags and offers a supporting arm. I wish I had half her optimism—I don't really see how theorising what *might* have happened will help.

In reception, we both wince at the scream of drills. The panelling is almost intact again. Our gazes travel first to the stairway door, then down to our bags, and finally meet in unspoken assent.

Daisy presses the lift button.

I refuse to think about crime fighting tonight. All I care about is a long, hot bath, and my outfit looking good as it did in the shop.

Oh—and Davy turning up.

FOURTEEN

'**W**ill I do?'
Daisy puts two fingertips on her lips and makes a smacking sound. 'Absolutely. You look fabulous, Sam. Oh... wait a minute.'

'What?'

Is there something wrong with my new clothes? I knew this top was a mistake

'I've just remembered, Davy's already organised the refits—so you won't need to go after all. That *is* the only reason you're meeting him tonight, isn't it?'

She ducks in the nick of time as a cushion zips over her head.

'Don't wait up,' I call from the doorway.

'Don't do anything I wouldn't,' comes the rejoinder.

Plenty scope there

I'd rather none of the staff see me. (Should that be "neither", since Logan's a partner, or does the gardener count?) It's stupid—but tonight it doesn't feel as though I'm the same person who runs this hotel. More like an imposter in her body.

I'm very compartmentalising. (So I've been told.) Which probably means it's good that, as Daisy pointed out, the business side of my relationship with Davy is up to date.

Leaving us free to... investigate the possibility of another side? Explore the wider interpretation of that word "relationship", even?

I'm in luck—reception's deserted. (As usual.) I'm out the door faster than our regulars come in at opening time.

It's a lovely night, no breeze, the dying embers of today's sun making my face glow—along with a generous expanse of exposed flesh further down.

I should never have let Daisy talk me into this top

The tarmacker's finished, and so long as I avoid those grey freckles that used to be potholes— I'm assuming the stuff they filled them with needs time to harden—I can stay on the drive. Not that walking on grass is a problem—unlike other women on a night out, heels are anathema to me. But I'd rather pretend to be Lady Mary leaving Downton Abbey for an assignation with a handsome Duke than Mariette Larkin cutting through the meadow to meet her gawky tax inspector.

I *am* worried about this motorbike business. Contrary to my previous rash claim, I've never ridden on anything with both an engine and less than four wheels. To be honest, the thought terrifies me—but I keep telling myself Davy drives his bike every day, and he's still in one piece.

Oh—it'll be fine

I think...

Seven thirty, he said—it's just after twenty past. I really should have kept him waiting—I knew

247

that, even without Daisy reminding me three times. But being late would mean not knowing if *he* was on time—a useful indicator of how important tonight is to him.

Smacking my wrist mentally, I resolve to stop overthinking this.

It's a drink—we're meeting for a drink.

Just a drink.

I know zilch about him (not that I knew much about Jake) and it may not go any further. But Jodie said instinct's our most powerful sense, and if she's right (and if my instincts are) then this might be the start of something—special?

I'm at the gate now, and it still isn't half past. It therefore means nothing that Davy's nowhere to be seen.

At twenty-five to, I text to see if something's held him up. There's no answer. Well, there wouldn't be. Not if he's driving.

At twenty to, I assume it's traffic holding him up.

At quarter to, I remember these are some of the quietest roads in Britain.

At five to, sat on a low, stone wall in front of the hedge, I worry in case my mascara's running.

At four minutes to, I realise that doesn't matter any more.

At eight, I get up, turn around, and trudge back up the drive.

FIFTEEN

'I'm going to kill him.'

'That's my job,' I snap back.

When I came back last night, Daisy was in the hotel kitchen schmoozing with Maggie, so I sneaked upstairs and into my bedroom (collecting a bottle of red en route)—and stayed there. There's no escaping her this morning, though.

She jumps up, parking her bum on the reception desk. 'Seriously, what's he playing at? I had him pegged as a decent sort.'

My phone's in front of me. For the millionth time, my eyes flicker to its screen.

Nothing.

Sitting back in the little-used receptionist's chair, it's a novelty to be looking up at my diminutive friend. And also, despite my angst, a relief to have those patches of dirty brickwork hidden behind new panels. Even if they are only raw plates of wood until the decorators work their magic. 'Maybe my deformity finally got to him and he changed his mind about dating Long John Silver?'

'Naw.' She shakes her head slowly. 'You obsess on that far too much—most people don't give it a second thought.'

Then she stiffens. 'What if he had an accident...?'

'On these roads?'

'Shouldn't you check? Just in case.'

'They'd want to know who I am. A first date that didn't even happen doesn't exactly make me immediate family—I think I'd get short shrift. Still, I hadn't really thought about him crashing his bike, or going down with food poisoning...'

Thanks, Daisy—screw my head up some more, why don't you?

I nod at the opening to the residents lounge. 'Have the decorators finished the restaurant? They were supposed to have.'

'Hopefully. D'you want me to check?' She bounces off her perch, then stops dead. Two men just walked through the entrance.

'Don't look so shocked,' I hiss. 'This *is* a hotel.'

'I think they're police,' she mutters. 'You can tell.'

'Rubbish.'

I paste on a professional smile as they approach. 'Good morning. May I help you?'

The older one brandishes a sheaf of papers. 'Miss Chessington? Detective Inspector Wilson, Donstable CID. This is Detective Constable Urquart. We have a warrant to search part of these premises.'

'A warrant? Why? Is this to do with my aunt's death?'

His eyebrows collide. 'Your aunt? What happened to your aunt?'

Daisy answers for me. 'We think somebody murdered her.'

Inspector Wilson's carefully composed expression crumbles, but only for a second. 'Ah, *that* aunt. The one Jodie's been bending my ear about. No, this is nothing to do with your aunt. We're looking for Logan Brown—is he here?'

Logan?

'He's not on 'til lunchtime, so I expect he's in his room. I'll buzz up and ask him to—'

Inspector Wilson's hand settles on mine and pushes the receiver back in its cradle. 'I'd prefer you didn't, Ma'am. Could you direct us to Mr Brown's room, please?'

I point at the lift with a finger that refuses to stay steady. 'Third floor—his name's on the door. What about this search warrant? What's that about?'

'Don't worry, Ma'am.' Constable Urquart's already on his way to the lift—Inspector Wilson turns in his wake, still speaking. 'The warrant is only for Logan Brown's room.'

The lift doors close, and I grab my mobile. Daisy gawks. 'Is that a good idea?'

'Relax...' it's ringing '... I'm not warning Logan. I'm phoning—Jodie? Is that you?'

When I put the phone down a few minutes later, Daisy's practically on my lap. 'Give,' she demands, eyes flaring. 'What did she say? Does *she* know what's going on?'

'Davy's in hospital,' I hear myself tell her. Then the voice I'm listening to shudders. 'He's in a bad way.'

Daisy puts a hand under my arm and eases me up. I hardly notice where she's taking me, too busy replaying Jodie's words in my mind, trying to make sense of them.

'Bit early is it not?'

The decorator's jibe pulls me out of my trance. He and his pals must be done in the restaurant right enough, because they're moving their stuff through to reception—via the residents lounge.

The joiners are way ahead of schedule—they completed all the work through here last night. Which means the decorators, as soon as they finish reception, can get straight on with both residents lounge and new snooker room.

That seemed such a big deal on Monday...

Daisy props me on a stool at our brand-spanking residents bar—this is what the painter's finding so amusing. The look she throws him turns his face scarlet. He grabs a can of emulsion and stares at the label as if his life depends on it, then scurries off towards reception in his workmates' wake.

With a satisfied nod, Daisy circles 'round to the serving side. Although no barrels have been hooked up yet, she already told me Maggie helped stock the optics last night. (No doubt they tested them, too.) Now, she thrusts a glass of amber liquid at me. 'Drink.'

The brandy burns my throat, but it goes down, and I welcome its spreading warmth. It thaws the chill in my chest, and I'm able to speak again.

'It... it was Logan,' I burble.

'What?'

Daisy comes back 'round to my side of the bar and hoists herself onto an adjoining stool. '*What* was Logan?'

In between gulps of brandy, I tell her what Jodie said. 'Davy had an accident on his bike—last night—on the way here.'

She waits, feigning patience, fidgety shoulders giving her away.

'There was oil on the road and Davy skidded. He took a terrible tumble—he has a broken leg, but it's the head injury his doctors are worried about. They operated to relieve pressure on his brain, and now... now he's in a coma.'

'Oh, Sam.' She wraps her arms around me, and my chin finds her shoulder. 'But what's Logan got to do with it?'

'It was Logan who poured oil at the end of Davy's road. That's why the police are here to arrest him.'

She draws back, looks at me incredulously. 'Jodie said that?'

I shake my head. 'No, she called it "circumstantial evidence". They found Logan's name badge near the oil spill...'

Daisy frowns. 'So they assume Logan did it. Because why else would Logan's badge—and by implication, Logan—be on Davy's road? Mm. I see where Jodie's coming from—it *is* a tad convenient.'

'Daisy.' I hold up a hand. 'I need to phone the hospital, find out how he is.'

'Sure.'

She hops off her stool. 'I'll give you some privacy.'

I manage a tight smile. 'Yeah, go beat up some more painters.'

Her face bobs into view again five minutes later. When she sees my phone lying in front of me, the rest of her follows. She trots behind the bar and grabs a bottle of beer. 'Need a refill?'

I slap a hand over my glass—I've got a spongy head already. 'All they would tell me is, he's stable—whatever that means. And that his mother's on her way from Glasgow—'

A cough draws our attention. Constable Urquart is standing half-in, half-out of the opening to reception. 'Miss Chessington, we need to ask you and your staff a few questions—individually. Is there somewhere private we can…?'

My mind races, then trips over its own thoughts. 'Daisy?'

She beckons Constable Urquart over. 'Want a beer? Only got bottled, I'm afraid.'

'I'm on duty,' he barks.

She shrugs. 'Well, there's wet paint all over the restaurant, and our decorators are setting up in reception. The *old* snooker room's full of joiners, and there's no furniture in the new one yet, so that leaves—here.'

She smiles sweetly and takes my arm to steer me towards the exit. 'If you change your mind about a beer, help yourself from the cooler.'

IT'S SUNNY AGAIN, SO WE DECIDE TO MAKE A BASE ON THE steps outside until they call us for questioning. As we pass through to reception the lift doors open, and two uniformed policemen (who might have been stormtroopers in a previous life) march out with Logan between them.

Daisy nudges me. 'He's handcuffed,' she whispers.

For a fraction of a second, my gaze meets Logan's—then his escorts hustle him away. His pupils were black against the stark whites of his eyes, but I also sensed confusion.

I don't know *what* to believe any more. I went from suspecting Logan of murdering both my aunt and his own stepfather to admiring his courage in standing up for Trudy. I even began to appreciate why Aunt Claire bequeathed him a share of the hotel. Until now, I've never thought this blundering, loveable oaf was capable of anything worse than "forgetting" to pay for the odd beer while he's serving.

Until now.

Surely it's reasonable to assume the name badge arrived at Davy's street attached to Logan—until it accidentally became *de*tached. Daisy felt it "a tad convenient"—but who would want to frame Logan? Why?

My fear and anger over Davy's condition are still expanding as fast as our business overdraft, making it hard to think, but a tiny jolt of clarity cautions me I shouldn't jump to conclusions.

'There goes Maggie,' Daisy mutters, fluttering her fingers at what bright sunshine has reduced to a bony outline. Through a propped open main door, we've got an unobstructed view of comings and goings.

Ten minutes later it's Rebecca's turn, then Daisy's.

When she re-emerges, Daisy jerks her head. 'They're ready for you now,' she says, voice alive with drama.

'How'd it go?' I ask, as we pass on the top step.

She pulls a face. 'The rubber hosepipes weren't much fun, but I stuck with my story... ouch.'

I leave her rubbing the shoulder I punched and pick my way through abandoned ladders and discarded paint trays. We've sent the decorators to give "The Cuppa Tea" some extra custom while this is going on.

DC Urquart's waiting. He steers me to a table DI Wilson has commandeered as his command post.

'Just a few questions, Miss Chessington. First, would you describe your relationship with Logan Brown?'

Funny question

'He's my business partner in the hotel, and we were also becoming friends. I've met his girlfriend, Jodie, too—but you already know that. I can't believe Logan would do anything like this...'

Wilson holds up a hand. 'Just answer the questions, please. It's been suggested that—Jodie notwithstanding—Logan had quite a fancy for you, Miss Chessington.'

'What? That's nonsense.'

'Was it not reciprocated, then?'

'There was nothing *to* reciprocate. Where are you getting this from?'

He settles back in his seat. 'From your own staff. Rebecca Perkins has observed Mr Brown developing a—crush?—on you. Possibly, in the light of recent developments, an obsession.'

Rebecca—she's lying. She has to be. I tell him that.

'Your opinion of Miss Perkins isn't high, I take it? Care to explain why?'

'No, that would be hearsay. But I *know* Logan—if all you've got is his name badge—'

I break off. He's shaking his head. 'We have more than the badge now—after searching his room, we seized a freshly stained jacket. It's on its way to forensics, but I recognise oil when I see it, Miss Chessington. Anyway...' he sits up straight '... you

257

were unaware of Mr Brown developing feelings for you, we've established that. Is there anything else you can tell me that might be helpful?'

'Not that I can think of.'

He pushes a card across the table. 'Call me if something occurs to you.'

He stands. 'We're done here—for now.'

SIXTEEN

I find Daisy in the kitchen, drinking tea with Maggie and Rebecca. Maggie rushes to pour me one, and Daisy raises her eyebrows, but my focus is on Rebecca. She startles and steps back when I rush towards her. 'What's all this about Logan having some sort of fixation on me?'

Rebecca turns, putting more distance between us as she places her cup on a worktop. 'It started that day Logan showed you around the hotel—since then, he's had a thing for you. It's been all "Sam this" and "Sam that"—his eyes never leave you.'

She swings to stare at me. 'You must have noticed.'

'I certainly haven't.'

'Oh.'

Her gaze drops. 'Remember last Saturday, when Logan dropped a glass in the bar? He was in a stinking mood after hearing that Davy guy ask you out...'

Now *I* take a step back, remembering. Logan *did* drop a glass, and his face *was* a picture—but then he winked at me. And smiled. Could that have been for show—was he actually boiling inside?

Rebecca flinches when I reach forward to pat her shoulder. 'I'm sorry, you were only saying how it looked. Maybe you're right—it would certainly explain—'

The words die in my throat and I flee, barely conscious of the startled faces watching me go. For once, I'm not thinking about the lift's antics as it hoists me away from everyone.

Just before I rushed out of the kitchen, an image of Davy popped up in my mind. He was lying in a hospital bed surrounded by beeping monitors, with tubes coming out of him. It was so vivid...

Stuff Logan—and *stuff* the police. None of that matters.

I *have* to see Davy.

WE COME TO A SCREECHING STOP OUTSIDE ABERDEEN Royal Infirmary, ignoring the man in a hi-vis jacket running towards us with both arms flailing. Graham quickly tells me he'll drive around until I call, and I jump out.

Daisy was in meltdown when I texted her from Graham's truck. I knew she'd follow, after my dramatic exit, but I'd already taken the lift. Instead of waiting, Daisy went pelting up the stairs. Meanwhile, I'd grabbed my bag out of the flat and started back down—in the lift.

I don't know how I expected to get to ARI—I *wasn't* thinking, is the answer to that—but I could have wept when Graham offered me a lift. He was mowing grass when I burst out of the hotel, and it must have looked like a pack of wolves was chasing me because he came tearing over.

We said little during the journey. I was preoccupied with recent explosive events, and he was—awkward. Now and again, I caught him glancing sideways. Mostly, though, his eyes stayed fixed on the road. He *could* have been treating me with kid gloves considering my near hysteria before—or was he wondering whether I know about his affair with Aunt Claire?

Probably both.

A friendly volunteer at the information desk turns out to be a star. She locates Davy for me, then gives directions even I can follow. At Davy's ward, however, the charge nurse is more reserved.

'What's your relationship to the patient?'

That's a hard one

I go with 'close friend', which isn't enough to get me in. When I start crying, she softens and ushers me into a large cupboard whose doorplate declares it's a "family room". 'I'll see if his mum will come and talk to you. What was your name again?'

She bustles off, and I slump on the smallest two-seater I've ever seen. There are folding chairs stacked against one wall, no doubt to accommodate *big* families (more than two members) though I can't imagine there's enough space to *un*fold them.

I feel... beaten. The nurses have made it plain I'm not getting to see Davy. As for his mum, her response when they say my name will probably be: "Who?"

I wonder about his dad—whether he's one of those men who blends into the background, or is Davy's mum divorced, maybe even widowed?

'Samantha?'

I jump up, losing my balance until I slap a hand against the wall. The crack of flesh on plaster makes both of us start.

'Are you alright, dear?' The tiny, grey-haired lady gives me a searching look.

'I'm sorry, you don't know me, but I know Davy, and...'

Then she does what I least expect. She steps forward and wraps her arms around me.

Despite having the stature of a bird, she hugs like a bear—reminding me of Daisy. When she draws back, leaving both hands on my shoulders, I see her eyes are moist. In a faltering voice, I ask: 'Is Davy...?'

The tight smile doesn't come easily. 'No change, duckie. He's holding his own, though. Are you that lass he told me about on the phone—the one with a hotel?'

He told his mother about me

My head nods of its own accord. 'We don't know each other very well yet, but...'

She sits on the midget sofa, drawing me with her. 'He's sleeping—ach, *they're* calling it a *coma*, but after getting smashed up like that it makes sense he would need a breather. That's what I think. I *told* him bikes are death traps, and he should get a proper car...'

262

We share a fragile laugh, and she pulls a cotton handkerchief from her sleeve and dabs each eye in turn. 'Anyway, they won't let you in, luvvie—I'm sorry—but as soon as he wakes up, I'm sure he'd love to see you. Give me your number and I'll keep you updated.'

'Have they said... when... how long...?'

Her lips whiten. 'No, they're being very vague. According to them, it could be hours, months, or even years.'

Then she brightens. 'But they did one o' them scan things and it seems his brain's still working. That's good, isn't it?'

'Very good.' I nod, trying to convince myself as much as her. 'Did you have far to come, Mrs...?'

'Geraldine,' she says firmly. 'I live on Skye, so yes... the journey's a bugger, but I'm here now, and I'll be staying until him through there sees fit to join us.'

Giving her hand one last squeeze with both of mine, I rise to go. 'Thank you for being so kind. Especially at a time like this.'

Howking my phone out, I add: 'I'll leave you my number...'

She stands too and hands me her own phone. 'Would you do it, sweetheart? I'm not very good with these things.'

Grinning, I assure her neither am I. Somehow, I get us into each other's contacts without wiping both phones. 'Tell him...' I start.

what?

'... I was here.'

It sounds so weak, but her arms go around me again. 'I will,' she promises. Then her eyes brighten, and she whispers in my ear. 'You're not missing much. Beggar snores like a chain saw, coma or no coma.'

ON THE WAY BACK, I TEXT DAISY AND TELL HER WHEN TO expect me. Then I turn to Graham. It's time to shoot the elephant standing between us. 'Graham, I know about you and Aunt Claire—please don't feel awkward about it. What two consenting adults do is nobody's business but...'

He's laughing

'Not you an' all,' he says breathlessly. 'I already got all this from Sadie. Me an' Miss Claire? I'm flattered, mind, but...'

'Graham, I saw a photo of you both coming out of the Station hotel in Aberdeen—your arm was around her.'

He shakes his head, concentrating on the road ahead. 'She sprained her ankle—not bad, like, but she weren't happy driving for a few days, so she got me to run her there that time to meet her fancy man. I had my arm 'round her for support—she was still having trouble walking.'

'Oh.' My mind blanks—then the million-dollar question pops into it. 'So—who *was* her "fancy man"?'

He shrugs. 'Dunno. Local gossips said it was one o' them snooker club boys, but they say a lot o' things and get it wrong as often. *I* never saw him—your aunt made sure of that.'

Jake must have jumped to the same conclusion as Daisy and me—and Aunt Claire couldn't deny it without revealing the identity of her real lover

We pass what's left of the journey in companionable silence, and I realise Graham's naturally quiet—before, when I thought it was awkwardness, he was just being Graham.

When we arrive, I can't help a smidgeon of satisfaction as Graham's truck glides over the new tarmac. Daisy's sat on the steps, reading her Kindle while she waits for us.

Graham grunts. 'Did a good job on them potholes.'

'You sound surprised?'

'Aye, well, thon lad you got to do it—he's a "half-a-job-Harry". There's folk 'round here haven't been right pleased with his work.'

I confess I'm also surprised—when I saw who was fixing the potholes, my heart sank. Davy's contractors obviously make a special effort for him—I've heard the way their tone changes when his name comes up. It turns out even Graham knows more about my almost-date than I do when he tells me

Davy's dad died years ago—he explains he knew Geraldine before she moved to Skye. 'Good wumman, that.'

When we draw up beside the steps, I lean over to hug my knight in not-so-shiny overalls. 'Thanks, Graham. You're a lifesaver.'

Daisy jumps up as I approach, and the urgency in her questioning gaze makes me flinch. A blanket of weariness envelops me and I hold up my palms. 'Nothing really to tell. I didn't get to see him, and he hasn't woken up yet.'

Her face falls. 'Will they let you know when...?'

'I met his mum—Geraldine. She's lovely, and promised to keep me in the loop. We've swapped numbers.'

'That's something.'

She takes my arm and we climb the steps. 'You worried me, running off like that. I thought you were having a breakdown...'

'Maybe I was—I never expected all these pressures when we decided to come here. All I saw was happy guests and cheerful staff, possibly the odd little problem with rotas or late deliveries—I didn't foresee investigating a murder or watching the police cart my under manager away in handcuffs. Any news on him?'

'Logan? No, nothing.'

The decorators in reception look 'round curiously as we whisk past, then we're in the residents lounge and I collapse on a plump armchair.

266

Daisy stays on her feet, looking down at me—she's got a question of her own about Logan. 'Do you think he did it?'

'No idea. The police seem to think so, but I'm having trouble picturing Logan dressing up like Tom Cruise in "Mission Impossible" and pouring oil in front of his love-rival's motorbike.'

'Yep, and... no offence, Sam, but Logan showed me a picture of Jodie, so unless it's *him* who needs glasses...'

She skips out of reach as I swipe the air between us. I know she's trying to lighten the mood, and it's worked—I'm laughing, for the first time since I came back last night. Still, I can't help thinking she's got a point...

Daisy grabs me under the elbow. 'C'mon, you *have* to see the restaurant. It's amazing.'

She's right—I did, and it is. Our decorators have done a wonderful job. They've turned our frumpy cafeteria into a vibrant brasserie.

'I can't wait until the new lights are up,' Daisy breathes. Then she falters, seems to search for words—not like her at all. 'Em... with Davy being... will it affect the renovations getting finished?'

Ah, right... Okay, good point

'I don't think so. He already instructed all the contractors—they know what they're doing and I know who they are, so I can't see why everything shouldn't proceed as planned.'

267

She nods. 'Yep—there've been guys carrying toolboxes in and out all morning. I've given up trying to keep track of them.'

Daisy's right—we *have* to be practical. *I* have to be practical. I need to remember, it's not like... the thing is, all my feelings about Davy are bound up in what *might* be and who I *think* he is.

I've only met the man twice.

Daisy squeezes my shoulder. 'He'll be alright, Sam. And for the record, I don't believe Logan caused his accident.'

'The problem is, who else could it be?'

She colours—instantly, I twig what she's thinking. 'Oh, come on. Jake's gone—and he doesn't even know about Davy.'

'I wouldn't be so sure—Rebecca could be keeping him in the loop. Those two were always a bit pally for my liking...'

'Daisy. I lived with the guy—give me credit for knowing he's not a homicidal maniac. Anyway, it would make no difference—Davy had nothing to do with why I threw Jake out.'

'Does Jake know that?'

Daisy's never happy without a few conspiracy theories on the boil. Her birthday's coming up—maybe I'll get her a tinfoil hat.

But now she's brought it up—thanks, Daisy—I've got yet another worry clamouring for space inside my head. Because, if Logan *was* behind Davy's crash, then the chances are he also blackmailed Aunt Claire—and lied about Jake's involvement.

Which would mean I've done Jake a terrible injustice.

SEVENTEEN

Next morning, I'm up before Daisy. That's not so clever as it sounds because, for the first time since I've known her, Daisy actually sleeps in.

She has a good excuse, though. Rebecca was mysteriously unavailable last night when we bowed to pressure and opened the new residents lounge bar to our regulars (AKA Daisy's Cairncroft Cowboys)— on the strict understanding it's a temporary rodeo until their saloon's ready.

With the hotel effectively closed for renovations, reducing our cash flow to zero, it wasn't an entirely altruistic decision.

So, with Logan also "unavailable", either Daisy or I had to take on the role of barkeep.

I owe her one

I leave her brewing coffee—and possibly considering the wisdom of accepting *every* drink foisted on her by our very own (and very grateful) Marlboro Men.

Picking my way down the now familiar but still unending stone stairway, I'm afforded both time and privacy to phone Georgina. She sounds bright and insists on telling me about her breakfast in minute detail. Then I get a list of the obstacles placed in her path by an unsympathetic NHS when she attempted to smoke on their grounds. When she pauses for breath, I steer her onto the subject she's trying so hard to put off and learn there's no change in Davy's condition.

'But no news is good news,' she insists, and all I can do is agree.

The decorators seem to have taken their construction colleagues' accelerated schedule as a challenge—they've started on the residents lounge already.

In our now classy (and unrecognisable) reception, the first person I run into is Rebecca. She's wearing a slinky red dress, whose length would be unremarkable in the sleazier parts of Soho, or even a shop window in Amsterdam. Complementing her outfit (or lack of it), her face has more paint slapped on it than the decorators used on reception's walls.

New boyfriend?

'Miss Chessington.' She hurries over. 'I was hoping to catch you—can I have a word?'

Oh, dear. After her "Grampa" tantrum, I did tell her... but I'm really not in the mood for this, whatever it is

She looks about, furtively, before continuing. 'I hope you won't think this is a liberty, miss, but I've got a message for you.'

I wait, and she colours under the makeup.

'Em... it's from Jake.'

That gets my attention.

'He was scared to contact you directly. Asked me to see if you would consider meeting him for a ... chat?'

On and off, Jake's been on my mind. I feel rotten about the way I treated him—*if* he's not guilty. But Logan's continuing absence makes it more and more likely Jake *is* actually innocent.

Rebecca's waiting for my reply, mouth half-open. 'Alright—I'll speak to him. Where's he been, anyway?'

She looks past me, and for a moment I expect Jake to tap my shoulder. 'Staying with me—well, with Grampa and me—at our cottage. We couldn't see him put out on the street...'

She leaves the accusation hanging. Then: 'He's going to wait outside the old stable block until nine.'

My first thought is:

Trust Jake to land on his feet

Closely followed by:

Let's get this over with

Nothing's changed about the way I feel about "*us*". He lied to me for so long I could never trust him again. However, in view of recent developments, it's only right I offer him his room and job back. 'Thanks, Rebecca. I'll go and see him now.'

She does something that might have been a curtsy, which isn't wise in a dress that short, and scurries off towards the kitchen. Simultaneously, the lift does its impression of a Jumbo Jet coming in to land and Daisy steps out—just as the landline rings.

'I'll get it,' she chirrups, skipping to the desk. 'Cairncroft Hotel, how may I help you?'

She even makes that sound threatening

I'm half-out the door when she calls: 'Sam.'

'What?'

She covers the receiver with her palm. 'It's the Edinburgh police—they've found your burglar.'

That's good news—I still have nightmares about being chased by that knife-wielding lunatic, and knowing he's behind bars is the closure I need. But it couldn't have come at a worse moment.

I admit it—sometimes I tend towards the compulsive-obsessive. I'm in a mindset for confronting Jake, and the idea of switching channels is just too daunting—I'd have to work myself up all over again. 'Say I'll phone back in half an hour—or take a message, if they prefer.'

I zip through the doorway before she can argue. The other reason for not putting this off is I don't want Daisy getting wind of it and trying to change my mind. She *is* over the top where Jake's concerned, so I'd rather tell her about re-employing him *after* it's a done deal.

The air outside is cool today—more typical of Scotland, summer or not. I check my watch—it's five to nine, and I'd better be brisk before Jake gets bored and leaves. Another reason for not letting myself get caught up with the Edinburgh police although, as I skirt the old well, I can't help wondering—are they simply keeping me informed or, more likely, do they want me to testify in court?

273

I could do without that

At the stable block, there's no sign of Jake. I curse under my breath, thinking he must have given up on me.

Then he steps through the doorway—I hadn't noticed it was open—making me yelp.

'Sorry, Sam. I didn't mean to scare you.'

'Well, you did.'

My mind clicks. 'That door's kept locked.'

'The handyman has keys for everywhere,' he returns, without a blink, and I frown.

'Yes, but I sacked you. You were supposed to leave your keys.'

He studies his feet. 'I forgot.'

'What were you doing in there, anyway?'

'Nothing—killing time until you arrived. *If* you arrived. Sam, listen to me, please…'

My palm swings up as I step closer. 'No, let me. Jake, I apologise—I may have acted hastily. There have been certain developments and in retrospect you didn't deserve to be thrown out like that. You can have your job back, and the room—if you still want them.'

'Sam, that's fabulous. Thank you. Hey, you've changed your hair. It looks great.'

He steps into my personal space, and I jerk backwards. 'Whoa. Too close.'

Ignoring me, he seizes my shoulders—and his eyes plead with mine. 'Sam, you know how I feel about you. Hear me out on this—what say we shoot off to Gretna Green, right now, and tie the knot?

Rebecca's grampa, bless his heart, will lend us his BMW.'

My mind reels. Has he lost *all* his marbles? 'Jake, leaving aside the obvious, you can't just turn up at Gretna and get married. Not any more. They changed that years ago.'

He nods, smiles a thin smile. 'That's true. They need at least 29 days' notice—but I've given them double that. Sam, I've been planning this for ages— back in Edinburgh, I took your birth certificate and passport from that box file you keep all your paperwork in and sent them to Gretna, along with mine—and a Marriage Notice form.'

I'm stunned—I never even noticed those documents were missing. Well, you wouldn't—not without looking for them.

I'm seriously starting to wonder about Jake's mental health

'I decided to go all out on a huge, romantic surprise, and sweep you off your feet. The ceremony's booked for three this afternoon, meaning we'd need to leave in the next hour. Please, please, please. Say you'll come—and that you'll marry me.'

He really has lost it. Has he forgotten that ghastly night at Carlo's, in Edinburgh? From the way his expression plummets, I think mine has already broadcast what I'm thinking. 'Jake, this is ridiculous. *We* are over. I don't want to marry you, and I'm wondering now whether giving you the job back is such a good...'

I break off as Jake's face changes. It contorts through frustration, reluctance, and finally... savagery?

Before the impact, I'm conscious of a flesh-coloured blur. Then Jake's fist crashes into my nose.

There's a loud crack, a searing flash in front of my eyes, and a nauseating blast of pain that makes me scream. Except it comes out as a whimper, muffled by blood pouring into my throat.

That's when, mercifully, my vision clouds and I pass out.

EIGHTEEN

I float up, out of darkness, into light. I'm lying on a hard surface staring up at wooden roof struts, arms crossed over my chest the way an undertaker would arrange them. Trying to move, I realise my wrists are bound. There's a musty smell. For a moment, my brain seizes, uncomprehending— then pain lances through the centre of my face, and I remember.

Jake hit me

The gurgling, keening noises I'm making sound as though they're coming from someone else. Turning, drawing my knees up and using two arms as one, I push myself into a kneeling position. Except—there's something wrong with my balance. I'm having trouble staying upright.

A glance down confirms what my other beleaguered senses are trying to tell me—the lower half of my left trouser leg's empty. Somebody's removed my prosthetic.

Jake.

'Welcome back, Sam.'

I didn't hear him come through the still open door. Struggling to hold focus, I see him as never before—this is the real Jake. The face I thought was handsome has a cruel twist, and his eyes are ablaze with darkness.

I've been such an idiot

277

The Jake I knew—he never existed.

Even his voice is cold, alien. 'It didn't have to be this way, you know.'

'Oh, I think it did, Jake.'

My mind slowly comes back online. 'All this business about getting married—it's the hotel you're after. It was never me you wanted—just my money.'

He nods, and a look of almost sadness crosses his face. Reaching behind, he pulls a huge knife from somewhere and crouches in front of me. A sob bubbles in my throat and I rock on my (only) heel, but can't get away from him—or the knife.

He grabs one of my forearms and saws at the rope around my wrists. My hands come free. Jake leans back, and I breathe again.

'Here.' The notebook he holds out has a pen wedged in its spiral. 'I need you to write a message for your weirdo friend.'

'Dream on.'

'Thought you might say that.'

Jake gets to his feet and I flinch, but he tosses the writing materials at me and marches off, disappearing outside.

Next moment, Rebecca flies through the doorway—and lands in a heap at my side. Jake comes up behind, kneels, and loops Rebecca's hair around his fingers. He yanks, and her head jerks back. With his other hand, he holds the knife to her throat.

Rebecca looks at me with wide eyes, her mouth drooping. 'Please, Samantha,' she gurgles. 'Please...'

278

His hold on her hair tightens, and Rebecca's face contorts with pain. 'Quiet. Sam, either you write that note, or I'm going to hurt her. Your choice.'

Not much of a choice. The back of my mind's wondering how he got Rebecca here so quickly. There again, how long was I unconscious for?

Grabbing notebook and pen from where they landed by my foot, I hold them poised. 'What do you want me to write?'

His lips purse. 'Dear Daisy, Jake and I have finally realised we're made for each other... Go on, start writing.'

I close my mouth and scribble down what he said.

'... and he's taken me to Gretna. Isn't it romantic? We'll be back later tonight, and I'll see you then. Love, Sam.'

Gaping at the words dancing before me, I speak slowly, enunciating every word. 'Jake, I don't know what sort of crazy plan you're hatching, but there is no way you can make me cooperate in a marriage ceremony.'

He grabs the notebook and pushes it into his trouser pocket, grinning. 'Good thing you've got a stand-in, isn't it?'

Rebecca's back on her feet—and she's grinning, too?

There's a bag lying in the doorway. I hadn't noticed it until now, a khaki-patterned canvas rucksack. Rebecca saunters over, reaches inside, and pulls out a dark wig—complete with blonde highlights. Carefully, she puts it on. 'We're the same height and build, Sammy-girl. Who's going to know I'm not you—at least in Gretna?'

'You... you're in this together?'

My lips mash against each other, and I snarl through them. 'Maybe you can fool the people at Gretna, but where does that get you? Nobody around here will be fooled for a millisecond.'   Jake has the temerity to look crestfallen. 'Once we're legally married, Sam, it won't matter—I never wanted it this way, but I'm afraid you'll be seeing your aunt sooner than you expected.'

My blood turns to ice. 'You... killed Aunt Claire?'

He shakes his head. 'How could I? I was in Edinburgh, with you, when the old goat popped it.'

'Rebecca, then...'

Rebecca laughs, and Jake frowns. 'Sam, it was just a brilliant piece of luck that Claire croaked when she did. I only planned on getting your flat—but when you inherited the hotel, *well*, that was a game-changer. It upped the stakes... in more ways than one.'

I'm scared to ask. 'What about Davy?'

'Oh, that was me.'

The pain is barely tolerable now, making my mind muddier by the moment, but I force myself to meet his gaze. 'Why? I don't see...'

He shrugs. 'I still hoped you'd come around. It would have been—solider—if *you* went to Gretna with me. Grizzly Adams got in the way. His tragic death was supposed to leave you looking for a shoulder to cry on—mine. Plus, that toerag Logan was responsible for your aunt kicking me out—I owed him one.'

He's insane

I turn to Rebecca. She's watching with a rapturous expression—reminds me of a feral cat. I hear desperation seep into my voice. 'Rebecca, think about this. Hasn't it clicked? Jake isn't leaving any loose ends—I reckon you're next for the chop, lady.'

She slinks up to Jake and drapes her arms around his neck. 'Naw,' she purrs. 'After three months of you, my Jakey needs me too much.'

Holding back the urge to vomit, I look down at the length of flat trouser leg trailing behind my left knee. 'You took my prosthetic.'

Jake holds up his palms. 'I'm going to tie you up again, but the leg's a little added insurance.'

He winks. 'Wouldn't want you *legging* it while we're gone. Don't bother looking for your phone, either—it's coming with us to Gretna. The GPS log will confirm it—you—went there.'

He's silent for a moment. 'Sam, I *am* sorry—I wish there was another way. I kept trying, right up to the end, but you've forced me to...'

He looks at his watch, then pulls out a length of cord and walks around me. 'It's time we hit the road. Put your hands behind your back, Sam.'

NINETEEN

'**A**w, isn't she sweet?'
Rebecca's voice pulls me from my doze with a jerk. I can't believe I fell asleep. I expected the pain from my nose to keep me awake, but it's dulled to practically nothing now. Through a grimy window, I see the sun's starting to set. Somehow, it's evening already—and the gruesome twosome have returned.

My right hand grips its fellow's wrist—Jake tied them behind my back before he and Rebecca left.

From somewhere, I summon an ironic grin. 'So—are congratulations in order?'

Jake cocks his head. 'For you too, Sam. After all, it's you I married—we're husband and wife, now.'

He leans closer and whispers. 'I wish you'd been there.'

I'm still trying to separate myself from sleep's sticky embrace. 'Jake, I feel like I've been dreaming. Did you really spill oil on the road, knowing Davy would skid on it?'

He looks at me curiously. 'Believe it, babe. Or not—it doesn't matter. I don't care—I'm about to become the owner of a redevelopment site worth half a million.'

Rebecca taps Jake's shoulder. 'Time's a wastin', honeybuns. Shouldn't we get on with this?'

My shoulders slump, and I let my eyes go blank. 'How does the next bit work? Are you going to slit my throat with your knife?'

'Sam, Sam.'

Jake scrabbles in his pocket. He brings out a tiny bottle and unscrews the cap, then shakes two triangular white pills into his palm. 'I'm not a monster.'

'What are those?' I grate, through a mouth drier than the Sahara.

'They're Es. Ecstasy tablets. You're going to swallow them. Then, I promise, you won't know anything about it when we drop you down the old well.' He glances sideways at Rebecca. 'How deep did you say it was?'

Rebecca blinks—I swear I felt the breeze. 'Twenty feet, maybe more. Deep enough, sweetie. Deep enough.'

Jake nods. 'See, there's no risk of you lying down there hurting—it'll be instantaneous.'

He takes a step towards me, and I flinch. 'Sam, don't worry. You won't feel a thing. After these, you'll soar like a kite. C'mon, babe—whether or not you swallow them, you're going down the well. Be sensible—enjoy one last rush.'

'And this is for my sake?'

He stops, scratches his chin. 'Largely—but it works for the plan, too. See, the story is, you and I came back from Gretna absolutely hyped—we sneaked over here to take some E, get us in the mood, like, but I fell asleep. When I wake up—*my darling bride*—where is she? I search, and I search, then finally I run to the hotel for help—and Rebecca says: "Have you checked the old well?" That's where we find you.'

He swipes his sleeve over dry eyes. 'I'll be inconsolable... and honestly, it won't all be acting...'

I scrabble back until my spine touches the wall, and splutter: 'I don't feel so good.'

Jake glances at Rebecca. 'Do you think she's got a concussion?'

Rebecca pouts, then a slow smile takes its place. 'What's the difference?'

Jake nods. He covers the remaining distance between us in an easy amble, crouches, and grabs my hair just like he did Rebecca's earlier—only this time for real. Jabs the pills at my mouth.

I make a desperate attempt to bite his hand, but he's too quick. 'C'mon, Sam. You're only putting off the inevitable.'

His eyes bulge when the fingers of both my hands latch on his wrist and twist. As Davy observed, opticians have *very* strong fingers. Jake drops the pills and rears back with a yelp of pain. 'How did you...?'

A voice—a very familiar voice, a voice so welcome it makes my insides run liquid—rings through the stable block. 'Stop right there, Jake—it's over.'

Craning to see past Jake, my heart leaps when Daisy strides through the open doorway. Clad in black jeans and denim shirt, everything about her exudes menace—not least the snarl contorting her normally angelic face.

Rebecca gulps, then launches herself at my friend. Daisy's response is a casual, sideways swipe of her fist.

Rebecca crumples to the floor—and doesn't get up.

Daisy's eyes set on Jake, still crouched in front of me, neck craned to watch her over his shoulder. She points a stern forefinger. 'You—we're long overdue to have words.'

Despite everything, Jake's expression shocks me. Lips retracting, eyelids slitted, he turns and leaps to his feet—then charges at Daisy.

She watches him pound towards her, lets her shoulders go slack, and it's probably only me who sees the tiny smile she's trying to hold back.

When Jake barrels into her, it's like a bowling ball hitting the last pin standing.

Daisy goes down, and Jake keeps going. In fact, he takes flight—a short-lived flight (the stable block isn't that big) which ends with him splattered against an unforgiving (stone) wall.

Daisy gets up unhurriedly while brushing off mummified stalks of straw as she glances at an unmoving Jake, now sprawled on the ground. She smiles thinly before looking around at Rebecca, who's still out cold, and the smile becomes a grin.

'Tomoe Nage?' I pipe up, struggling to my (one) foot. I've been to all Daisy's judo gradings, and she always tests me afterwards.

'Or "stomach throw" in English,' she drawls. 'Very effective against amateurs.'

Turning to a sudden influx of uniformed police, headed by Jodie, Daisy and I say in unison: '*You took your time.*'

TWENTY

Jodie drops to her knees, facing the paramedic
appraising Jake. 'Hell, Daisy. We're going to
need an ambulance for this one.'

She motions to a second paramedic, bent over
Rebecca. 'How's she?'

'Mild concussion it looks like.'

Now Jodie glares at Daisy. 'The ambulance
was for Sam, but there won't be room for her.'

Daisy just shrugs and turns to me. 'Nicely
played, Sam. Cutting it fine with your "panic
phrase", weren't you?'

'Yeah—you know, we should have come up
with something better than "I don't feel so good".
They both looked at me like I was crazy when I came
out with that. Oh, but you should have seen Jake's
face when he realised my wrists were untied.'

'How's the nose?' Jodie checks.

'Still tolerable, thanks. Those co-codamols did
the trick, but my head's swimming—it feels as
though I've had a half-dozen of Jake's E tablets.
Hey—has anybody found my leg yet?'

Jodie motions to a constable. 'Arnott. Go and
check the suspects' car—see if you can find... um...
it.'

'Yes, ma'am.'

I slump back, careful not to crack my head
against the stone wall. One policeman is standing on

a plastic block, removing the naked bulb from its hanging lampholder. 'Did you get it all?'

He holds out the bulb and grins. 'James Bond stuff, this. Yes, we got everything. Sound *and* video—this little beauty transmitted the whole show to our van in real time. Made for good watching—it beat last night's "Line of Duty" hands down.'

Daisy squats beside me. 'You *sure* you're alright?'

'I'll be fine.'

I will be—I'm flying high, and it's not just the codeine. Earlier on I thought it was the end of me—but, at this moment, I've never felt so alive. Near-death experiences have a reputation for leaving survivors with a delicious sense of euphoria—which reputation, I can now confirm, isn't exaggerated. Still, I remember with a chill, if it hadn't been for Daisy—which reminds me: 'Who gave you permission to put a tracker on my phone?'

Daisy's cheeks turn pink. 'I did it ages ago. You know what you're like—I need to keep an eye on you.'

'What do you mean, "what I'm like?"'

'You're hopeless,' she says simply. 'If your car broke down miles from anywhere, you'd have no idea what to do—for example.'

'Daisy, I don't *have* a car. And anyway, in that scenario, I'd use the same phone you were tracking to call a breakdown service.'

'Yeah, well... good thing I did. When I found that note behind the flat door, it was obvious something was badly wrong. You were still a bit "head in the sand" about Jake, but running off to Gretna with him? Not likely. Certainly not voluntarily. Especially not while Davy... and, after hearing what the Edinburgh coppers had to say...'

Davy—thinking of him drags my mood down again. Poor Davy—in a way, his coma's my fault. If he hadn't met me... I shake those thoughts away and return to Daisy's last words. 'Yes, what *was* that about, with the police in Edinburgh? You started telling me before, but then Jodie announced we were running out of time and hustled you out.'

'Well, I made them leave a message, like you told me. That burglar you had? He must have run past the shop down from your old flat and got caught on its security camera—that's how they identified him. Took them long enough... anyway, the burglar was Jake's brother.'

'What? Jake never said he had a brother.'

'Oh, yes. Right pair of shysters they are—no strangers to the police, either. It was a setup, Sam. The idea was to get Jake back in favour. Make you feel beholden to him. So, when they checked on the brother's brother—that's Jake—his probation officer told them...'

'Jake's got a probation officer? That means—'

'Yeah. He's done time, has our Jake. Him *and* his scabby brother. So, the address his probation officer had for Jake was—wait for it—*your* address. The same address that was burgled.' She giggles. 'Understandably, they thought you should know.'

I sit quiet for a minute, letting that sink in. Who *was* that man I lived with for three months? Then I remember another question that's bugging me. 'Thing I don't understand, Daisy, is by the time you checked that tracking app my phone must have been on its way to Gretna. What made you come here?'

Uh-oh. Going by that look, the spirit of my old maths teacher is still around

'The app doesn't only tell me where your phone *is*, Sam—it also says where it's *been*. I saw you'd gone straight from the hotel to here, hightailed it over to search for clues—and found you.'

Jodie steps closer. 'Then Daisy phoned me...' she arcs her arm in a regal wave '... and we organised all this. Just in time to record Jake's confession. Good job, Sam.'

She crouches between Daisy and me. 'Thanks—from Logan, as well as me.'

The moment's broken when PC Arnott runs up, clutching my leg. (What I like to call the "bionic bit".)

'It was in the boot,' he burbles, thrusting it at me and looking confused by a sudden wave of laughter.

Everyone graciously looks away while I strap the prosthetic on. Oh, that feels so much better. Unlike my poor nose...

A low moan escapes before I'm able to stop it and Daisy leans in, tilts her head. 'That nose getting sore again?'

I nod, and Jodie jumps up. 'Constable Arnott,' she bellows, then to us: 'He'll take you to hospital faster than we can get another ambulance here.'

Daisy ignores Jodie's accusatory glance. 'I'm going with her.'

I feel a rush of love for my pal as she helps me upright, her arm under mine while I hobble to the waiting police car. If it wasn't for Daisy, I'd be at the bottom of that old well now. I'm so glad she's by my side, her gentle grip reminding me I'm not alone...

'Sam, you go in the back. Oi, Arnott. Can I ride up front and work the blues and twos?'

TWENTY-ONE

'**Y**ou look like a panda.'
I *was* grateful to Daisy for making me breakfast. Looking back, I ate practically nothing yesterday—hardly surprising, then, that I'm vacuuming the full English she put in front of me. But my goodwill is rapidly evaporating. 'It's not funny.'

I have two absolutely huge black eyes. Not to mention the white butterfly plaster stretched over my nose, holding a plastic cast in place.

And my latest co-codamol tablet is wearing off.
'Sorry, Sam.'
She doesn't LOOK sorry

Somebody knocks at the door and it's more than timely—another comment like that and even Daisy's judo skills wouldn't have saved her. She springs up, disgustingly bright this morning, and I hear her say: 'Come on in.'

Oh, no. I'm not ready for visitors—Daisy's quite enough.

But when she brings Jodie and Logan through to the kitchen, my mood softens. Jodie was an absolute star yesterday, and Logan—what a nightmare he's been through. I feel terrible for doubting him. I don't think I ever *really* believed he was the psycho Jake and Rebecca made him out to be, but I'm ashamed that I never *completely* dismissed it as a possibility.

Logan starts when he sees me. 'Heck, Sam. You look awful.'

Okay—you can go now

Jodie's elbow spears his ribs and I nod my appreciation. 'He was desperate to see you,' Jodie explains. 'But maybe I should just take him back to his cell.'

'Sorry, Sam.'

Unlike Daisy before, I think he really is. 'I assume you're officially off the most-wanted list?'

'Yes, thanks to you. That's why we came—so I can tell you how grateful I am.'

'Pshaw. Good under-managers are hard to find.' Logan grins, and a swell of joy fills my chest now there's no doubt he's who I thought he was, after all.

Unlike Jake.

Daisy excuses herself to the bathroom, and Jodie watches her go with a quizzical expression. 'What drives her, Sam? She wouldn't strike me as a violent person—if she wasn't so good at it.'

The more I get to know Jodie—the fonder I'm becoming of Logan's girlfriend. Despite her hard-boiled detective act, she has a compassion that looks beneath the surface—my difficulty with answering her question is that Daisy's a metaphorical iceberg. Glancing at the door, I speak softly. 'She won't talk about her past, but there's something there, something that happened—something she had to guarantee could never happen to her again.'

Jodie nods thoughtfully, and Logan scratches his head but wisely keeps quiet. The sound of taps running has all three of us looking anywhere but at each other. Daisy bounces back in, then freezes—her gaze jumps around the sudden silence. 'You talking about me?'

Logan comes to the rescue. He beams at Daisy—'We wouldn't dare.'

Daisy rolls her eyes, and Logan turns to me. 'I just saw Aunt Maggie—she told me about moving into the hotel. Sam, she's over the moon—that was a really nice thing you did.'

I look away, embarrassed. I'm glad Maggie's happy, though. Last night, sometime after opening a second bottle of wine, I remembered shelving our plan to move her in until we were sure she wasn't involved—and felt a bit guilty for doubting her. I wouldn't have been up to it today, but Daisy promised she'd ask Maggie on my behalf. Knowing the wrong was going to be righted sooner rather than later went some way to easing my conscience.

Jodie's hand flickers across the breakfast bar and snags one of my hash browns. 'Rebecca confessed to taking Logan's spare badge and slopping oil on his jacket—she used her housekeeping keys to get into his room. So, he's totally in the clear. Any word on Davy, Sam?'

When she said Davy's name, my heart slammed. 'No, nothing new. His mum's with him, and the doctors say all we can do is wait—and hope.'

Logan dips his head. 'Poor Davy. I can't imagine...'

Jodie rescues me. 'Inspector Wilson gave the go ahead for your aunt's exhumation this morning. We're hoping to have PM and toxicology results in a few days.'

Daisy glowers. 'But you don't think Jake and Rebecca were behind her murder?'

Jodie shrugs. 'No reason for them to lie. Far as they knew, Sam wasn't going to tell anyone—and we aren't certain it *was* murder, but after everything that's happened, my inspector's no longer prepared to assume she died of natural causes.'

Daisy's expression says she'd still rather blame Jake, regardless. After giving the floor a thorough inspection, her head snaps up. 'While I've got you and Logan together, Sam, we need to do prices for Herbert—I should have sent them yesterday.'

'Herbert?' Logan murmurs, looking at me.

'One of the snooker club members—Daisy's busy selling him seminar space. I'm not sure we have proper facilities...'

Daisy cuts in. 'I'll sort all that out.'

Logan's face brightens. 'Oh, you're talking about the pharmacy chain.'

Nodding, Daisy turns to him. 'I was forgetting—he's your uncle.'

I feel my jaw drop. Suddenly, it's obvious...

TWENTY-TWO

'They didn't waste any time.'

Daisy's right—Aunt Claire's body was exhumed first thing Monday, and the toxicology results came back this morning. Finally, we know how she died.

'So,' Daisy clarifies. 'This stuff's definitely a synthetic drug, factory-made. Not one of Maggie's plants.'

'No—absolutely nothing herbal about it,' Jodie tells her. 'It's also tasteless, odourless—and at twice the normal dosage, lethal.'

We're holding a summit in my sitting room, where Jodie and Inspector Wilson are updating us on the investigation into what's now officially Aunt Claire's murder. Jodie leans forward. 'Your gut feeling was right, Sam. Soon as toxicology identified the drug, we got a warrant to search MedPharm's computers. Herbert's wife, Dinah, ordered in that same drug a week before your aunt's death. Strangely, she can't account for its whereabouts.'

Daisy lets go of a frustrated hiss, and I throw her a sympathetic smile. 'Don't blame yourself, Dais'—there's no way you could have known.'

She looks at me with wide eyes. 'It's not that— I'm thinking about what I was going to charge for their seminar.'

Jodie coughs. 'Anyway, like Graham told Sam, Claire was having an affair with one of the snooker club members. Herbert, we can now confirm. Jake had it all back to front—Herbert and Claire arrived at and left the hotel separately so Graham wouldn't see who Claire met. Claire, of course, went along with Jake's assertion rather than admit to Logan she was involved with his uncle—even to the point of paying Jake's first demand. Then he got greedy.'

The snort's out before I can catch myself. 'It was more likely the thought of Sadie's reaction that made Aunt Claire cough up initially—and I don't blame her.'

'What *about* Sadie?' Daisy asks. 'Why did she think Claire and Graham were doing the dirty? Do you suppose Jake told her out of spite?'

I wouldn't put it past him

'Who knows? Maybe she was suspicious when they both vanished for the better part of a day. You could always ask her...'

Even Daisy flinches at that. 'Pass.'

I turn to Jodie. Sadness wells in my chest and the words come out in a croak. 'So, Dinah admitted everything? Including...'

'The boss got it all out of her,' Jodie answers, looking at Inspector Wilson.

He shrugs. 'It wasn't difficult—Dinah's a fragile type, and I think she assumed we already knew. I just asked a lot of open questions until we had the full picture.'

298

The door opens, and Maggie sticks her head around. 'You ready for afternoon tea?'

I nod, and Maggie wheels in a trolley packed with sandwiches and pastry nibbles, and a stand of freshly piped cream cakes.

Jodie's eyes widen. 'Wow. I can feel the weight piling on just looking at that.'

'Enjoy,' Maggie trills with a wave of her hand, and turns to leave.

'Maggie,' I call, pointing to the empty chair beside me. 'Please, join us.'

Maggie looks flustered. 'Are you sure, Miss?'

'Of course. Sit yourself down.'

She blushes and reaches for a plate. 'Very well, Miss. Erm—I thought you'd like to know that I've been on to the estate agent and put my house up for sale. I'm so grateful to you for offering me a room— and fair lookin' forward to it.'

Whoops—forgot about that

I've grown fond of Maggie. Her motherly presence was a comfort while I came to terms with Aunt Claire's loss.

Which is why this is so hard. 'Maggie, the police have your sister, Dinah, in custody—and she's confessed everything.'

I draw a huge breath. 'Maggie, how could you?'

Maggie turns chalk white.

Inspector Wilson rises and stands in front of her, hands clasped behind his back. 'Margaret Brown, I'm arresting you for the murder of Claire Chessington. You do not have to say anything...'

INSPECTOR WILSON AND A FEMALE CONSTABLE TAKE Maggie away, and everyone else heads for the bar to tell Logan. Well, that's part of the reason...

'Another,' Daisy demands, slamming her glass on the bar-top.

Logan lifts the gin bottle, his eyes glassy. 'I still can't believe it... Aunt Maggie? I'd never have believed she was capable...'

When I nudge my own glass, Logan reaches for the vodka. His double brandy lies untouched. 'It seems the fling between my Aunt Claire and your Uncle Herbert escalated into something else— Herbert announced to Dinah he wanted a divorce. She didn't take it well...'

'She took a bottle of sleeping tablets,' Daisy puts in.

Logan downs his brandy in one as I carry on. 'Her sister—Maggie—found her. Maggie called an ambulance and later, after Dinah had her stomach pumped, Dinah told Maggie *why* she tried to kill herself.'

I pause for a swig of vodka and Jodie takes up the story. 'Maggie says the only way she could be sure Dinah wouldn't try again was to come up with a plan to stop Herbert from leaving. She was convinced it was infatuation more than love, and reckoned if she removed Claire from the equation...'

'... Herbert would settle down and Dinah would have no reason to top herself,' Daisy finishes for her.

Still looking bemused, Logan pours himself another brandy. 'So... they cooked up this scheme? Dinah got the drug, and Maggie gave it to Claire in a cup of cocoa?'

Daisy sniffs. 'Maggie also made sure it was Rebecca's grampa who did the death certificate—because there was no chance of *him* calling for a post-mortem.'

I nod and study my hand—it's trembling. When I had my flash of inspiration, it was based on the rumours that Aunt Claire's boyfriend was a snooker club member—and how easy it would be for a pharmacist to obtain poison. Herbert, in other words—or a jealous wife who also happened to be a pharmacist. But to find out Maggie... 'Maggie was part of this place. It feels like, oh, I don't know—like finding out Santa Claus isn't real.'

Daisy looks aghast. 'Who told you that?'

Despite myself, I giggle. Only Daisy could make me do that right now. A ringtone makes me scrabble in my bag. Pulling out the phone, I stare at its screen. 'Davy's mum,' I whisper.

Daisy stiffens. 'Go on, then. Answer it.'

'I spoke to her less than an hour ago. Something must have happened.'

'She'll ring off,' Daisy warns.

'Okay.'

301

Raw fear grips me and my thumb hovers over the green button. I couldn't feel more trepidation if this phone were an unexploded bomb.

Which, effectively, it is.

Two Months Later

B eth puts down an enormous platter of nibbles beside the coffee flask. 'Let me know if you need anything else.'

'We will,' Daisy calls after her, and grabs a bacon and cheese pastry. She points with her cup. 'Beth's no Maggie, but she's a wiz with snacks—and the ready meals.'

Lifting a prawn croissant, Logan shakes it for emphasis—oblivious to spots of mayonnaise spattering his shoulder. 'And a brilliant baker, too.'

'Her saving grace,' I put in. 'She's great with everything snacky—which is pushing up the bar takings since we started doing pub grub. We *have* to get a proper chef as well, though. Even with the extra discount Daisy squeezed out of Kim, ready meals aren't profitable enough.'

We're having a board meeting in my flat. (Actually, that should be "our" flat now Daisy's moved in properly.) Strictly speaking, only Logan and I are "board" members, but Daisy's probably the most enthusiastic participant at these gatherings.

Today, the latest management figures cast a solemn shadow over proceedings. With the renovations complete and various marketing strategies deployed—the hotel's bank balance is zero. (Actually, it's a lot less than zero when you take the overdraft into consideration—but let's not go there.)

That *is* after paying all three of us a wage—but at slightly under the going rate for a paperboy.

'Things *have* improved—drastically,' Logan points out. He hasn't stuttered for ages—strangely, his diction's rebirth dates from the moment he was released from Donstable police station's holding cell. Maybe that awful experience re-calibrated something inside his head, and everyday stresses don't seem so stressful any more.

'There's a vast improvement,' I agree. 'We have guests—thirty per cent occupancy, on average—and bar takings have soared because of the gaming machines and Beth's snack menu. We *are* making money now—rather than losing it—just not enough for the three of us to live on.'

Absent-mindedly, Logan brushes at his jacket and manages to relocate most of the pastry flakes onto his trousers. 'Talking of the bar, Daisy's Wild West theme has been a big hit. "Refried beans" is the unlikeliest bar snack I could have imagined, but it's beating crisps and nuts hands down.' He wrinkles his nose. 'We need better ventilation in there, though...'

Daisy giggles, and I thank my lucky stars she and Logan are covering the public bar between them. I've bagged supervision of our new (upmarket, and definitely more sedate) watering hole in the residents lounge. Trouble is, it's a bit *too* sedate... like the rest of the hotel, if you don't count the "Last Chance Saloon".

A deliberate cough from Daisy makes me look her way as she holds up a clutch of papers. 'These are the results from my survey...'

'In a minute.'

Daisy's got a bee in her bonnet about some survey she conducted on the guests. My worry is how voluntary their participation was... 'We either need to borrow more for extra marketing, or come up with alternative strategies.'

'Whichever way we go, it'll mean taking on more debt,' Logan points out. 'Like you said, our existing income streams are barely sustaining us—there's nothing left to fund new ideas.'

'Any costs we can cut—?'

'STOP.'

Daisy jumps to her feet, cheeks shining. 'Will you listen to me? This is important.'

I look at Logan, wait for his eyebrows to drop, then refocus on Daisy. 'Alright, tell us then.'

'Good.'

She picks up her notes and starts pacing. Logan catches my eye, and I shrug. She's determined to have her say—might as well get it over and done with.

'I've been investigating how the publicity surrounding Claire's murder has affected business. First of all—sorry, guys—it's our highly publicised notoriety that's bringing guests in. Nothing to do with the marketing.'

Ouch. I look at Logan—he looks straight back. We never thought of that. If Daisy's right, all our advertising efforts have been money down the drain.

Daisy gives that a moment to sink in, then continues. 'So, all these guests heard of us because the previous proprietor was murdered. It's not so surprising—anything ghoulish catches people's attention—but interestingly, I discovered our current guests are reluctant to admit that's why they came.'

She slaps the page she's reading from. 'Although "Let's go see where somebody got murdered" prevailed, that was only after lots of soul searching. In other words, these guests were nearly too embarrassed to come—what does that tell us?'

Logan's chin jerks up—nobody told him there'd be a test. Being more familiar with Daisy's methods, I'm ready with an answer. 'The adverse publicity is holding us back?'

Her lip curls and she shakes her head. Both palms float up and beat the air in front of her. 'NO. I've just told you—that's why they *came*. The bigger picture is, there must be loads *more* people out there who considered coming for a butcher's—but chickened out. It's basic psychology—most folk go along with whatever they perceive to be the prevailing herd instinct. What we have to do is change the minds of all these potential guests who've heard about us and fancy a gander, but can't get over how that makes them look—transform their rubbernecking into a concept convention has no quarrel with. The whole "murder" thing has to become herd-friendly.'

'She's losing me,' Logan mutters, and he has my sympathy.

After all that, the gears in my head are definitely labouring—but I sort of see where she's going. 'Alright, Daisy. *How* do we make people feel comfortable about indulging their morbid curiosity?'

She waves her papers frantically, eyes alight. 'By bringing it out in the open and offering a peer-approved route into our already-famous crime scene. We re-name the hotel—maybe call it "The Murder Hotel"—and do "Murder Weekends". We don't just legitimise their fantasies—we offer an opportunity to act those fantasies out.'

Logan looks at me. 'Murder Weekends?'

Pulling a face, I slap both palms against my cheeks. 'Would it hurt to give it a go? We've tried everything else.'

'S'pose not,' he says, not sounding like he means it.

'Alright,' I tell Daisy. 'Let's do it.'

'Yayyyy,' she whoops, and launches into a tap dance.

Privately, I can't see this going anywhere, but it'll keep her occupied while Logan and I come up with something better. 'Okay, you do the research, find out what hosting "Murder Weekends" involves, and we'll meet again next week to take it further. I'm afraid that's it for today, folks—there's somewhere I have to be.'

Daisy dips her mouth to Logan's ear, but being Daisy her whisper's clearly audible.

'She's picking Davy up from physio...'

EPILOGUE

The Donstable Gazette

20TH OCTOBER, 2021

MURDER HOTEL MAKES A KILLING!

Since the former Cairncroft Hotel changed its name to "The Murder Hotel", traders in the area have seen a sudden influx of visitors - together with a welcome surge in profits.

Samantha Chesswell, senior partner at The Murder Hotel, told our reporter she's astonished by how popular their newly introduced murder weekends (where participants play the parts of characters in a murder mystery) have become.

The "Murder Weekends" have been extended to include "Mid-Week Mysteries", but even with this increase in capacity, Miss Chesswell says the hotel is fully booked until well into next year.

PUBLISHED EVERY WEDNESDAY
BY DONSTABLE PRESS LTD

SAM & DAISY ARE BACK IN:

THE CAIRNCROFT DETECTIVE AGENCY

STAND DOWN, THELMA & LOUISE...

Sam and Daisy have made a success of The Cairncroft Hotel.
Where do they go from here?
If it was up to Daisy, well—she's always wanted to be a private investigator
... and Daisy usually gets her way

In The Cairncroft Detective Agency, Sam and Daisy set off down a new path - but this time, have the girls bitten off more than they can chew?

The Cairncroft Detective Agency is a cozy murder mystery, the next in series after "The Murder Hotel", and with a (now trademark) twisty, high-tension ending

I also write "The Con Woman" series of thrillers

Meet Dawn and Roger – jet-setting siblings who also happen to be con artists.

When David dumps Dawn, he wasn't expecting her to kidnap his brother-in-law. Dawn says it's "business" – but Roger questions her motives.

Brother-in-law George doesn't have an opinion, being blissfully unaware of his own kidnap... but that changes when a second crew snatch him from under Dawn and Roger's noses. Now the siblings find themselves switching sides – racing to rescue George before the new kidnappers run out of the fingers they're chopping off to make their point.

☆ ☆ ☆ ☆ ☆ **Loved this book! Action packed, twists and turns, thriller, smart and interesting characters... you will enjoy this well written book...** Amazon.com reviewer

ALSO BY A.J.A. GARDINER

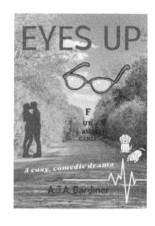

Comedy meets drama in this cosy, heart-warming tale of a man, his dogs, and his dreams.

Join Mark as he struggles with zany patients, gets fleeced by his ex-wife, and makes a friend called "Shovelhead".

Sometimes Mark's ahead, mostly the world tramples him into the dirt— but so long as he has his dogs to go home to, his caravan (which IS his home), and now Diane, Mark's optimism never falters.

Well, hardly ever…

"Eyes Up" is the story of a home-visiting optician, written by—a home-visiting optician!

AUTHOR'S NOTE

Thank you for choosing this book—I hope you enjoyed reading it as much as I enjoyed writing it.

As an aside – my other book, "Eyes Up", was originally published under a pen name (Mark Rogers) but, since retiring from domiciliary practice to write full time, I no longer have to worry about offending my former paymasters and am happy to take credit for the opinions expressed by Mark. I hope you'll decide to try it.

The best way to be kept informed of new books etc is to join my readers' club—when you'll get a free **Ebook** called "When Sam met Daisy", a short story telling how the girls met—which you can do by typing the following into your browser:

https://ajagardinerwriter.co.uk/free%20book/

I maintain a mailbox for reader feedback, and would love to hear from you—it's at:
alistair@ajagardinerwriter.co.uk

Sincerely,

A.J.A. Gardiner

First paperback edition August 2022
ISBN: 9798844467714

Printed in Great Britain
by Amazon

39071364R00182